ABANDONED

BITTER HARVEST BOOK THREE

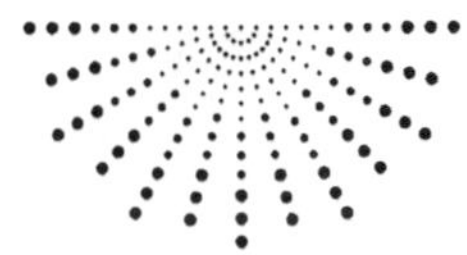

ANN GIMPEL

Edited by
KATE RICHARDS

CONTENTS

ABANDONED

BITTER HARVEST, BOOK THREE

Dystopian Urban Fantasy
By
Ann Gimpel

A runaway spell is the most dangerous weapon of all.

Recco misses his cozy lab and well-organized veterinary clinic, but ten years as a Vampire stripped him of any illusions. Life is done handing him everything he wants. He could rail against fate—which never bought him much—or suck it up and keep going. Defeating the Cataclysm broke Vampirism's hold on him, though. Even better, it threw Zoe square in his path and kicked open the door for him to bond with a wolf.

When Zoe left Ireland for a visiting professorship in Wyoming, she assumed she'd be home in a year. She didn't factor in being trapped by the Cataclysm and scratching and clawing for everything from food to air clean enough to breathe. She's a very different woman now. And not one she likes all that well—or even recognizes some days. A rotten sailor, she never imagined she'd end up on a ship.

In a world with few choices, evil runs rampant and none of the old rules apply. Darkness stalks the ship. Harsh and ruthless, it blocks them at every turn.

BORROWED TROUBLE

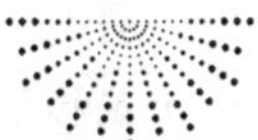

Zoe Seisyll lurched from one side of the generous galley to the other, compensating for the motion of the ship. She was alone in the stainless-steel kitchen running behind *Arkady's* dining room because it was her turn to prepare the evening meal. The beginnings of biscuits spread before her. Half the dough was shaped into rough circles. The other half still sat in an enormous mixing bowl. Back before the Cataclysm, *Arkady* had been home to as many as sixty passengers and a sizeable crew, which explained the industrial-sized pans and cookware.

She flexed her fingers, coated with cornmeal, flour, powdered eggs, powdered milk, and enough water to hold it all together. Maybe focusing on her hands would drive the infernal song from her head. The elusive mix of chords mocked her as usual, slipping away before she could identify their origins.

"Och, and I brought it on myself," she muttered.

Zoe adored music. She played guitar and piano passably well, and could hold her own on the flute. Cooking and singing went together like old, cherished friends, and she'd been deep into an Irish folk tune when the discordant melody intruded.

The one she hadn't been able to get out of her head from a few weeks after they fought the Cataclysm. Not for long, anyway. Whenever she gave in and hummed or sang anything, she rarely got away with it. On the occasions she did, her victory was short-lived. The aberrant notes always intruded, ruining one of her favorite escapes.

Aye, Why music? Any other intrusion wouldna be quite so hard to stomach.

Her mind voice was thick with the brogue from her native Northern Ireland. She'd spent nearly as much time in Scotland, so her speech held hints of both accents, something that had confused folk in the U.K., many of whom amused themselves by placing wagers about her origins. When she'd taken a visiting professor position in Wyoming, everyone there chalked her up as a Brit. Or, God forbid, an Aussie.

No self-respecting U.K. native would ever make such a mistake, but to North Americans, British-type accents all sounded alike.

She swallowed a snort and plunged her hands back into the dough, working on autopilot until three pans of cornmeal biscuits were ready for the waiting oven. Popping them inside, she set a mental timer for fifteen minutes. At least the jarring music in her mind had fallen silent. It was like the intruder knew the moment she let her guard down, waiting in the wings to pounce when she was vulnerable.

The worst part was it killed the spontaneous joy she'd always taken in music.

Moving to the sink, she rinsed her bowl and her hands. Something about the eerie melody was familiar, and unsettling enough she always tuned it out before she could identify it. A knee-jerk reaction to unpleasantness. She perched on a three-legged stool to wait until the biscuits were ready to rescue from the ovens but was too antsy to sit still.

A quick tour through the pantry identified other items to add to dinner preparations. It was too early in the day to do much more than get the biscuits done, though. No point wasting electricity keeping a casserole hot for hours. Everything on the ship was generator powered, and those generators required fuel. The scent of warm cornmeal wafted through the kitchen, comforting and reminiscent of home.

Aye, home. Is aught left of it?

She rolled her shoulders back and stood straighter. No point thinking about Belfast or the family she'd left behind. Parents, aunts, uncles, cousins. She'd never meant to be gone forever. Her plan had been a one-year visiting professorship at the University of Wyoming. Their offer included full access to newly excavated Native American settlements and the expectation of several research papers in prestigious journals. Journals already lined up and anxiously awaiting her impressions—and her photos.

Definitely a career-making move, and one almost guaranteeing the offer of a full professorship after she returned to Queen's University in Belfast.

Even with all that, she'd negotiated until the university in Wyoming sweetened the pot by offering to underwrite her travel and living expenses. Zoe would have been a fool to refuse what was any archaeologist's dream. Plus, she'd gotten herself into a wee pickle, and leaving Belfast for a time seemed prudent.

Once her visa was squared away, she'd moved into a cozy cottage walking distance from the campus in Laramie. Soon afterward, she'd been delighted to meet Aura MacKenzie, another Shifter, who was also a history professor. Aura had introduced Zoe to the local Shifter pack, and her concerns about carving out a secondary home in America evaporated—

The smell of almost-overcooked biscuits sent her flying to the ovens, mitt in hand. She pulled the pans out, thanking all the bloody saints she'd gotten to them in time, and turned off the oven. They had sufficient supplies on *Arkady*, but it didn't mean she could ruin an entire batch of anything daydreaming. Their food stocks wouldn't last forever. Between now and then, they had to figure out a way to resupply.

She located cooling racks and stacked the pans atop them. Wisps of the eerie, haunting melody were back. Zoe shivered and didn't dig any deeper. Something about the song drew her to the restless ocean churning beneath the ship's hull.

Had it followed her from Ushuaia?

Worse, had she done something wrong during their group incantation to defeat the Cataclysm? Wrong enough to absorb some of its fell energy?

No point borrowing trouble.

The corners of her mouth twisted into a grimace. Her grandma had been partial to the phrase. Thinking about the old woman was bittersweet. It was hard to long for someone she'd probably never lay eyes on again. Painful and a waste of energy.

Zoe arranged the rest of her dinner preparations in a neat row and left the galley, intent on layering up so she could spend some time out on deck. She trotted up the stairs to the corridor leading to her cabin and let herself inside the small, neat space. One bunk ran beneath the porthole; another sat at right angles along the back wall. A small desk and chair were the only other furniture in the room.

She flipped the duvet into place to cover her unmade bed with its rumpled sheets and pulled gear from one of the cabin's many closets. Because this boat had ferried tourists through polar regions, it held a full complement of cold-weather clothing, saving the passengers from packing bulky gear on long transoceanic flights.

Zoe stepped into thick black trousers and an insulated red jacket she zipped to her chin. Red waterproof bibs came next. Followed by knee-high Wellingtons and a weatherproof rust-colored parka. She tugged a woolen hat over her head, before snugging the parka's hood into place, and stuffed her hands into fluffy down mitts. After a quick glance at her tarot deck and a few magical accoutrements—mostly gemstones—she'd hung onto through her years in Ushuaia, she felt guilty. Maybe her time would be better spent immersing herself in chasing the intrusive song to its roots.

I won't be outside for long, she promised herself. *Only enough to clear my head.*

Before she could overthink her decision, she trudged out of her cabin and along the corridor to the first door leading outside. The ship had a million doors and almost as many staircases. She supposed they'd been placed strategically to maximize safety, but things like insurance companies were part of the Old World order.

None of that mattered anymore, and maybe the demise of things like insurance companies was one of the plusses. No one to bail you out when you fucked up meant you were a hell of a lot more careful.

Cold hit her like an unyielding wall after the ship's warmth. Her first full breath stuck in her throat, making her gasp, and she buried her nose and mouth in the parka's neck ruff.

Zoe walked mindlessly. She started to hum, but cut it off fast. For once, the marauding melody didn't insert itself. After a while, she wrapped her arms around herself in a feeble attempt to preserve her body heat. Icy wind cut through her layers of clothing, and sleet stung her face. The cold air searing her lungs was clean, though. A welcome counterpart to the years she and eleven other Shifters had been trapped in Ushuaia, wondering what was going to kill them first. A marauding Vampire or tainted air and water.

Years ago, Aura had talked her into joining their group on a trip to the tip of South America. At the time, it sounded like quite the adventure, and it occurred during a week when the university was closed for one of many U.S. holidays. The Shifters had planned to harness the power of an eclipse, something that would have enhanced their Earth-linked magic. Except the eclipse never happened. Instead, a spell gone bad had imprisoned them at the ass end of the Earth.

She pushed past the chill leaching into her bones and strode briskly from deck to deck, covering a familiar pathway. She tried to get outdoors as much as she could, but foul weather had kept her inside the last two days. Her coyote had pitched a right fit at the confinement.

"Better?" she asked her bondmate and picked up the pace.

"Yes." The word held a grudging tone.

Zoe waited. After twenty plus years, she knew better than to argue—or cajole—her bond animal into anything. The strategy never worked.

"What happens after this McMurdo place?" the coyote asked.

"Depends what we find there." Zoe was hedging because she didn't want to break the news about a blue water voyage that could take a month or better. For some reason, the coyote hated water—or maybe it was the combination of water, cold, and being stuck in a small space. She tried a different tack. *"Before we left Ireland, you enjoyed our jaunts in those little boats I used to rent."*

"Those were different, and you know it. How can you compare a sunny afternoon when we'd spend an hour or two within sight of land to this? Everything here is white or gray. It's unnatural. I miss green and trees."

She gave up on telepathy—the coyote would hear her either way —and chose not to mention most of their sailing time around the British Isles had scarcely been under sunny skies. It had been green, though. A byproduct of incessant rain. "What bothers you most?" She channeled a thread of magic to her feet before her circulation shut down entirely.

"All of it."

"Could you narrow it down?" Zoe reached the sixth deck and reversed course. Clouds the color of hammered pewter boiled across the horizon, limiting vision to fifty yards. Wind ripped at her, pushing her first one way, and then another.

"I assumed when we defeated the Cataclysm and left Ushuaia the world wouldn't be quite so hostile." The coyote yipped, wistful and somber.

"We all hoped for much the same." Zoe sent warm thoughts inward.

"What have we encountered so far?" the coyote demanded, not mollified by her attempt to soothe it. Without waiting for her to reply, it kept right on talking. *"Four reluctant Shifters. A mad priest.*

Demons. Vampires—that apparently aren't all dead yet. An evil dark mage—"

"I know all those things. I was there too," she cut in. "Goddammit. This is hard enough without you cataloging all the bad shit. Besides, the men made peace with their bond animals, so at least that part is on its way to being fixed."

A vicious blast of wind chopped sideways. She gripped a nearby railing with her mitten-clad hand just before her booted feet slipped on icy metal risers. A quick blast of magic kept her upright.

"What's wrong?" She repeated a variant of her earlier question and hustled to the next deck down. "It's not like you to be such a pessimist."

"I want forests. I want you to shift so we can run and I can hunt." Rather than petulant, the coyote's words were sentimental, as if it were bidding farewell to a life it figured was gone forever.

Zoe constructed her reply carefully. "You can have those things. Just not with me right now. Nothing has changed in the special world you share with the bond animals. My feelings wouldn't be hurt if you retreated there to roam."

"Really?"

"Really," she reassured her bondmate.

"What if another wicked mage shows up? And you need my magic to strengthen yours?"

"I have a feeling you'd know. No matter where you were." Caring and gratitude for the coyote tracked from her toes to her head. Its last bondmate had died in a bloody skirmish during the First World War, and it had always blamed itself for not keeping its human partner safe from the shrapnel that had torn him to bits.

Wars had been simpler then. At least they'd had beginnings and ends. Winners and losers. Not anymore. From the time a magical barricade trapped them inside Ushuaia, they'd fought an amorphous enemy. One without defined boundaries that was a magnet for evil. Zoe shivered and set her teeth together to keep them from chattering.

They'd fought Vampires too, but they were pikers in the evil department. Nowhere near as daunting as demons or powerful mages. Besides, Vamps seemed to be on their way out. The battle against the Cataclysm had paved the way for them to lose their fangs and, if they chose to do so, welcome a bond animal.

Zoe broke into a shambling trot. Perpetually cold outside. Stifling heat within. She reminded herself it was good to have choices. Any choices at all. Those years in Ushuaia hadn't offered much in the way of alternatives. She'd spent most of her time helping humans survive and avoiding Vampires.

She burrowed deeper into her parka, shielding her eyes from blowing snow with one hand. It might be cold out here on deck; at least it wasn't claustrophobic. They'd been en route from Antarctica's Palmer Peninsula to McMurdo Research Station for the past week. Between pack ice that had surrounded the ship—and forced them to slow down—and storms blowing up out of nowhere, their progress hadn't been as brisk as they'd hoped.

Or as Viktor and Juan had hoped, she corrected herself. They were the only ones who actually knew anything about sailing a ship as large as *Arkady*. As she'd recently reminded her bondmate, she'd done her share of piloting skiffs and day sailors in the murky zone where Scotland and Ireland were separated by the Irish Sea. Those experiences had scarcely prepared her for a three-hundred-foot-long vessel.

Vik and Juan had parceled out tasks, training the rest of them as fast as they could, but the ship's array of instrumentation was daunting. Zoe doubted anything as prosaic as sitting down with an instruction manual would be sufficient to teach her the basics of what she needed to know. Guiding *Arkady* required years of hands-on practice. *Sailing for Dummies* wouldn't cut it.

"There you are," sounded from behind her.

Zoe spun to face Ketha, a wolf Shifter and seer, who was also Viktor's wife. "Here I am," she agreed, surprised by how flat and hard the words sounded.

Ketha had slung a parka over her tall, slender frame. Dark hair shot with red and gold streamed around her, tossed by the wind, and her golden eyes held a worried cast. "Is something wrong?"

Zoe choked on a groan at the memory of what she'd dragged out of her coyote by asking the same question.

Ketha grappled with her parka hood with one bare hand. Clearly, she hadn't expected to remain outside very long.

"Come on." Zoe trotted twenty feet and yanked the first door she came to open. "You're not dressed to be out here."

"Judging from how white your skin is, neither are you," Ketha retorted and dove through the door Zoe held for her.

"My skin is always white. 'Tis an Irish redhead's curse."

"Looks like frostbite to me." Ketha stopped in the long corridor spanning Deck Three and turned to look askance at Zoe. "Och, sure and ye've a wee bit of Scots blood too, lassie."

A laugh bubbled from Zoe's belly. Ketha had a quirky optimism, and it was impossible to remain annoyed with her. "Drop the brogue, sweetie."

"I speak Gaelic," Ketha protested.

"Aye, but it doesn't translate well when you pretend you were born on the old side of the Atlantic."

"North America is every bit as old. It's not why I came hunting for you. We could use your archeology skills."

Zoe frowned. "Why? Surely you didn't unearth any pot shards or strips of fabric or bits of buildings for me to examine."

"Yes and no."

"Equivocate, why don't you?" Zoe rolled her eyes and hustled down the corridor to her cabin. "You may as well come on in and tell me what's going on while I ditch some of these clothes. I'll cook if I keep all these layers on."

Ketha followed her into her cabin and pushed the door shut. "What do you know about genetic blends?"

Zoe unzipped her parka and slung it over a hook next to the door. Next, she toed off the Arctic Pac boots so she could get out of her bibs. "By genetic blends, do you mean two species not normally associated with one another?" Ketha nodded, so Zoe went on. "You're the microbiologist. Why ask me?"

Ketha laid her parka on one of the bunks and settled next to it. "I didn't mean on a cellular level. What I was fishing for was evidence —and it can be anecdotal—of beings not explainable by any normal selection process."

"Do you mean mythical creatures? Like the Phoenix? Or Selkies?"

"More like Gryphons since they're a mix of eagles and lions."

"Ah." Zoe unhooked the bibs and stepped out of them, hanging them next to the jacket. Once she'd stuffed her feet into slippers, she perched on the bed catty-corner to Ketha's. "And you'd be asking this, why?"

Ketha blew out a tight breath and stretched out fingers she'd rounded into fists. "We've been at this for the last two days. Ever since the weather turned to shit and lab time was about the only avenue open to us—"

"Who's us?"

"Karin, Recco, Daide, and me."

Zoe nodded. It made sense. Karin was an MD, and the two men had been veterinarians before being turned into Vampires. Courtesy of the standoff with the Cataclysm, they were Shifters now.

"Go on." Zoe made come-along motions with one hand.

Ketha pressed her lips into a thin line. "You know how Karin's first evaluation yielded unrelated bits of genetic material?"

"Yeah. And we figured the dark mage shaped the protoplasm to his liking when he created those impossible animals."

"Exactly. Well, the unrelated DNA strings are there, but there's more. We've checked it nine different ways—except it feels like a hundred—and we keep coming up with the same result."

Zoe leaned forward and rested a hand on Ketha's knee. "You don't have to justify yourself to a jury of your overeducated peers. This is only me. I don't need the run-up. What'd you find?"

"Something truly ancient. It's made up of archaea. Odd thing is, they're arranged in an intelligent fashion. I've never seen anything like it. Never read about it, either."

Zoe culled through her memory. "Those are what? Some kind of amoeba, right?"

"Not exactly. Amoeba have a cellular nucleus, and these don't. Archaea are the oldest, simplest single-cell organisms. The original building blocks of life. They're a type of prokaryote, and they date back three and a half billion years or more." She stopped to take a measured breath. "I'm here to ask you to generate a list of possibilities."

Zoe got to her feet and clasped her hands behind her as she covered the distance to the door and back again, stopping in front of Ketha. "So you have a microscopic piece of…of something. And you want me to come up with a list of everything that used to live in this neck of the woods millions—or billions—of years ago? Without the Internet or access to textbooks?"

Ketha opened her mouth. Zoe held up a hand before she said anything. "Archaeologists are exactly like any other scientific discipline. We have areas of specialization. Mine was Native and indigenous peoples. I had colleagues who fell in love with the polar regions, but I only spent one summer there."

The hopeful look on Ketha's face folded in on itself. "Damn, I miss libraries and my collection of scientific journals. This could be the find of the millennium. A sentient prehistoric creature that migrated to Antarctica before the continent turned into nature's icebox."

"How did you get from prokaryotes arranged in unusual ways to a sentient prehistoric creature?"

Ketha screwed her mouth into a grimace. "Bit of a leap, eh? It's why I'm here. I was hoping you might have relevant information I could feed into figuring this out."

"I understand it's important," Zoe said, picking her words with care. "I'm not blowing you off, merely cautioning you this isn't exactly my area of expertise. I'll try to remember what I can, and I'll ask my bond animal. It's one of the older ones. Have you asked Juan what his mountain lion remembers? It wasn't one of the first Shifters, but it wasn't far removed from them, either."

"Grand idea. Ashamed I didn't think of it first." Ketha jumped to her feet, snapped up her parka, and headed for the door.

A blast of discordant music rocked Zoe. The timing couldn't be accidental. "Did you hear that?" she demanded.

Ketha pulled her hand away from the door latch and turned to face Zoe. "Hear what?"

"It sounds like a five-year-old pounding the flat of both hands on a keyboard."

"Fascinating. Do you think something is trying to communicate with you?" Ketha skewered Zoe with troubled eyes. "Have you heard it before?"

"Aye, I have. 'Tis so unpleasant, I've always shut it down afore it had a chance to be more than annoying."

Ketha screwed her face into a reprimand. "When were you going to get around to telling the rest of us about this toddler piano player?"

"Skip the lecture. I told you now. I was worried maybe I'd brought a piece of the Cataclysm along with us. I hoped it would go away. I—"

"Sorry. I was way too harsh. There might be a connection between my tissue sample in the lab and whatever is singing to you."

Zoe rolled her eyes. "It's another really big stretch."

Ketha rolled her eyes back and squeezed Zoe's shoulder. "When you have no fucking idea what you're dealing with, no idea is fantastic enough to discard out of hand. I'm going back to the lab."

"I'll see if I can remember any of the legends unique to the poles."

"Good woman." Ketha pulled the door open and left at a quick pace.

Zoe stepped to the sink long enough to sluice water over her face and then sat at the desk and pulled paper and a pencil from the top drawer.

"Monsters from the North and South Poles, huh?" she muttered and cleared her mind.

It didn't take long before her eidetic memory regurgitated materials she'd studied during a long-ago summer spent above the Arctic Circle, researching the Inuit and the hunter-gatherer forbearers of Scandinavians. She stared at the page centered in front of her, stabbed her pencil onto it, and began to write.

Adlet: A type of werewolf with the upper body of a man and the hindquarters of a wolf.

Keelut: Evil earth spirit that takes the form of a large, hairless black dog...

2

ODDITIES

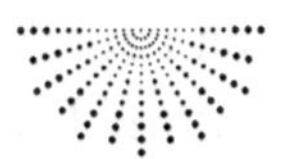

Recco—Ricardo Cardoza, except it had been so long since he'd heard his full name, he wondered if he'd even respond to it—hunched over a microscope in the makeshift lab on Deck Two. The room had originally been a common area for the ship's crew, and it was about twenty feet by thirty. Three tables were bolted to the floor, and several straight-back chairs lay scattered about. Half rested on their sides on the floor, a byproduct of rough seas.

The stained sample beneath Recco's dual eyepieces twitched. He stared harder, and it did it again. A rippling motion from left to right and back again.

Impossible.

He had to be imagining it. Dead tissue didn't move. Straightening, he squinched his eyes shut to give them a break before bending low over the scope one more time. Shades of blue and red stared back, quiescent, looking like they were supposed to this time. He waited through a count of ten, but nothing changed.

"Hey, *amigo*." Daide walked up behind him. Diego Vegas had been Recco's practice partner since they graduated veterinary school twenty some odd years before. When they'd stopped being

15

vets because the world imploded, they'd stuck it out as Vampires. Daide's dark hair was chopped to uneven lengths; some strands hit chin level, others brushed his shoulders. Tall and lanky, his stark bone structure—high cheekbones and a squared-off chin—revealed Native blood. He twisted until his dark eyes were trained on Recco's face.

"Hey, *amigo*, what?" Recco countered, taking in the other man's black pants, stretchy red top, and puffy vest.

"You were muttering in Spanish. Did you figure anything out?"

Recco pushed to his feet and gestured to his vacated chair. "You tell me. Take a look."

Nodding, Daide perched on the chair and adjusted the optics to his liking. They'd had plenty of arguments over the years about Recco's tendency to ratchet the focus on one side to compensate for a slight astigmatism.

Over on the other side of the room, Karin stumbled to her slipper-clad feet and raised her hands over her head, rotating her upper torso. Medium height, she looked as if she'd once had a pleasant roundness. Ten years of short rations in Ushuaia had yielded the same gauntness they all sported. A pair of fuzzy green sweats hung low on her hips, and she'd stripped out of her jacket to a silver long-underwear top.

"I sat for way too long," she muttered. "I'm taking a break. Anyone feel like coffee?"

Recco crossed to where the wolf Shifter stood, not wanting to disturb Daide's concentration. "Coffee would be great," he said. "Daide likes tea."

"Yes. I remember. While I'm gone, I'll hunt Ketha down. No idea what's taking her so long. All she was going to do was see if Zoe had any ideas to shed light on those odd prokaryote patterns."

"Black with two sugars," Daide called without looking up. "None of that chai crap for me."

"Got it." She made a smothered snorting sound. "Who knows? I might have a future as a waitress if the world ever sets itself to rights." Karin's lined face split into a warm smile. White hair fell in curls to waist level, and her copper eyes radiated a keen intelligence. Schooled in traditional Western medicine as well as magical interventions, not much rattled her.

"Back in half an hour." She walked purposefully through the open doorway.

Recco returned to Daide. "Well?"

Daide straightened. When he angled his head to look at Recco, his forehead was drawn into a mass of confused wrinkles. "The dye colors are changing. Did you add something to the original stains?"

"Nope." Recco shook his head.

"The structure is clearer than it was before. I didn't realize prokaryotes could even do this."

"You mean join together to form something more complex than a single-celled organism?"

"Yeah. It's kind of what I guess I mean." Daide pushed heavily upright. "Maybe Karin is onto something, and we could all stand a break. Granted, my science is rusty, but none of this makes a whole lot of sense."

Recco shrugged. "Nothing has since that fucker, Raphael, turned us into Vampires. Why should this be any different?"

Daide narrowed his eyes. "You asked me to look through this scope for a reason. Was it because the colors were different?"

"No. I could have sworn the sample moved. Twice." Recco sucked in a tight breath and waited for Daide to ask what he'd been smoking.

"Moved, how?" Daide's question was carefully neutral.

Recco offered him points for not laughing his head off—or running out of the room to escape what had to feel like a plunge into madness.

"You know"—Recco spun one hand in a small circle—"rippled from side to side. Kind of like you'd expect from a live tissue sample."

"Might explain the colors changing."

Recco fell back a pace as understanding drove a wedge into his midsection, forcing breath from his lungs. "You think it's alive."

"Pretty much has to be. Dead things don't move. And if it's turning into something, it would absorb the stain differentially. Ergo, the color shift." Daide dusted his hands together. "Mystery solved."

"For some reason, it doesn't make me feel any better." Recco sifted his fingers through his hair. It fell past his shoulders and had escaped the rubber band he'd tied it back with.

Ketha walked through the open door. "What doesn't make you feel any better?" she inquired brightly, followed by, "Where's Karin?"

"That's the easy question," Daide replied. "She's getting coffee and looking for you."

"What's stuck in my craw is the cell cluster seems to be... changing," Recco muttered.

"Changing how?" Ketha asked.

"Reproducing. Growing. However you want to label it. Even the stained portions aren't the same."

Instead of asking more questions, Ketha crossed the room to the microscope she'd been using. It was one of the ones they'd taken from the lab in Grytviken and was far more sophisticated than their other instruments. Bending, she gazed through the eyepieces, but not for very long.

"This slide has changed too. Not much more than it was doing before I left, though."

Recco hunted for words that wouldn't be offensive. "The alteration doesn't seem to bother you. Why not?"

"Magic is afoot here. I'm more used to it than you are, and I'm curious to see what we end up with." She angled her head to one side and looked from Recco to Daide. "Brace yourselves. The plot thickens. Something is singing to Zoe."

"What do you mean, singing? Is she all right?" The words escaped before Recco could stop them. He cared about Zoe. A lot. So far, they hadn't done much more than share coffee and conversation, but worry for the red-haired coyote Shifter filled him with a crawling sensation. The same sense of creeping doom that had snuck in when the clump of cells slithered beneath his eyepieces.

Ketha quirked a dark brow and sent a pointed look Recco's way. "She's fine. Researching mythological creatures in her cabin if you want to check for yourself."

Heat rose from Recco's chest, and he trotted back to his workstation before Ketha picked up on the flush. It had to have added a tint to his coppery skin. "I'm going to make up a few fresh slides."

"I'll do it," Daide said.

"Great. You make slides, and I'll hunt down Karin. She could probably use a hand if she's bringing back drinks for all of us." Ketha moved briskly toward the door.

"Wait." Recco followed her. "Do you see a connection between whatever is happening with the prokaryotes and the music Zoe is hearing?"

Ketha adopted a thoughtful expression. "I floated that with Zoe. It's a stretch, which is the same thing she said. Way things have been going, we can't afford not to turn every single rock over. Back soon, and then we can kick this around some more." She hustled out the door.

"What are you thinking, *amigo?*" Daide asked.

"The truth?"

"Of course. Otherwise there's no reason to answer."

"I'd like to scoop up every cell of what we salvaged from the deck and chuck the entire mess into the ocean."

"How would it help?" Daide walked closer, his dark gaze never leaving Recco's face.

"Separation. At least whatever is morphing into God only knows what won't be on this ship."

"Remember the albino fur seal pup?"

Daide's question came out of left field, and Recco blinked

stupidly as he shifted gears. "Of course, I remember. It was a long time ago."

"The mother rejected it," Daide went on. "Rightly so, because it had almost no chance of survival. Its color would have made it a target for every predator in the waters around Ushuaia."

Recco pressed his lips into a thin line. "You told me I was a fool when I took it and fed it and raised it. Once it got to be a few months old, I introduced it to the sea." He swallowed hard. "Damn thing didn't last two days before a leopard seal ate it."

Daide turned his hands palms upward. "I rest my case."

"I'm not seeing the connection."

"You can't circumvent nature. Tossing the samples won't change the outcome. It's impossible for us to make certain we've obliterated every single cell. Some will remain inside the freezer—and in this lab. Hell, for all I know, some will drill back through the ship's hull." Daide shook his head. "We're in the middle of something, and it has to play itself out."

"How can you be so sure?"

"I have no idea, but I am. Before you go see how Zoe is doing"—Daide winked broadly—"can I switch topics?"

"Sure." Recco ignored the visiting Zoe suggestion. "What's up?"

"Did Viktor talk with you about training us to do more of the navigation?"

"No, Juan did, and I thought it was an excellent idea."

Daide angled his gaze to the clock sitting high on one wall. "We're supposed to be on the bridge at sixteen hundred."

"Not a problem. I'll be there. It's a couple of hours from now."

A harsh, grinding noise reverberated in the pit of Recco's guts. "Fuck. More pack ice."

The deck canted from port to starboard and back, its movement more pronounced.

"Listen up." Viktor's voice crackled over the PA system. "We're headed closer inland to ride out this storm. My plan is to tuck *Arkady* in between Siple Island and the continent. There used to be a year-round ice shelf there, so it's a risk, but one I'm willing to take."

"Not thinking you'll need survival gear," Juan cut in. "Put your outside clothing on and your pack boots and life vest, anyway. Don't forget warm hats and your mitts. Tuck anything you can't live without in your pockets. We'll let you know when you don't need them any longer."

"Move to the bridge as soon as you're dressed," Viktor added. "So we'll have everyone in one spot."

Recco hurried back to the microscope he'd been using and tucked it into its padded case. Daide did the same with the other three instruments. Opening the storage closet, he set them inside.

"See you on the bridge," Daide said. "In full regalia."

"No kidding. Hope they have a few windows open, or we'll bake in there."

"Better than being dead." Daide loped through the door and vaulted up the nearby stairwell with Recco on his heels.

Karin met them partway down. "The microscopes—?" she began.

"We took care of them," Daide reassured her. "Better get duded up."

Karin chuckled. "Science first. Safety second." Turning, she trudged back up the risers.

"No." Daide's tone was somber. "If you put safety second, you might not be around to keep the science part going."

Recco turned down a side corridor that led to his cabin. He dressed fast, since everything hung on hooks, and he'd layered up and down so many times, it had become second nature. He started for the bridge and then detoured, heading for Zoe's cabin. It was probably ridiculous since she had to be dressed and gone, but he knocked on her door anyway.

"Come in," she called.

Recco pushed the door open, awkward with his mitten-clad hands.

Zoe sat at her desk surrounded by sheets of paper. Closely

written script punctuated with drawings covered them. Her eyes widened. "Why are you dressed for the Zodiacs?"

"Didn't you hear Viktor and Juan over the PA system?"

"Nay. I had it turned off so I could concentrate." She closed her teeth over her lower lip. "The sea's been getting rougher—"

Zoe leapt to her feet, eyes wide with apprehension. She was tall and thin like the rest of them. No one had survived the Cataclysm years with any meat on their bones.

"Awk. Christ." Her soft brogue rolled over him. "Sure and we're not sinking, are we? Wouldn't there have been warning horns or something?"

He hustled toward her. The ship lurched, and the door slammed shut behind him. "No. We're sheltering in the lee of some island. They want us dressed for outside in case…"

"We hit submerged ice or rocks or a berg." She saved him the trouble of soft-pedaling the truth and grabbed clothing off her bed, dressing fast. "Where are we assembling?"

"Bridge. Where else?" He smiled. No matter how dangerous things were, being in the same space with Zoe made his heart light. "Bet you were one of those who turned your cell phone off too."

"Busted. All the time. It was such an annoying little bugger." She zipped into her parka and stuffed her feet into Pac boots. "It's a relief we're meeting on the bridge."

"Why?"

"If things were really bad, they'd have us wait at the gangway to load into the rafts. Could you gather up my worksheets and stuff them into a drawer, so they don't end up scattered to hell and back?"

He scooped the papers into a pile, opened a side drawer, and dropped them inside. "Looks like a lot of work," he ventured while she tucked her bright curls beneath a woolen cap.

She trained her soft, brown eyes on him. "Not so bad once I got rolling. I'm one of those with an eidetic memory. Once I hit the right spot in my brain, material automatically downloads."

Recco thought about the endless hours he'd spent memorizing anatomy and physiology from dozens of species. "You're lucky."

She nodded. "Aye. I know. I'm ready."

Another long, growling howl filled the air as the hull scraped against something. "Crap. That didn't sound good." A worried look pinched the edges of her eyes into pinwheels.

"Not as bad as you think." Recco tried to project a confidence he wasn't certain of. "The hull has two layers, so you get a reverberating effect when anything hits the outer portion. Come on." He extended a hand, and she grasped it, awkward with her padded mitts.

Three flights later, they emerged on Deck Six. Climbing the stairs had required both hands as they clutched railings spanning every stairwell and corridor on the ship. He'd kept Zoe in front of him so he could catch her in case she slipped.

"Doing okay?" he asked once they cleared the last of the stairs.

"Mostly grateful I got over being seasick." She opened the door leading into the bridge, and he followed her through.

It looked as if they were the last to arrive.

Aura hastened to Zoe. "Where were you? I was very close to going after you." With her blonde hair, green eyes, and sharp cheekbones, she projected a simple elegance that transcended the thick, nondescript clothing.

Zoe tossed her hood back. "I had the PA system turned off. Sorry."

While Aura hugged Zoe, clucking over her, Recco trotted to the windows. Hail, sleet, rain, and snow took turns pounding the glass. The windows were steamy on this side. Even if they hadn't been, visibility was almost zero.

He moved to where Viktor and Juan huddled over the wheel. "Tell me to get lost if you need to concentrate, but how the hell can you tell where we're going?"

"Combination of luck and skill, mate." Viktor grinned; it didn't reach his eyes.

Boris d'Costa, one of the passengers they'd picked up on their ill-fated stop on King George Island, moved away from the back of the bridge. Average height, and far too thin, he had long, tangled black hair, a scraggly beard, and deep-set dark eyes. "If we hold to this heading," he said, "we should make the strait with a cushion on both sides."

"Thanks." Viktor nodded brusquely. Tall, broad-shouldered, and green-eyed with tawny hair, he would have cut an impressive figure in any setting. Right now, he looked like one of the ancient Vikings sailing his boat into the teeth of a roaring storm.

Juan tossed a puffy, orange coat at Viktor. "Put this on, *amigo*." Built similarly to Viktor, Juan was very blonde with shrewd hazel eyes. Both men's cheeks were covered with stubble.

"What? Don't fancy saving me from drowning again?" Viktor stuffed his arms into the survival coat.

"I'm not going to bother answering you." Juan tapped Boris's shoulder. "Let's go over those calculations one more time. I want to make certain we didn't screw this up."

"What you mean"—Boris inclined his head—"is you want to make double damn sure I followed your directions."

"Yeah. That too. *Andale, amigo*."

The two of them walked to the chart table, heads bent in conversation.

"Anything I can do?" Recco asked Viktor.

"Since you mentioned it. Here." Viktor pulled a two-way radio from a cabinet built into the wall behind him. "Take this, go outside, and tell me if we're on a collision course with anything."

Recco took the radio, checking its operation. "Don't you have instruments that do the same thing?"

"You bet, but I'm old-fashioned. You're my insurance policy."

"Presuming I can see my hand in front of my face." Recco turned to go.

"Take these with you, mate. They'll help." Viktor dragged a set of goggles from the same place he'd gotten the radios. "Check in with me once you're in position, and then every few minutes."

Recco met Viktor's direct green gaze. "Even if I see something, will you have enough time to institute corrective measures."

Viktor shrugged. "Maybe. I've only lost one ship. Not planning to sink another. Now, get moving, or I'll assign the task to someone else."

Zoe joined Recco when he was halfway out the door. "I heard most of your conversation. Would you like some help?"

Her willingness to abandon the warmth of the bridge for the raging storm touched him to the bottom of his soul. "You don't have to—" he began.

"I know, but I want to. Besides, two of us have a better chance of keeping the ship safe, and I can sense magical forces better than you." She dangled goggles in front of him. "I came prepared."

"I have a feeling prepared is your middle name." He kicked his hood back far enough to position the goggles and snugged the parka around his head once more.

"Busted again." Zoe mirrored his actions with her goggles. "I swear, you must have a spy who's been watching me and reporting back to you. Wow. The wind is romping."

Recco draped an arm around her shoulders, stabilizing her as they moved outside on one of two side decks that wrapped around the bridge. He keyed the mike to let Viktor know he was in position. It chirped as Viktor did the same from inside.

The amber-tinted goggles did help, making it possible to see something beyond a gray cloud bank. *Arkady* nosed forward exceedingly slowly. Waves slapped the ship from both sides, boiling around them. The air was thick with cold salty spray. Ice floes surrounded them, banging against the hull.

"Must be Siple Island over there." Zoe pointed at a land mass rising out of the mist.

Recco stared ahead, willing his eyes to greater sharpness. "Never mind the island. The ice dead ahead is solid, isn't it?"

Zoe leaned into him and bent forward. "Not quite solid."

"Yes. I see the same opening." Recco keyed his mike and held the radio directly in front of his mouth so the howling wind wouldn't drown out his words.

"Ice. We need to move maybe five degrees toward the continent."

"Damn it. I'll be right there. I'll angle to portside first, and then I need to see for myself."

Recco opened his mouth to tell Viktor to hurry; the whining shriek of metal hitting ice obliterated his words.

He and Zoe were thrown forward and then back. Somehow, he kept hold of her and the radio.

Viktor lurched outside, cursing in German. "Lucky for us, global warming weakened the ice shelf, or I'd never have tried this. Hang onto something," he yelled at Recco and Zoe. "It's going to get rough cutting through it."

Recco had a hard time imagining it getting much rougher, but he kept his thoughts to himself. Zoe's face—what little he could see of it—had turned into a rictus of fear. She didn't escape into the bridge, though.

"You've got guts, I'll give you that." He aimed his words near her ear.

"Och, aye," was followed by a spate of Gaelic.

"What'd you just say?"

"Ye doona want to know. Thank all the bluidy fecking saints we're still moving. I've read about boats getting stuck in pack ice."

Recco had too, and none of it was pretty. "Come on," he urged. "Let's count off landmarks as we pass them. You go first."

She tilted her chin at a defiant angle and pointed with a mittened hand. "The huge boulder."

"Good call."

"Your turn."

"Come on, woman. Give me a break. I can't see shit."

The radio crackled. "Talk with me, mate," Viktor urged. "It's why you're out there."

"No obstacles in our immediate path," Recco reported. "We're maybe halfway into the ice."

"Keep talking," Viktor urged. "The depth sounder only goes so far, and it only paints the area beneath the hull."

Zoe shot a pointed glance his way. Apparently, Viktor's explanation didn't set well.

Recco adopted what he hoped was a reassuring expression. "Hey. There's your boulder. I call the next one. The black obelisk rising out of the mist."

"Did you feel that?" she asked in a strained voice.

Her question caught him off guard. Did she think he was stupid? "Of course I feel the ice we're moving through."

"Not what I meant. Something's out there, and it has nothing to do with ice and water. Not directly, anyway."

Understanding sank in, and his gut tightened. Her bitter-fruit expression hadn't had anything to do with Viktor's comments. "Do you know what it is?"

"Nay. I used telepathy to sound an alarm. Between all of us, mayhap we can figure things out afore whatever is lurking blows up in our face like the bastard mage who killed Rowana back on King George Island."

3

SAIL ON BY

Zoe wanted to slap her hands over her ears. The infernal music was back, but it came from inside her head, so blocking her ears wouldn't help. Ice grated, harsh and strident. It made a hell of a racket but didn't come close to drowning out the discordant notes.

"Does this have something to do with the music Ketha mentioned?" Recco trained worried dark eyes on her face.

"Sure and she shouldn't have told you about it."

The radio crackled to life. Before Viktor could say anything, Recco beat him to the punch. "Almost through the ice shelf, *amigo*."

"Are we past the narrowest waters?"

Zoe peered through the murk, grateful for the goggle's green-tinted lenses. "Looks like it." She angled her mouth near the radio.

"I'm going to drop anchor in about five hundred yards." The radio crackled once again and quieted.

Between the storm that didn't seem much better here than it had on the open ocean side of Siple Island and the music, Zoe longed for a good, stiff belt of whiskey, followed by enough additional shots to make everything fade into an alcoholic haze. She wouldn't actually blitz herself into oblivion. Not now, but she craved a break. From everything. She was an academic, for chrissakes. Not a bloody warrior queen.

The door to the bridge whooshed open, slamming against its stops. Ketha, Karin, and Aura crowded onto the small platform. Recco moved aside to give the women room to stand next to one another and wrestled the door back into place.

Zoe wanted him standing next to her, the comforting bulk of his body shielding hers. It was pure indulgence; she had work to do. Work that had nothing to do with what may well be a one-sided attraction. Recco enjoyed her company. She was certain of that, but not of his reasons. For all she knew, she might remind him of a kid sister or a favorite female cousin.

A shock wave buffeted her as the women joined their magic.

Ketha's eyes—about the only visible part of her face—rounded. "Holy shit. You weren't kidding about the kid and his keyboard."

"Might be a she." Zoe tried for humor but didn't get very far.

"What do you mean, kid? Or keyboard, for that fact?" Karin asked. She skewered Zoe with her copper eyes. "Do you know where the cacophony is coming from?"

Zoe shook her head. "Nay, and 'tis way worse."

"Worse than what?" Karin pressed. "Must mean this isn't new. Why didn't you mention it before?"

"Same thing I asked," Ketha said in a dour tone.

"Not important." Aura wrapped a protective arm around Zoe. "Let's see if we can track where it's coming from."

"Aye. You can all flog me later," Aura muttered. Wind whipped the words away before anyone could have heard them. She opened herself as far as she could to the other women's magic, merging, blending, weaving strands together. The concentration helped. She imagined the Shifters' magic forming a shield between her and a headlong plunge into madness.

A shudder racked her, followed by another. Until the thought formed, she hadn't realized how frightened she'd been the music presaged a descent into a place where her wits would desert her. Permanently.

The music stuttered, almost as if it sensed it faced more than her. Who knew? Maybe it did. The discordant notes engendered an eerie sensation; she laid it aside and dug deep. Whatever this thing that had dogged her was, now was the time to force its hand.

So long as it doesna rear up from behind some psychic veil to smother us.

"Stop it." Her coyote's voice rang with censure.

Zoe choked back a tart reply. Her bond animal was correct to condemn her. So were Ketha and Karin. She should have—

A piercing squeal followed by a series of thumps halted her descent into self-pity.

The anchor chain.

When she peered over the edge of the hanging balcony, she saw two people hunched over the anchor's housing three decks below. Bundled as they were, it was impossible to determine who'd drawn the short straw.

"I don't get it," Aura muttered. "The music's coming from two separate places."

"No," Ketha corrected her. "Three. Below the hull, from inside the ship, but several decks down, and from there." Raising a mittened hand, she pointed at the Antarctic mainland, swathed in ice and gray misty clouds.

"I don't think so," Karin said. "The primary source is out there." She jerked her chin at Antarctica's land mass. "The rest is reflection meant to confuse us."

Zoe focused on glaciers cutting into the thick ice sheet at intervals. They might have been beautiful, if she'd been able to see the colors in the ancient ice. The song's pitch and cadence altered abruptly. No longer angry noise, it transformed into a fetching melody. One Odysseus might have lashed himself to the mast to avoid as he skirted the Sirens' island.

Recco angled his head to one side. "Is this what you've been hearing?" he asked Zoe.

She opened her mouth to tell him not exactly, except words gushed from him before she could figure out how to explain what seemed impossible.

"If it's the same thing"—his voice vibrated with awe—"it's beautiful. We have to—"

"Oh no, we don't," Zoe spoke up, frightened to her bones for Recco. She wanted to break free of the line she and the other women had formed but didn't dare. Their magic was stronger together, and the current version of liquid notes was far more lethal than its forerunner had been.

Sweet. Seductive. Mysterious. Alluring… Zoe shut off the flow of her thoughts before she wrenched free and dove over the rail to merge with the beauty vibrating around her.

"Go inside." Karin's voice was laced with compulsion and directed at Recco. "Make sure the other men don't pay any attention to the music."

"Why?" Recco smiled softly, his chiseled lips parting in a hard-to-resist expression. "I'm a vet, remember? I understand how to communicate with things that can't talk. Whatever this is, it's approachable. I'd know if it meant us harm."

"Inside. Now," Karin echoed, upping the ante on her compulsion spell.

Recco turned and unlatched the door, sliding through.

"Jesus." Karin blew air through her clenched teeth. "For a minute there, I didn't think he'd obey me, and I funneled enough magic into my spell to fell an ox."

"Just because he went inside doesn't mean he'll stay there," Zoe muttered.

"Oh, he'll remain for a while. At least until my magic lets go of him," Karin retorted. "Meanwhile, we have a tiny window and a whole crapload of things to figure out."

"Only one creature has such an effect, but how could Sirens be here?" Aura demanded, her voice rough.

"Exactly what I was wondering." Zoe bit off the words to keep from sinking under the spell of the music. It sounded like Beethoven, or maybe Brahms, absorbing, soothing. All she had to do was let down her guard, and all would be well. The music would wrap around them, take care of them, make sure they found shelter…

Ketha tightened her hand around Zoe's upper arm hard enough to hurt. "You're not helping."

"Sorry." Zoe shook herself from head to toe to regain focus.

"This…thing. It wants something from us," Karin said.

"Yeah, like our humanity." Ketha curled her lips into a snarl, baring her teeth in a gesture reminiscent of her wolf.

Zoe ground her teeth together to keep them from chattering. The implications of what was unfolding froze her to the marrow of her soul. "The music, it didn't change until we got here. Must mean there's a reason for us to go ashore."

"Where, ashore?" Aura demanded. "The island or the mainland?"

"I'd vote for the mainland, although I couldn't tell you exactly why. Not that it matters. Viktor and Juan will never go for it," Ketha said.

Zoe wasn't so sure about that. Recco yearned for a face-to-face with the music's source. Longing had streamed from him—until Karin cloaked him in her spell. The men aside, Zoe was having a hell of a time not giving in to the music's charisma. Was it worse for the men? She dug the Siren myth out of her memory.

Dangerous creatures, they lured sailors into shipwrecks along Greece's rocky shorelines. No one agreed exactly which islands they inhabited, but no one disputed their existence. Sirens in myth were always half female, combined with feathers and avian lower bodies. They played a variety of musical instruments, the lyre being favored. When a man heard their song, he had to follow the music. Once it happened, he was lost—

"One of those maps on the wall at the back of the bridge marks the location of all the research stations down here," Aura said. "I say we go inside and study it. If there was a settlement nearby, maybe something important is there. Something we can't afford to overlook."

"And I say we sail on by," Ketha countered. "Worked for Odysseus."

"I don't know about visiting any more outposts," Karin broke in. "The last places we've stopped have all turned into disasters." Her tone grew fierce. "We lost Rowana. I do not want to sit over another of your bodies and bid your bond animal farewell."

"None of us want that," Zoe agreed. She straightened her back. Her body had been bent like a bow angled toward where the music was strongest. The tune shifted to something lively like Grieg. No less compelling, though.

"Even if we go ashore, what will we find?" Aura demanded. "A modern-day version of the Pied Piper of Hamblin playing a flute in an ice cave?"

"If 'tis flutes you're after, I vote for Pan." Zoe broke away from Ketha and Aura and tugged the door open. The heat of the bridge stole her breath but jostled her brain back into action.

She waited until the other women were inside and made a grab for Ketha's arm. "Wait a minute. You wanted me to come up with mythical creatures, obscure combinations—"

Ketha spun one hand in a "get on with it" gesture and unzipped her parka with the other.

"Sirens. Of course." Karin's voice cut like a knife before Zoe could get any words out. "They were women and birds."

"Precisely," Zoe said. "'Twas what I was about to point out."

Shock twisted Ketha's face into uneven planes. "Surely you're not suggesting the tissue samples we've been looking at come from Sirens?"

Zoe shrugged. "I have no idea. Cellular identification is your bailiwick, sweetie."

Aura clapped her gloved hands together. "The map. Let's look at it first." She moved briskly past the small anteroom into the bridge. "Crap! Goddammit!"

Zoe hurried forward. Viktor stood at the wheel like a man transfixed, the sole inhabitant of the ship's command center. Recco, Daide, and Juan weren't anywhere to be seen. Neither were the seven other women. Or the small group they'd picked up from Arctowski research station.

Ketha crossed the space in a few strides. She pried Viktor's hands off the wheel and magic flashed, turning the air around them blue-white.

"Come on, Vik." Ketha grasped his shoulders and shook him. He continued to stare straight ahead. She whipped back a hand and slapped him hard enough to leave a red mark on his cheek.

A shudder racked him, and he clasped Ketha's gloved hands. "You're dressed for outside. Why?"

"Because you sent some of us out there to lay eyes on the strait. Don't you remember?"

He squinched his green eyes shut, and then opened them, forehead creasing into worried lines. "Yeah. Now I hear you say it, I do." He looked around the bridge. "Where is everyone?"

Zoe, Karin, and Aura had closed on them. "I suspect they've launched a Zodiac," Aura said. "We have to take the other one and follow them."

"A Zodiac? Nah. Someone has to remain with the ship." He dragged a hand down his face, distorting his features. "Why do I feel like I'm coming off a two-week drunk?"

Zoe scanned him with magic. Relief coursed through her. At least the ones who'd left hadn't spelled him into zombie-land, which left the music's source as the most likely culprit. "Because the thing making the music wanted you right where you're standing."

A growl emerged from Ketha, followed by another, and she closed a protective arm around her husband.

"What music?" Viktor frowned. "I thought I might have heard something, but it was gone so fast, I was certain I was mistaken."

"Thank the goddess, it doesn't want you." Ketha looked as if she'd tear anything threatening the man she loved from stem to stern and feed the bits into a fire.

Viktor shook loose from her grasp. "What doesn't want me?" He snapped his fingers under her nose. "If I'm going to launch the other raft, I need to know what's going on."

Zoe sucked in a jagged breath and felt like she'd swallowed glass shards. "The quick and dirty version is I've heard this bizarre music since we defeated the Cataclysm. It wasn't all that annoying—or frequent—in Ushuaia, nor anywhere on this voyage until a few days ago. Then it was discordant, blaring, jangling. Hard to push aside. So I was grateful it didn't bother me verra often."

She stopped to take another breath. "Once we got here, to this stretch of water between the continent and Siple Island, things changed. Suddenly, the noise shifted to music."

"We think it's Sirens. Or something related to them," Karin said.

"Sirens?" Viktor raked a hand through his hair. "Like in Greek mythology? The ones who promise knowledge and your every dream fulfilled—just before your ship pitches up on rocks?"

"Same ones," Ketha concurred.

Viktor skinned his lips back from his teeth. "Maybe it's me they're after. I did lose a ship to rocks at the front end of the Cataclysm. No music, though. Not much fanfare. Only a storm straight out of Hell."

"If they wanted you, we wouldn't have found you here at the wheel," Karin said, sounding grim.

"Anyway," Zoe went on. "Ketha came to me a couple of hours ago wanting archaeological information about creatures straight out of myth. Sirens fit the bill since they're women, and birds too."

Viktor angled his gaze at his wife. "I thought you were studying tissue samples from those things we killed on the deck. The weird animal mixes conjured up by the wizard—or whatever he was—from Arctowski."

"I was."

"I'm not seeing a connection between them and Sirens, but it doesn't matter. If the others really left the ship, we have to follow them before whatever lured them draws them beyond where we can bring them back."

A tortured moan tore from Aura. "Juan. He has such a good heart—"

"And a hell of a lot of strength," Viktor interrupted. "Get those layers zipped up and I'll meet you at the gangway if the other raft is gone. If it's not, we need to turn the ship inside out hunting for everybody."

"Won't be a problem. They're not here." Aura's voice was brittle with anxiety. "I checked with magic a moment ago." She pounded one mitt into the other. "I swear, if anything harmed Juan, I'll make it sorry it was ever born or hatched or transmogrified."

"Haven't heard that word in a while." Karin shot a pointed look at Aura.

Viktor zipped his flotation coat to his chin and grabbed a hat and mittens from a small, open cabinet behind him. "Gangway. Five minutes tops." He bolted out of the bridge.

"Sometimes I'm glad he spent those years as a Vampire," Ketha mumbled.

"Why would you say such a thing?" Zoe jumped in to defend Viktor.

"It makes all this supernatural crap an easier sell." Ketha latched her parka together and hustled toward the door at the back of the bridge.

Zoe glanced at the glowing instrumentation. All the dials and gauges looked like so much gibberish to her. They'd dropped anchor, and presumably Viktor would have made any needed alterations.

"Get moving," her coyote prodded, an undercurrent of something she couldn't interpret in its voice.

She hastened after Ketha, Karin, and Aura. *"Do you know what's doing this?"* she asked her bondmate. *"Is it truly Sirens behind the music? We're a long way from Greece."*

The coyote hesitated long enough, she figured it was one of those questions it wasn't going to answer. Risers flashed by beneath her feet. The ship still canted from side to side as waves slapped its hull, so she grabbed the handrails on both sides. Now wasn't a good time to trip and add an injury to all their other problems.

"I'm not certain. Its magic is strong. More potent than the sorcerer we fought during the last skirmish."

Zoe's stomach twisted into a hot, painful knot. The bastard who'd first boarded their ship and then blown up a research station, trapping Rowana and several others in a magical hell, had been plenty powerful.

"Zoe! Move it!" blasted her from below, and she realized she'd come to a stop halfway between Decks Four and Three.

She hurtled downward, muttering apologies, and pushed through the door Karin was hanging onto.

"Is the music still hammering you?" Karin's question held sharp edges.

A sinking feeling joined all Zoe's other misgivings. "No," she said dully. "I can't hear it anymore, but then I wasn't paying attention until you asked me." She squeezed her eyes shut for a moment. They felt hot, gritty, and tired. As if she hadn't slept in weeks. "Where did it go? It can't be gone."

Karin's normally kind expression twisted into something harsh and feral. "No. It only means it's busy. The song did its job. Over a dozen of us raced to its summons. It doesn't need us anymore." She hesitated. "I'd venture to guess we were spared because we were the ones whose magic could have fought against it."

Bile splashed the back of Zoe's throat. She swallowed, and it burned going down. "By that token, 'twill will give us hell if we try to land a raft."

Karin's copper gaze turned to burnished amber, reminiscent of her wolf's eyes. "You're quick, woman. It's one of the things I've always appreciated about you."

They reached the gangway. Ketha and Aura were already at the bottom, and the raft with Viktor manning it was pulling into view. The ocean heaved in great gray waves washing over the gangway's platform. It creaked and swayed alarmingly.

Viktor tossed a rope to Ketha, who wrapped it around a cleat.

"Not so tight," Viktor yelled, and Ketha made adjustments. Viktor motioned, and she and Aura tumbled into the raft as it moved up and down in the swells. Seas like this had nearly been the death of Viktor. His raft had flipped, and he hadn't been wearing a life vest in rough waters. Magic had been afoot then. Magic that had whispered in his ear, telling him to swim toward the ocean bottom.

Magic was afoot, now too. Dark, fell power full of greed.

Zoe did her best to clear her mind of negativity and followed Karin down the ladder. A Karin muttering in Gaelic as she timed her leap into the raft.

"Hurry," Viktor shouted at Zoe. "Sea's getting worse."

Worse was one word for it. The one she would have chosen was impossible. She'd never been the best of sailors, and her chest constricted with fear as she watched the raft bob four feet above her head before it plunged into a trough.

"We can do this," the coyote said. *"We have to. Turn things over to me."*

Zoe could barely breathe around the thick place in her throat. She was shaking so hard, it was an ordeal to remain on the platform, but she didn't think her legs would carry her back into the ship, either.

"Give me your body," the coyote shrieked. *"Now."*

Certain death was imminent, that, life jacket or no, she'd sink beneath the frigid waters of the Antarctic Ocean, Zoe relinquished her control over her human form. They wouldn't be shifting, but her bond animal would be the one pulling the puppet strings that determined what happened next. It was a leap of faith, but she trusted her coyote. Loved it beyond measure.

Her body flew through the air and landed hard in several inches of water on the bottom of the Zodiac. Karin grabbed her by the arm and pulled her onto a pontoon. "Finally. I thought you'd never get the nerve to leave the platform."

"I didn't. It was my coyote."

"Thank it for me," Karin said and focused her next words on all of them. "Listen up. Whatever has the others in thrall will fight us every step of the way. I'm going to build a ward. Funnel your magic in and join mine. No matter what, keep power flowing. We can worry about recharging our batteries later."

"If there is a later," Ketha muttered.

Zoe wished she hadn't heard Ketha. *"Thank you,"* she told her bond animal.

"Welcome. Our magic will make the difference between success and failure. We couldn't remain on the ship."

More bile erupted from her rebellious stomach. Zoe ignored it and threaded magic outward, doing her damnedest to make a bulletproof weave with the other Shifters.

Grim-faced, Viktor edged the raft toward shore.

Magic bubbled around them and forged a path through the turbulent waves, making the going not much easier but at least doable. Zoe narrowed her focus to her part of their mutual spell. If she thought about what lay ahead, fear would rise up and choke her. As it was, each breath was a pitched battle.

"You can do this," the coyote spoke up. *"Believe in yourself. You come from Irish warrior stock."*

"Och, 'twas centuries ago."

"Doesn't matter. Your blood kin are in there. Channel their energies."

4

SING A SONG OF...

Recco blinked stupidly at the interior of the bridge. How the hell had he ended up here? Zoe was still out on the quarterdeck. She needed him. He spun, intent on returning outside until he remembered Ketha and the others were there. Their combination of magics far outstripped whatever he could offer with his neophyte skills.

Besides, they'd sent him away. He drew his brows together, trying to remember. His mind felt sluggish. As if he'd been drugged. Had Zoe chivvied him back inside? Or had it been one of the other Shifters? If it was Zoe, it didn't bode well. Meant she saw him as weak and ineffectual—

The fog crowding his brain exploded, and all thoughts of Zoe fled. The enticing music was back. He glanced around the bridge. Viktor stood in his usual place at the wheel, thousand-yard stare in place. He often looked like that, so Recco didn't pay it much heed.

Juan beckoned to him from near the door; Recco hustled to his side. "What's going on? You do hear the music, don't you?"

"*Si, amigo.*" The sharp planes of Juan's squared-off jaw and chiseled cheeks split into a blissful smile, almost as if one of the gods had blessed him with his spirit.

Juan held the door, and Daide pushed past, along with Boris, Ted, and Sasha—refugees from Arctowski—and all the women. Most of the women were Shifters, but two were human. They'd come from the Polish research station.

"Go on. Follow them. It will be fine." Juan was still smiling like one of the faithful on his way to holy communion.

"Why? Where are we going?"

"To meet whomever summoned us." Juan gave him a gentle push, and Recco slithered through the open doorway, feeling like he was sleepwalking. It seemed right in some ways, and very wrong in others.

"Isn't Viktor coming?" Recco asked.

"Nah. I tried. He can't hear me."

Recco knew he was forgetting something. Whatever it was, the overlooked item hovered at the edge of his consciousness—provocative, enticing—but he couldn't get a grip on it. When he tried harder, something sharp stabbed him between the eyes. The discomfort was so real, he flinched and swatted the air, shocked to find it devoid of pointed objects like knives or ice picks.

What the hell had jabbed him?

Juan dropped a hand on his shoulder, propelling him toward the stairs. "I'm going to launch a raft. Wait with the others at the gangway."

Recco wanted to ask something. Recognized it was important to dig deeper and not leap into an unknown intent on claiming them. Words jammed together deep in his throat, strangling him. He clawed at the neckline of his parka in an attempt to get more air.

Oblivious, Juan swept past him, his Arctic Pac boots making slapping sounds on the linoleum-covered stairs. Recco followed more slowly. It would take time for Juan to get the raft into the sling affair that lowered it into the water. A flash of memory appeared and was gone, but not before Recco identified the ice sheet the ship had plowed through. Had they truly moved beyond it into open water? If they had, why not slog down the gangway and jump onto the ice?

Probably lots of reasons. Who knows how thick it is. On the other hand, the raft can't sail through ice—

The music made his spirit soar. He felt purified, and confused. Why was a simple exercise in inductive logic so hard? He stopped at the landing for Deck Four and rubbed his mitten-clad hands down his face. The rough fabric hurt, but it also yielded a brief flash of clarity. The music might be beautiful. It was also why he couldn't think.

He'd reacted to it when he was outside with the women. It was when they'd sent him packing. They must've viewed the melody as a threat, and they'd been trying to protect him. It made him feel about three inches tall. He was a man, goddammit. Men took care of women. Not the other way around.

Annoyance bit deep. Fine. They'd banished him. He'd prove them wrong, by God. He'd figure out what the fuck was going on with whoever was behind the tantalizing song. Driven by a combination of humiliation he hadn't been deemed competent enough to remain with Zoe and the others and a need to demonstrate he was better than they believed, he loped to the gangway.

A long, low laugh bubbled through him, counterpart to the music. Juan ground his jaws together. Had he been played by a skilled puppeteer manipulating marionette strings in the background?

Before he could dissect the thought, it crumbled to nothingness. He made a grab for it; his mind went blank, lulled by trilling notes. The others were climbing down the gangway, on their way to Juan and the Zodiac. A quick glance downward to check for ice made his skin crawl. Not only was the area around *Arkady* clear, the seas had quieted. Alarmingly so. How could the waves have altered from a raging inferno to one-foot swells in less than half an hour? Weather patterns changed fast here, but this was ridiculous.

"Bondmate!" thundered through his skull.

"No need to shout. I never went anywhere."

"Yes. You did. I've been trying to break through since you entered the bridge. Pay attention, or you'll sink back into the trough."

"What trough? What are you talking about?" Recco reached the bottom of the gangway and stepped onto the Zodiac's pontoons and then into the raft.

"You all right?" Juan eyed him, hazel eyes flaring with suspicion.

"Fine, *amigo.*" Recco looked away and grabbed a seat on a pontoon.

"Perfect. Do not let them suspect you're not a hundred percent onboard with their plans."

Recco glanced about the raft. Seven of its occupants were female Shifters from the crew who'd been trapped in Ushuaia. Tessa, Moira, Becca… His normally sharp reasoning capacity was buried in layers of cotton batting. *"The women,"* he started and then tried again. *"Where are their bond animals? Why aren't—"*

"They're with me. Same problem."

"What problem?"

"Do things seem normal to you?" the wolf countered.

For some reason, the question gave him pause. Recco started to answer automatically, say everything was fine. The time-worn phrase pinged sourly off his common sense. *"I guess not. What's wrong with everyone?"*

"Same thing that was wrong with you until five minutes ago."

"You're being pretty cryptic."

The wolf didn't comment.

The roar of the Zodiac's motor pounded Recco's ears, accompanied by harsh grating as the craft moved through ice parting ahead of them. He glanced over a shoulder, and alarm sluiced through him along with a metallic taste he associated with adrenaline. The path opening ahead of them closed as soon as the raft moved through it. Ice stretched between them and *Arkady.* Whether it was robust enough to walk across was anyone's guess. It didn't matter. There'd been about a fifty-foot gap of open ocean around the ship. Manageable to swim if the water remained quiescent, but he had an uncomfortable feeling the same mechanism chopping a path through the ice would ensure returning to the ship turned into a death sentence.

"Are you going to say anything else?" he demanded.

"Safer if I don't," his wolf responded.

Juan's head snapped up from where he manned the craft. Confusion screwed his face into a shocked expression. "Jesus. What are we doing out here?" His gaze skittered from one of them to another. "Aura. Where is she?" He stared at the ice, still splitting to offer them passage, and his face morphed from shock to horror. His mitten-clad hand shook where it rested atop the tiller, and the Zodiac bounced from one side of the ice channel to the other.

Recco intuited the other man's thoughts. He wanted to turn the raft around, except it was impossible, the channel far too narrow. The engine must have a reverse setting, though. Why wasn't Juan using it?

The other occupants of the Zodiac barely blinked. They were clearly caught up in the music's spell. The same trance had snared him when he stood on the quarterdeck with Zoe. At least the women's magic had been strong enough to fight back. Had Juan's mountain lion broken through? Was it what brought him around?

Recco started to ask in clumsy telepathy, but he was afraid he might endanger them further. Clearly, his wolf viewed any type of communication as risky. Maybe a method not reliant on magic might be safer. He wished he knew more about how magic worked. Now wasn't the time for a crash course, even if his bondmate were up to the task.

Recco moved across the raft and settled next to Juan. He started with an innocuous question so the others wouldn't pay any attention to them. "How can you tell when we've reached land?"

Juan regarded him through eyes narrowed to slits, as if he were delving for ulterior motives. When he replied, his voice was gruff.

"In this instance, it will be when whatever is cleaving through the ice quits."

"What happens then?"

Juan inhaled audibly, harsh and ragged. "I have no idea."

"Seems to me," Recco went on, hoping to hell the music maker wouldn't rise through the ice and kill him, "once we're over land, we could spin the raft around." The words were no sooner out than the same ice pick between the eyes sensation he'd experienced inside the ship, blasted him. Except this time, it was worse by a factor of ten. A headache bloomed, pounding through his skull. He dropped his head into his hands, hitting pressure points as best he could, given his thick mitts.

"Of course we don't want to turn the raft around. Where's your spirit of adventure, *amigo*?" Juan's jaunty tone held a frayed undernote, as if he was holding himself together by the thinnest of margins.

Colors flared in front of Recco's eyes as the peak of the pain subsided. Christ. No wonder his wolf had cautioned him against talking. At least the other abominations they'd faced hadn't toyed with them. It was all-out war from the gate. This time he felt like a cornered mouse facing off against a pissed-off cat that wasn't in any hurry. He squinted, meeting Juan's gaze, and the other man shook his head in a small, barely perceptible motion. Hope flared. At least two of them had broken free of the Kool-Aid everyone else seemed to have drunk.

The Zodiac's bow bounced against a shallow ice shelf.

"Looks like this is the end of the line," Juan said in his best tour guide style. "I'll get out first and secure the anchor rope with ice screws." He dug in the wooden box next to him and extracted ten-inch long silvery bolts with threaded ends and flattened tops. Next, he killed the motor and tilted it into the raft where the propeller wouldn't drag.

Boris tossed a leg over the side of the raft.

"Hang on!" Juan said. "This time, you'll all exit the same way I do.

Ice is solid beyond the bow. If you go over the edge, you may end up in water to your waist."

"Thanks." Boris's reply was muted, as if he were talking from underwater.

"Not the weather to get wet," Juan agreed in the same cheery tone as he crossed to the front of the raft and vaulted over the pontoons, rope in hand.

"Oh, it's not so bad." Ted spread his arms expansively and draped one around Boris. "This is almost balmy for Antarctica."

Recco held onto a neutral expression. The calm seas and the lack of wind had to be products of magical manipulation, which meant they could shatter between the space of two breaths. A gradually rising expanse of white spread before them. Once they were all out of the raft, he and Daide helped Juan drag it onto the ice.

Daide elbowed him. "You're quiet."

Recco shrugged. "So are you. So what?" Everyone except for the three of them had taken off across the frozen headland, presumably guided by the same force that had lured them off *Arkady*.

A gust of wind battered him in the ass, and he ground his teeth together. "Guess it's our sign to get moving."

"I'd feel better about this if I had some idea where we were going," Daide spoke up, sounding like himself.

"When you got into the raft, it didn't matter to you." Recco tested the waters, curious what his friend would say.

Daide lowered his voice. "My coyote showed up."

"Funny. So did my mountain lion," Juan said. "It was like being doused with a bucket of ice water straight out of the Amundsen Sea." He twisted a corner of his mouth downward in a pained expression. "I'm appalled I left the ship at all. Doubly so without Aura."

Recco braced himself, but nothing attacked them. No one rolled on the ice clutching their heads. Maybe the thing couldn't split its attention, and at the moment it was focused on the group moving briskly toward god only knew what. He remembered the blast of wind. "We have to follow the others. Last thing we need is to draw attention to ourselves."

Juan straightened from where he'd secured the raft to the ice screws. "Yes, and we need to shut up. My bond animal was most specific about it."

Recco slipped and slid, running across the slick surface until he caught up with the tail end of the line. Daide flanked him on one side, Juan on the other. The music was back, except this time it lacked the mesmerizing effect. Magic boiled around the group. If he looked through his psychic view, colors collided in a mass of wicked-looking sparks. Was the alien magic doing its damnedest to keep theirs at bay?

The vista was oddly hypnotic, drawing him into kaleidoscopic imagery until an urgent growl from his wolf refocused him. A sense of urgency surrounded him. "We're getting close," he mumbled.

"My take too," Juan said.

"We may shift," his wolf said. *"If I commandeer our body, do not fight me."*

"Understood."

Recco wanted to stop and strategize. Anything unusual—like not moving in the same direction as everyone else—would be a dead giveaway three of them weren't playing in the same court, though. The magic they faced had to be both ancient and powerful. Right now, they held the element of surprise. It wasn't much, but he couldn't afford to be picky. Or ignore any potential advantages.

The distant roar of a Zodiac reached him; he exchanged pointed glances with Juan and Daide. It had to be Viktor and the women. Or at least the women. Viktor had been sunk deep in some kind of trance.

Juan touched a finger to his lips in the universal sign for silence. The other raft had a chance—so long as whatever wanted them badly enough to go to all this trouble didn't notice it. Once it was discovered, the channel in the ice would close, crushing the Zodiac—

"Have faith." His wolf punctuated the words with a snarl. *"We can more than match any power conjured up by the other side."*

Recco wanted to know what the other side was, but he'd find out soon enough.

Dead ahead, the undulating plain of ice and snow developed a definite upward cant. At the head of the line, Boris and Ted took turns kicking steps in steepening snow.

Recco glanced over one shoulder. At least their trail would be easy to follow. They'd dug a trench in the snow as they traversed the tundra. Should they slow down to increase the odds of connecting with whoever rode in the second Zodiac?

Probably not. Any divergence from what everyone else was doing would draw attention to them. Ketha, Zoe, Karin, and Aura were safer if the music maker's attention remained focused on Boris and Ted and the others a few yards ahead.

Light flashed, yellow edged with black, and a section of the hillside directly in front of Boris vanished. One moment it was there. The next, a gaping maw stood. The music swelled, pounding against Recco's resolve to ignore it. Warm, seductive, tantalizing, enchanting. All he had to do was walk through the hole in the ice, and every dream he'd ever had would come true.

He'd never want for anything again. Ever. Never have to worry about the Cataclysm's destruction. Or Vampires. No. He'd remain here. Safe. Protected. Every need met. The secrets of the ages revealed.

Daide closed a hand around his arm and gripped hard.

Recco understood. He had to be strong. Had to wrench his focus away from the insidious suggestions eroding his determination. Breath rasped in his throat as he forced his lungs to inflate.

Boris hesitated, and decorative multihued lights flared around the yawning hole, almost as if their host recognized the need to make the entrance less threatening. Boris leaned into Ted, wrapping his arms around him. Angling his head, he kissed his lover squarely on the mouth. Normally, the men kept their relationship subtle. Not anymore. Sexual heat flowed from them, surrounding them in red-tinged concentric circles. Maybe one of the music's promises had been they'd never have to hide their connection from the world again.

Footsteps thudded from behind Recco. How the hell had the second raft's occupants caught up so fast? He started to turn. Juan hip-butted him from the other side, no doubt as a warning to do nothing to alert the music maker others would join them soon.

Boris and Ted's kiss deepened. They clung to each other as green, blue, and black light washed over them. At least the men's passion was buying all of them time. The longer they stood at the brink of the opening, the more convinced Recco became they couldn't go inside. If they did, the alien magic would swallow them whole.

And they'd never, never leave.

Daide still gripped him, so he slithered closer and positioned his mouth over his friend's ear. "We can't go inside."

"Tell me something I don't know," Daide mouthed back.

Juan stepped next to Recco's other side. "We can't—" he began.

"We know," Daide said.

The lights flashing around the hole in the ice brightened until Recco couldn't look directly at them anymore. Ted and Boris were still kissing, grinding their bodies together. Breath rose around them, turning the air steamy.

Amid shimmery flashes, two women emerged from the ice. Naked. Perfect, with high, full breasts. Silver hair shot with gold fell to their feet. When Recco looked closer, he saw the bottom half of their bodies was avian, covered with glittery, jewel-toned feathers. Silver eyes regarded the men, and magic flowed from long, tapering fingers, winding around Ted and Boris.

Juan crossed himself. "Holy fuck. You'd think nothing would surprise me after ten years as a Vampire, but those are Sirens. Anyone who's ever gone to sea knows about them."

"Hell," Daide muttered. "Anyone who's read the classics does too."

"What are they doing here?" Recco stared at the duo. "I thought they lived in the Mediterranean."

"Who knows?" Juan replied. "Maybe the Cataclysm displaced them too."

"It didn't displace their destructive nature." Recco swallowed back distaste.

A third woman joined the other two. She held a golden lyre set with gemstones between her hands, plucking the strings. Each note developed a life of its own, and Recco felt himself sinking back into the pit where nothing mattered except ensuring the music never stopped.

"Welcome." The third Siren's word formed a harmonic with her music.

"Yes. Welcome," the other two said in unison. "We've been so lonely."

"I'll bet." Juan squared his shoulders and took a step forward. "Hell of a life with no ships to wreck."

The third Siren tossed her head back and laughed. It made her breasts jiggle, and Recco fought against a wave of lust that brought his cock to full attention. "I'll take you, little sailor." She focused her unearthly gaze on Juan. "I adore men with spirit."

Magic buffeted Recco from behind, and Aura bounded between their small group and the Sirens. He spun to see where she'd come from and discovered the group they'd left on the boat. He clamped his jaws tight to avoid feeling too relieved. It helped they were all here, yet he couldn't drop his guard. Power boiled around him, the air prickly and electric with it. If he wasn't vigilant, the enchantment would sweep him into its maw.

Aura opened her mouth; a wild growl bounced off the ice, echoing crazily. "He's mine," she announced, teeth bared, just before she shifted to her mountain cat amid the cacophony of ripping fabric.

The Siren dropped the lyre to the frozen ground. A riff of discordant notes followed as if the instrument resented such rough treatment. The air around the Siren rippled, and her arms turned to wings. Spreading them to better than a six-foot span, she faced off against the snarling mountain lion.

With a feral, grunting howl, Juan shifted too, joining his mate. Screeching and hissing, the two cats sprang on the Siren. Recco edged closer, wanting to help.

"Stay back, amigo," Juan's voice echoed in his head. *"I've got this."*

"No, we have this," Aura corrected him and closed her jaws over a wing, crunching through feathers and bone. The Siren shrieked her outrage and pain.

If their situation hadn't been so desperate, Recco would have smiled.

5

ALL THAT GLITTERS IS PROBABLY GOLD

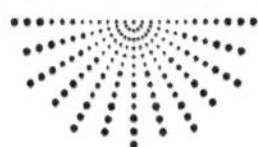

Zoe borrowed heavily from magic to push the Zodiac to greater speed. They had to catch up with the first group. Had to. If the Sirens got their hands on them, they'd ensorcel everyone, making rescue much more difficult, maybe even impossible. She eyed the jagged pathway through the ice. It still held vestiges of the magic that had made it.

The ocean pitched and heaved against the narrow channel, and they hit the waves head-on, bucking their way toward where they could exit the craft. Salt spray coated Zoe's lips; it burned cold when she breathed in.

"Ward yourselves," Karin ordered in a terse tone.

"Aye, this isn't Shifter magic," Zoe said.

Viktor grimaced. "I still cannot believe I stood by while everyone filed out of the bridge. Christ! Those Sirens command powerful magic."

"You spent years at sea, and you're only now figuring that out?" Aura stared at him.

"Never paid much heed to something I didn't believe in." To his credit, Viktor didn't sound defensive.

"Makes sense," Aura muttered. "Sorry, didn't mean to put you on the spot."

"Back to the Sirens," Ketha said. "Viktor is correct. Their magic is strong, ancient, and it might be hard to second-guess them. It's why we must be as invisible as we can for as long as we can."

"There's the other raft." Aura pointed. "Didn't take long to locate it."

"Magical battles never last long, either," Karin noted sourly. "I hope to hell we're not too late."

Zoe pushed power ahead of her, and then reeled it in just as fast. Nothing like a blast of magic to alert whoever was stumbling around on the ice-shrouded continent.

Ketha sent a pointed glance her way, and Zoe nodded curtly while mumbling, "Sorry."

Viktor was already out of the raft, and the women piled after him. With all five of them dragging the Zodiac, it slid out of the water and onto the ice shelf easily. Viktor tied it off to the other raft after a brisk tug on something drilled into the ice.

"What are those?" Zoe asked, pointing.

"Ice screws. Normally, I'd never secure one raft to another's tether, except we have to hurry."

"We shouldn't hurry so fast we run square into whatever's happening ahead." Karin tugged her hood tighter. A shudder racked her. "It's far from cold, but the closer we get to the supernatural source controlling things, the more creeped out I am."

Zoe moved to her side. "Not much choice other than to tip our hand. Nothing to hide behind here. No trees. No bushes. Not even much in the way of boulders. If we leverage magic to ward ourselves, it's no different from posting a sign warning we're on our way. Unfortunately, I don't see any alternative. If we don't ward ourselves, they'll discover us even sooner."

"She's correct," Viktor said. "Speed is our friend. The faster we reach the others, the more help we'll be." A troubled look rippled across his face. "The music must've spelled them. God only knows what we'll find."

A vicious blast of wind chopped from the side, and it took all Zoe's strength to remain upright. She threaded magic around herself, fearing if she didn't, she'd make no progress at all. Instinctively, she latched a hand around Karin's upper arm.

"Form two rows," Ketha said. "Viktor and I will be the front one."

He draped an arm around her, and they surged into stiffening wind. Aura took hold of Zoe's other arm, her fingers cutting like pincers. "Weave our power together." Her words were almost lost in the howl of a storm that had blown out of nowhere.

"Aye, not much to lose displaying our power," Zoe muttered. "The bastards know we're here." Her own stupidity stabbed her. She'd known about the music, but had chalked it off as unimportant and been played for a fool. Maybe if she'd paid closer attention—

"Heed what's happening now," her coyote said, its tone pointed.

Recognizing good advice, she refocused her attention on the terrain in front of her boots. The ice was knobby, or travel over its slippery surface would have been a gargantuan task. Gale-force gusts stiffened by the moment, the wind baying like a wounded animal, pathetic and compelling.

"Hope we don't have to go very far." Rather than fight to be heard over the howling, shrieking wind, Aura switched to telepathy.

Karin didn't reply. Neither did Zoe. They needed to conserve every scrap of power they could. According to her coyote, she'd originated from sturdy warrior stock. When she tried to latch onto a calm confidence, it eluded her. The only emotion churning through her, turning her guts to water and her knees to jelly, was fear.

Because she couldn't obliterate her terror with reason, she glommed onto its energy. Fear was fight or flight. The latter was out of the question. If she ran back to the Zodiac and curled into a paralyzed ball of nerves, she'd never be able to face herself in the mirror—or anywhere else. The years in Ushuaia had been a proving ground of sorts. They'd forced her into survival mode, but she and the other women had never faced anything this bad.

Until we fought the Cataclysm.

She hadn't known how horrendous it would be until she was in so deep the only way out was to power on through. And she'd had plenty of magic—and backbone —to do her part.

The memory added steel to her spine. She stood straighter as she, Karin, and Aura battled forward, fighting for every step. She aimed for a balance point where she funneled enough magic to make progress possible, yet not so much as to drain her reserves away to nothing. She squinted against the wind and wished she'd had the foresight to bring goggles. Bits of ice and grit stung her eyes and face.

Unremitting white spread before them, and the land wasn't flat anymore. They were moving uphill, when they weren't slipping backward. The phrase *one step forward, two steps back* pounded through her head, encouraging in an odd way since they were making better progress.

Viktor and Ketha had pulled ahead. When they came into view, they weren't moving at all. Zoe borrowed from her coyote's senses, scented the wind for changes, and wished she hadn't. A bitter, dark magic thrummed around her, and the infernal music started up again. Harsh and tantalizing by turns, it promised everything she'd ever wished for. Surcease from their endless battles, predictions of normalcy, whatever normal was. Even though she recognized its soothing stream of images as bullshit, she was inexorably drawn into its spell.

"If I was anywhere except inside, I'd bite you," the coyote growled.

Its words shattered the hypnotic trance that had snared her, and Zoe braided more magic into her wards. She gripped Aura and Karin tighter. "Still here, right?" The words tore from her in a rush.

"Hanging on by my toenails," Aura grunted.

They caught up to Viktor and Ketha. *"We're close enough to attack,"* Ketha murmured, keeping her mind voice low.

"How do you know?" Karin demanded, not bothering with telepathy.

Viktor turned until he faced them, leaving Ketha staring into a gray void studded with ice crystals. "Every once in a while, the mist parts. The surface dead ahead steepens, and there's an opening— maybe a cavern. Everyone is huddled in front of it, like they've been bewitched or something."

"How far?" Karin asked in a strained voice.

"Closer than you might think. Maybe fifty yards. The snowy surface and the storm flatten out the light, and it's tough to judge distance."

"Shit." Ketha angled her head over one shoulder. "Two Sirens sashayed out of a hole in the mountainside."

"We have to get moving. Now." Karin's voice held a desperate edge.

Ketha tilted her head, scanning forward again. "Hang on. They don't seem to be in any hurry, so we shouldn't be, either. Oho. Number three just emerged."

Zoe let go of Karin and Aura to push between Viktor and Ketha. Shielding her eyes from the glare of daylight on snow, she stared ahead and willed the vapor to part for her like it had for Ketha. Lyre music reached her, provocative, enticing. Each note developed a life of its own as it swept around her, through her.

Like a curtain being drawn back, the mist fell away.

Her heart thudded hard against her chest as she stared at the tableau. It might be a trick of the light like Viktor suggested, but the group stood far nearer than fifty yards. The Sirens were beautiful and terrible. She'd never seen a mythological being before. Closest she'd come was the Archangel, Raziel. Maybe they all contained the same unearthly combination. A mixture that made you want to race forward and throw yourself at their feet, while everything within you rebelled and shouted to run the other way as fast and as far as your legs could carry you.

As if someone had turned up the sound along with the visual, the

Siren with the lyre purred, "Welcome." Her words formed a harmonic with notes plucked from the lyre's strings.

"Yes. Welcome," the other two said in unison. "We've been so lonely."

"I'll bet." Juan squared his shoulders and took a step forward. "Hell of a life with no ships to wreck."

Zoe sucked air through her teeth. The cold made them ache, but at least Juan wasn't under the Sirens' spell. Had any of the others broken through? She leaned forward, muttering prayers the bond animals had managed to punch holes in the music's compelling enchantment.

The third Siren tossed her head back and laughed. It made her breasts jiggle, and Zoe wanted to throttle her. "I'll take you, little sailor." The Siren focused her eerie silver gaze on Juan. "I adore men with spirit."

Magic blasted from behind Zoe, and Aura bounded from their small group to where the Sirens stood. She opened her mouth, and a wild growl bounced off the ice, echoing crazily. "He's mine," she announced, teeth bared, just before she shifted to her mountain cat amid the din of ripping fabric.

The Siren dropped her lyre to the frozen ground. A riff of discordant notes followed as if the instrument resented such rough treatment. The air around the Siren rippled, and her arms turned to wings. Spreading them to better than a six-foot span, she faced off against the snarling mountain lion.

With a feral, grunting howl, Juan shifted too, joining his mate. Screeching and hissing, the two cats sprang on the Siren.

"That's our cue, mates. Watch yourselves. Out of the first group, Juan is fighting on our side. No telling about the rest of them." Viktor leapt forward with Ketha, Zoe, and Karin on his heels.

Zoe kept her gaze trained on the Sirens. They were naked and perfect, and she didn't see how she could raise magic against them.

"Your reluctance isn't standing in Juan or Aura's way," her coyote

pointed out acidly. *"How do you suppose creatures like them have survived for millennia?"*

She winced. Once again, her bondmate was spot-on in its observations. *"Should we shift?"*

"Not unless we have to. Those two are stuck in their animal forms until they get back to the ship. Their clothes are ripped to shreds, and no one can be naked in this weather and survive."

The two mountain lions snarled, hissed, and bit. Zoe expected the other Sirens to dive in and help their fallen sister. Instead, they stood and stared, gape-mouthed, as if being attacked was so far off their radar screen they had no idea how to react to it.

Magic arced from Zoe's fingertips, shredding yet another set of gloves. She added her power to Karin, Viktor, and Ketha. Together, they fashioned a protective arc around the mountain cats. Where the Siren's blood spilled onto the snow, iridescent red-gold rivers formed, creating a song of their own. The music sang to Zoe not unlike the Sirens' song. Pain sluiced through her.

They were killing something sacred. One of the mysteries.

"Och, enough." She spoke aloud to steady herself. That *mystery* would have been quick enough to bind all of them on the seventh continent forever. What had the one said? *We've been so lonely.*

How the hell had they ended up here in the first place?

Juan and Aura raised bloody snouts from the fallen Siren. Light flared around her prone form. Red. Gold. Blue. Violet. Each flash of light bathed a part of what was left of the Siren in eerie relief—right before it shimmered into nothingness. Within the space of ten heartbeats, the snow was as pristine as if nothing had ever lain there.

If the mountain cats' mouths weren't rimmed with blood, Zoe might have thought she'd imagined everything. The lyre sat in the snow, exactly where the Siren had dropped it. Moving slowly, as if something inside her had broken, another Siren picked up the lyre. She held the instrument in front of her and teased its strings. Two notes evoking all the sadness in this world and every other fell from the instrument.

Tears gathered behind Zoe's eyes, freezing as soon as they dripped onto her cheeks.

Both Sirens opened their mouths. Zoe girded herself for shrieks and wails. Instead, a song without words floated through the still, cold air. Crafted in a minor key, it summoned images of all the pain Zoe had known through her life. Every loss. Every death. Every wrong turn where she'd shed tears for her ignorance—or her stupidity.

"Watch it." Her coyote was back. *"Their grief is as dangerous as their joy."*

The mountain lions paced back and forth leaving big paw prints and claw marks in the unending white. Aura yowled. Juan howled. Were they regretting their part in the Siren's demise?

Knowledge intruded. The longer they remained here, the less likely they'd ever leave. While she still had free will—and it was eroding fast—Zoe strode forward on feet that had turned to blocks of ice.

"Enough." She shouted directly into the Siren's faces. For good measure, she grasped the lyre and yanked hard on it. She'd expected the Siren to try to hang onto the instrument, but she didn't. Zoe stumbled backward. The lyre was warm in her hands, soothing her icy fingers.

She'd always adored music. The lyre wanted playing, and she settled her fingers over its strings.

"Bad idea," Ketha shouted. "Don't."

"But it wants me to play it." Zoe pedaled through a warm river sending bits of suggestion into her mind. The only important thing was the lyre. The goddess had made sure it ended up in her hands. She had to play it—

A determined yank unbalanced her. She fought to hold onto the lyre. She was its new mistress. Out of all of them, it had chosen her.

She curled her fingers around the shiny wood set with gemstones. Wood that fit her hands as if it had been made for her.

"Zoe!" Karin's voice cut like a whip. "Let go. That fucking thing has you in thrall. If you play as little as one note, you'll be lost."

Recco grabbed her shoulders from behind and hooked his arms through hers. She couldn't fight against pressure from both sides. The next time Recco jerked backward and Karin forward, the lyre slipped from her grasp.

"Nay." The keening howl shooting from her mouth shocked her, but she couldn't shut up. "'Tis mine. *Mine.* Give it back."

Karin threw the lyre into the snow and closed on Zoe. "Listen to yourself." She clutched Zoe's forearms hard enough to hurt. "The lyre's power is insidious. It's cut you off from your coyote." Copper eyes stared into hers. "Don't believe me? Go ahead. Try to raise your bondmate."

Recco drew her against the solidness of his body, still holding tight. She struggled. He didn't let go. The pull of the lyre was strong. It called her from where it sat, end down in a softer patch of snow.

Voices rose and fell around her, not making much more sense than the Tower of Babel. She shook her head hard, trying to clear her thoughts of the lyre. Had it truly had her in its clutches?

"You're all overreacting," she muttered, but her words lacked conviction.

"Your coyote," Karin pressed. "Sometimes our bondmates can't survive competing magic when it's this strong."

"Don't be ridiculous. I've been bonded to it since I was a girl." Zoe bristled. Why the hell was Karin being such a bitch?

"Do what she says." Recco's deep voice rumbled against her ear. "We need to get out of here. First, you have to locate your bond animal. If you don't, you risk leaving its essence here for the Sirens to eviscerate."

"How could you know?" She tried to turn and look at him, but he held her too firmly.

"My wolf told me."

Raw sincerity ran beneath his words, and it knocked the last of the lyre's sneaky suggestions out of her sluggish brain. Suddenly afraid what she'd find, Zoe turned her magic inward, seeking her other half. For long moments, the place her bondmate dwelt was empty, much as it was when the coyote retreated to the animals' special world.

"Please." Naked pleading began in her heart and arrowed straight into her soul. "I'm sorry. Come back to me. I never meant to—"

"I know. I know. I'm here." Weariness underscored the coyote's words. *"I failed you. I understood the danger, and I was helpless to intervene. The lyre contains magic far stronger than mine."*

"Not your fault." Zoe reached deep. *"I love you."*

"We have to be more careful next time."

Zoe sucked in a ragged breath, grateful there would be a next time. This had been far too close a call. Relief shot through her, so poignant she felt the quick, hot bite of tears—except this time they were genuine. They coated her cheeks with ice, and she sagged in Recco's arms. "You can let go," she said. "I wouldn't touch the lyre again if it held a king's ransom."

He let go and stepped aside. Worry for her had carved deep lines into his austere features.

"It contains far more than any royal ransom," Karin said. "Those gems are worth millions, and the lyre is solid gold."

"Gold? It felt like wood in my hands." Zoe glanced at where the Sirens had stood. The spot was empty. "Where'd they go?"

"We were just kicking that question around," Ketha said. She walked to Zoe's side. "Welcome back to the land of the living, sister. For a while there, you started to look like the Sirens. Lucky for you, I was scanning with my third eye. Otherwise I'd have missed the start of the transformation."

Shock hit Zoe like a blow to the midsection. "Feathers and all?" At Ketha's nod, her stomach clenched into a hard, painful knot. "So 'tis how they make more of themselves."

"As good a guess as any," Ketha replied sourly.

Viktor sidled to where they stood. "We should leave while we can. Everyone is free of the music's spell—at least for now."

"Yes. Leave," echoed around them.

"Leave. Leave. Be gone."

"Be gone, and be cursed for you have forever altered something man has no right to tamper with." The message held none of the beauty of the Sirens' earlier words. None of their grace, and also none of their hypnotic pull.

As if it didn't want to be left out, the lyre began to play on its own. Sour, bitter, discordant notes spewed from it until it belted out a reel that would have shamed a blind drunk.

The rest of the group had already left for where the rafts were, slipping and sliding as they tried to run. Recco gripped one of her arms, Karin the other. Zoe started to protest she could manage on her own, but the lyre snagged her gaze out of the corner of one eye. Even though it spit poison, it still glowed softly, and she understood full well it was begging her to tame it, save it from itself.

Nay. 'Tis only one more trick to hold me here.

Zoe dragged her gaze in a semicircle and let Recco and Karin guide her away from the place that had almost sundered her bond with her coyote. Anger burned bright. She ached to run back and stomp the lyre into splinters, all the while recognizing it as folly. The instrument was scarcely wood like it wanted her to believe. Gold wouldn't break apart, no matter what she did.

"I'm going to throw you in the Amundsen Sea when we get back to it," Karin muttered.

"It's not polite to help yourself to my thoughts," Zoe retorted, trying for a scrap of dignity.

"It is if my intrusion saves your life."

When they reached the rafts, the one with the mountain lions and half a dozen others in it was already on its way back to *Arkady.* Zoe wondered why the Sirens were letting them leave. Maybe their magic wasn't bottomless.

"Why didn't they fight back harder?" she asked Karin.

The other woman shook her head. "I have no idea, but I'm not in the habit of kicking a gift horse in the mouth, either."

Recco snorted and helped them into the remaining raft. Daide and everyone who hadn't snatched a ride on the first raft looked more than ready to leave. "It's look a gift horse in the mouth," he corrected her. "You can tell how old a horse is by its teeth, so when you looked in its mouth, you could tell how much of a gift the horse actually was."

"I knew that," Karin muttered, followed by, "Goddess preserve me from veterinarians.

"Of course you did." Zoe stuck up for her friend and settled against a pontoon. The adrenaline was fading, and she felt as if she could sleep for days.

"When we're back on *Arkady*"—Ketha skewered Zoe with her gaze—"I expect a full recounting of exactly what happened back there with the lyre." She hooked a thumb at the rapidly receding shoreline.

"How about if I take a nap first."

Ketha shook her head. "Absolutely not. It will dull your memories."

"Okay. You're on." Zoe swallowed hard. Reliving shame wasn't at the top of her list. Maybe after she'd detailed her swan dive from grace, she could put it behind her and find a way to move forward.

TEAM PLAYERS

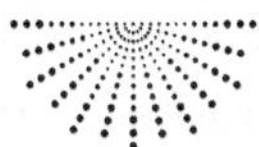

Recco marched from one side of his cabin to the other, shedding outerwear as he went. He'd always liked things neat and hung his red jacket and black bibs in their customary place. His mitts and hat lay atop the desk, so they could dry. He'd had to toe off his boots to remove the bibs, but he slid his feet back into them. He unzipped his fleece jacket, stopping shy of getting rid of the insulated garment. It wasn't particularly warm in his cabin. He kept it on the cooler side on purpose.

He smothered a snort. He and Daide were mirror opposites in terms of their preferred methods for arranging things, something they'd butted heads over for years. Daide would wait until the end of a busy clinic day and then sort instruments into the sterilizer, while Recco took care of business after each patient. They'd ended up with enough equipment to fill two veterinary clinics, but at least they never ran out of anything.

Their clinic had been looted in the first months after the Cataclysm. He and Daide had been Vampires by then, and protecting their turf hadn't been high on their lists. Survival—and avoiding blood as long as they could—overshadowed everything. By the time he'd finally settled into being a Vampire for long enough to be rational again, his first stop had been their small clinic tucked into Ushuaia's hills. The sight of broken windows and the splintered front door told him all he needed to know, but he'd gone inside anyway. Not much was left, so he'd torched the remains.

It was a turning point, one that made it clear his old life was gone. Looking back bought him nothing except pain—and anger.

He was still pacing. Six steps in one direction, and then back again. It had been damned hard to bid Zoe farewell at the top of the gangway. She'd held such a trashed, defeated look, it made his heart hurt. He hadn't wanted to intrude, not that he would have had much choice in the matter. Ketha and Karin had settled Zoe firmly between them and rushed her off somewhere.

Protectiveness surged. He got it under control fast. Before his wolf could chastise him. One of the surprising factors to this Shifter business had been the bond animals not only knew one another, but their relationships had developed over hundreds of years. Maybe thousands. They shielded their own with a fierceness bordering on obsession.

And now I'm one of them.

The thought warmed him and made him wary at the same time. This was way more serious than signing on with the military, something he'd done as a young man fresh out of high school. This commitment was for life, and he'd damn well better be worthy of the honor.

An approving woof sounded from his wolf.

Recco stopped at the sink and bent low to sluice water over his face, drying it with a nearby towel.

"Thanks," he told his bondmate and draped the towel back over its hook.

"No need to thank me. You're making progress."

Praise from the animal was so rare, Recco savored it. A glance out his porthole told him the storm was still raging. Viktor had been going to move the ship to put some distance between them and the Sirens. Whether he'd accomplished it or not remained to be seen.

Recco hadn't heard the screech of the anchor chain, but it didn't mean much. The wind squealed like a herd of Banshees on the loose, obliterating almost everything.

Recco sat in the room's only chair, knowing he wouldn't remain there. Too edgy to sit, he wrestled with an uncomfortable in-between place, one he recognized all too well. Exhausted, but too keyed up to sleep. Having something to do would help settle his racing thoughts. They bounced from the lyre to the Sirens and back to Zoe.

His physical reaction to the Siren had shocked him. He'd read about them yet hadn't been prepared for the wave of lust that sucked him into its hungry maw. And it hadn't been only him. Ted and Boris had practically had sex in front of everyone. If he'd been by himself, he wasn't under any illusions about the outcome. One of the Sirens would have waggled her hips his way, and he'd have succumbed.

"You underestimate me," his wolf said dryly. *"I'd have forced a shift before I allowed any of those sex-mad bitches access to our body."*

"Good to know."

Recco dragged his hands through his untidy hair and walked out the door. He wasn't certain where he was headed until he took the stairs leading down to Deck Two. After swinging by the empty galley and snapping up a piece of leftover cornbread from breakfast, he trotted to the lab, chewing thoughtfully. The door had been propped open, and Daide bent over one of the microscopes.

"Hey there." Recco strode to his side. "Find anything interesting?"

Daide straightened. Dark circles etched beneath his eyes, and he scrubbed the heels of his hands down his face. "I'm afraid I'm not present enough to do much good here. It beat hanging around my cabin, bouncing off the walls, though."

"You too, huh?" Recco hooked his boot into the bottom of a nearby chair and pulled it close, settling into it.

"Did you stop by the bridge?"

Recco shook his head. "Nah. If Juan or Vik needs us, they'll let us know. I'm not even sure they moved *Arkady*."

"They did, but not far. You can't see shit out there, so I looked on a map. This channel has several islands to the south. We still have land masses on both sides, but we're not as protected as we were." Daide arched his back to the accompaniment of cracking bones.

Recco slapped his shoulder. "You never did have the patience for lab work."

Daide smiled crookedly. "Busted. I guess we don't have many secrets."

"After all the time we spent in the same office, *amigo*? You must be kidding. You're worse than a wife."

"Nope. You were the wife. Always cleaning up after me." Daide chuckled, but his mirth faded fast. "I may have been staring at the slide on the stage"—he tapped the microscope—"except all I can think about is what an easy mark I was for those creatures. Did you —? Er, were you—?" Color rose from the open neck of his dark-green, fuzzy jacket.

"Hot to trot? Yup. They'd have had me like a trussed pig."

Daide made a face. "Not a very attractive visual."

"My wolf informed me it would have taken over before the Sirens ravished me or ate me for dinner."

"Aw geez. Yours too?" Daide twisted so he faced Recco directly. "My coyote started giving me hell the moment it broke through the enchantment."

"When exactly was that?" Recco was curious since his wolf had punched through before he'd even left *Arkady*.

"Not until after the first Sirens showed up. I swear, it was like a pitched battle inside me." He rubbed his midsection. "The pain was excruciating, like someone had cut into me without anesthesia. Something about Juan and Aura shifting seemed to give my bondmate what it needed. I'm not certain, but I believe it's when everyone shook off the spell that dragged us off the ship in the first place."

Recco exhaled sharply, inhaled, and did it again. "I actually figured it out before we left the ship. Juan did too, once we were in the raft. We kept quiet."

"Why? You could have helped the rest of us."

"My wolf said it was dangerous to do anything other than lie low."

"Did it say why?"

"No. I figured it didn't want to draw the Sirens' attention any closer than it already was. If they looked too intently and realized two of us had escaped their spell, it might have destroyed our slender advantage, assuming we had one. I wish I understood more."

"You think?" Daide set his mouth in a hard line and regarded Recco intently. "At this rate, I assume we'll make McMurdo. It's not far. What are your thoughts about the women's plan to sail all the way to Siberia?"

An undernote in Daide's question activated Recco's internal alarm system. "Why are you asking?"

Daide looked away. "It's not that I don't want to be a team player and all, still it seems to me McMurdo is as good a stopping point as we're likely to find. If the rest of the world looks like the part we've seen so far, the odds of us transiting the globe south to north aren't good." He scowled.

Concern for his friend stabbed Recco, and he leaned toward him. Before he could open his mouth to ask what was wrong, Daide continued. "Damn. My coyote just called me a coward." A defiant expression blazed in his dark eyes. "Maybe I am, but I prefer to label it as practical."

"None of this is second nature, *amigo*. Hell, I never got used to being a Vampire. Resigned, perhaps, yet neither of us embraced it." Recco took a measured breath. "The way I read things, we need time —and practice—to come to terms with our new abilities, except we don't have either. So we're constantly forced into spots where we're reacting—and making mistakes."

The strained expression around Daide's eyes deepened. "As

usual, you called it. I made a bunch of assumptions before we left Ushuaia. None of them have played out, and I'm not liking where the ball ended up."

Recco rolled his eyes. "What a mish-mosh of mixed metaphors. How the hell did you deal with our transition to being Vamps?"

"Enough familiar was left, I only looked at the parts I wanted to."

"You know, I was thinking about our clinic before I came down here. When I saw it in ruins, it was a moment of truth for me. This might sound hokey, but it symbolized our lives. They'd never be close to the same, and I stopped expecting things to change."

"Even if I'd seen it, it wouldn't have helped. You've always been the practical one of the two of us. I was the dreamer."

"We have complementary strengths." Recco shrugged. "Probably why none of our various attempts at domesticity lasted. The women always felt they were competing with a bond you and I developed in vet school."

An emotion Recco couldn't interpret rippled across Daide's face. "That life is gone. I can't look back—at any of it. Today proved it. I have to seat myself squarely in the middle of now, or my ability to be any help to anyone—including myself—will be compromised."

"A Zen approach never hurts." Recco jerked his chin at the microscope. "What were you looking at when I got here?"

"The stained slides from earlier."

"The ones with the archaea on them?" Recco stood and angled his head around Daide's shoulder to peer through the eyepieces.

"Yeah. They're pretty much the same."

Recco adjusted the optics for his vision and examined the red and violet-stained sample. He waited. Nothing so much as twitched.

Daide butted his shoulder into him. "Let me get up so we can trade places."

"It's all right." Recco lifted his head and stepped away from the microscope. He glanced at his chair, and then remained standing. It helped him think.

"I recognize your look," Daide said. "Talk to me."

"All this"—Recco swept his arms wide—"is familiar. Examining cells for things that shouldn't be there. Crafting decisions predicated on the outcome of what we find—"

"We haven't operated that way for a long time," Daide broke in. "We couldn't."

"Maybe not, but the second a semblance of a lab showed up, we glommed onto it."

Daide nodded. "Sure. It makes perfect sense since it's what we believe in. What we were trained to do."

"Our attraction to science-based decision-making is understandable," Recco agreed. "What if it's a waste of time?"

Daide drew away as if Recco had slapped him. He opened his mouth, shut it with an audible *clack*, and crossed his arms over his chest.

Recco smiled grimly. "Heresy, yes? How could any scientific line of inquiry be a waste of time? We spent our lives basing almost every important decision on answers we got from the lab. It's not the same world out there."

"The laws of physics can't have changed," Daide sputtered.

"Maybe not. Nothing we've faced since we defeated the Cataclysm has had any relationship to what's on this slide." He moved close enough to tap the innocuous sliver of glass mounted on the instrument's stage. "Yet we've clung to what we know."

His wolf howled, startling him, and Recco jumped.

"What?" Daide stared.

"I must be on the right track. My wolf gave me the rhetorical equivalent of a high-five."

"Ketha and Karin wouldn't agree. If they weren't busy doing whatever they're up to with Zoe, they'd be here glued to microscopes exactly like us." Daide frowned. "They have a grasp of the magical world, so maybe there's a nexus where the two intersect."

"Don't throw the baby out with the bathwater?"

"Something like it." Daide shrugged. "I wish—" He shook his head. "Doesn't matter."

"You'd like it better if we had an instruction manual. I would too. It was the one plus about Raphael. He not only turned us, he made damn good and sure we understood the fine points about being Vampires. Except he crammed them down our throats."

Daide snorted. "The lessons didn't stick, or he'd have had a more loyal cadre—"

Ketha and Karin barreled into the lab. "How are our samples?" Ketha demanded.

"They look normal again," Recco replied, followed by, "Will Zoe be all right?" He wasn't certain how the last five words snuck out, but he couldn't call them back.

Ketha sent a speculative glance scudding his way. "She's fine. Sleeping, with a small assist from us."

"Why was she the one snared by the lyre?" Daide asked.

"An excellent question, and not one I have a ready answer for," Karin replied. "Out of all of us, she probably has the most musical talent. It may be why the lyre targeted her."

"Would the Sirens have had a way of recognizing her affinity for music?" Recco furled his brows.

"Probably." Ketha closed her teeth over her lower lip. "We don't know much more about them than you do."

"Would the bond animals know?" Daide cut in.

"Have you asked your coyote?" Karin narrowed her eyes.

Daide looked uncomfortable when he got to his feet and faced Karin. "Mostly, I'm afraid to ask it much of anything. It's temperamental. I was grateful when it returned, and I haven't wanted to risk alienating it."

Karin placed her hands on her hips. "You weren't listening very well when you and I worked together. You have entirely the wrong attitude. The bond is one of equals. We have different skills, and you approach your coyote the same way you face Recco. As a valued partner." She took a measured breath. "To answer your question more directly, my wolf doesn't hold knowledge about the Sirens. Each bond animal has its own strengths—and its own information base. It's possible Juan's cat might understand the Sirens' magic because it's so ancient."

"Have you asked it directly?" Ketha spoke up.

"When would I have had a chance?" Karin countered.

"True enough." Ketha slid into the seat Daide had vacated and peered through the binocular eyepieces, clearly intent on taking her own read on the material on the slide. "Did you check all of them?" she demanded.

"Nope. Only that one," Daide said. "I'd planned to be more thorough, but Recco showed up."

"Sure. Blame me." Recco tried to joke. Daide shot him such a pained look, he switched focus. "All of us don't need to be here. I'll run up to the bridge."

"We stopped there first," Karin said. "Viktor and Juan were poring over nautical charts."

"Yeah. They're worried about pack ice surrounding us," Ketha muttered, not looking up from the microscope. "At least at the point we were there, they'd pretty much decided to risk the storm and keep the ship moving."

Recco nodded and walked briskly from the room. An unsettled sensation landed like a brick in his guts; he ignored it. He might not know much about ships, but he'd studied plenty of maps. And he'd lived in Ushuaia long enough to have witnessed bays filling up with ice. Rather than focusing on all the places he wasn't much more than dead weight, he tried for a more positive spin and ran solutions through his mind.

On his way up the stairs, he paused on the landing for Deck Three. He wanted to stop by Zoe's cabin. The women had said she was asleep, though. She'd been through a hell of an experience, and it was better not to bother her. Besides, who knew if she'd even welcome him? She'd thrashed like a cornered animal when he'd pinned her in place to keep her from strumming the lyre.

He'd been close enough to feel the thing's magic, except what was directed at him had ordered him to let Zoe go. Prickly heat had traveled up his fingertips to his shoulders, shooting unpleasant jolts of burning pain into his joints. He flinched at the memory, and kept moving.

Time enough to approach Zoe later, after she was rested.

He trotted smartly up the remaining sets of stairs until he reached the bridge. Pulling the door open, he walked through. Viktor and Juan were still huddled over the chart table, deep in conversation.

"Can I help?" Recco asked, adding hastily, "With anything at all. I like being busy—and useful."

Viktor straightened. "How about helping Juan with the anchor?"

"Sure. I take it we're leaving."

"No choice," Juan said. "This storm's not going to blow itself out for at least another day, maybe two. We can't wait it out. We'll be stuck in several feet of pack ice if we don't keep moving."

"That's the key, then?" Recco met his gaze. "Forward motion?"

"It's our primary weapon," Juan clarified. "But it's far from absolute. We could still end up mired in ice. There won't be an easy way to get to McMurdo if this keeps up. For all I know, the part of the Ross Sea next to the continent might be frozen solid now."

"Isn't the base manned year-round?"

"It used to be," Viktor said, "and the Americans have an icebreaker. It may still be operational. Or not."

"What if it's not? After Arctowski, I'm wondering who will even be at the base." Recco felt he was asking too many questions, but it was the only method he had for gathering information.

"So are we," Viktor murmured. "I've been trying to raise them on the radio. It runs off satellites, so I'm not surprised there's been no response."

"Once we get closer, we should be able to use shortwave radio," Juan spoke up.

"How close is that? Sorry to be a pest. I like to understand how things work."

"You won't like my answer," Juan said. "Shortwaves can broadcast over thousands of miles. Before we relied on satellites, they were our main way of communicating at sea."

"What am I missing here?" Recco narrowed his eyes. "If shortwave is as efficient as satellites, wouldn't they get through?"

"If someone is on the other end with a radio on, and they're actively hunting for broadcasts, sure," Viktor said. "There are a bunch of unknowns, though. Radios require electricity, either directly or via batteries."

"After ten years, most batteries would be defunct, even the lithium ion type," Recco said.

"Exactly," Juan said. "And we have no idea if McMurdo has any generator capacity left. They'd have run through their fuel supplies long ago."

"Maybe." Viktor shrugged. "Arctowski had plenty of biodiesel, and even though they couldn't finesse it, it's not hard to retrofit generators to run on other fuels."

"Lots of questions. Very few answers," Recco murmured.

"About the size of it, mate," Viktor replied. "The anchor?"

"On our way." Juan snapped off a sloppy salute.

Recco followed him out of the bridge. "Do you suppose whoever was at McMurdo abandoned it?"

Juan shook his head. "A more likely scenario is they're all dead."

"How?"

Juan stopped on the landing for Deck Five and turned to face Recco. "Ten years is a long time. Survival hangs by a thread here. My first bet is the generators failed, and whoever was left froze. Second guess is a fire knocked out a big part of the facility, and whoever wasn't burned, froze." He clattered down another set of risers.

"So you're not holding out much hope?"

Juan glanced over a shoulder and grimaced. "This is what hope looks like, *amigo*. An empty research station is far better than if monsters have taken over the installation. My advice to Vik was we should skip it entirely. Why risk stopping since we can't raise anyone on the radio?"

It was a good question. Why wasn't Viktor paying attention to Juan's recommendation? Rather than get in the middle of something, Recco said, "I'll meet you out on deck. Got to stop for my coat and gloves."

"Put your bibs on," Juan instructed. "And a life vest. The way the wind is whipping, I'll be fully duded up too. No point taking chances when we don't have to."

Recco gave him a thumbs-up sign and ran for his cabin. He appreciated Juan's quiet competence, and he didn't want to keep him waiting. As he threw on clothes, an idea formed. They'd all gather on the bridge after dinner and talk about the pros and cons of stopping at McMurdo. Get everything into the open and go with majority rule.

CHOICES

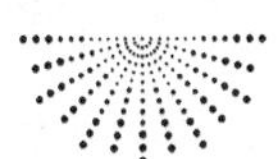

Zoe started from a deep sleep at a staunch knock on her door. Aura pushed it open and walked to her bunk. "Rise and shine, sleepyhead. Dinner is in a quarter hour."

"Ugh." Zoe rolled over and groaned. Her head pounded, and her eyes felt scratchy even before she tried opening them.

The mattress tilted and sank when Aura sat next to her. Firm hands rubbed her shoulders, and healing magic swirled around her, counterpart to her fatigue—and her guilt. No matter what Ketha and Karin had said, recounting her ensorcellment at the hands of the Sirens' lyre only made her feel worse. Nothing she'd come up with ameliorated even a scrap of her crushing sense of responsibility.

She should have slit her own wrists before she allowed anything to steal her judgment or her free will.

"Hmmm." Aura's fingers dug deeper.

"Hmmm, what?" Zoe's words were muffled by her pillow, so she flipped over. "Never mind. Go away. I'll take a quick shower and be along presently." She offered a smile, one that didn't fool Aura.

Green eyes zeroed in on her face until Zoe wanted to shrink into herself. "Goddammit. Don't look at me like that."

"Like what?" Aura's voice radiated innocence.

"Like I'm some variety of intriguing relic you uncovered on one of your history field trips."

"Do you want me not to care?" Aura dropped her hand back onto Zoe's upper arm, and her eyes never left Zoe's face.

The question was laced with compassion and warmth. A dam rose, cracking open, and Zoe blinked back tears. "Do. Not. Be. Kind. It only makes things worse."

"Would you like it better if I read you the riot act?" Aura arched a brow.

"Probably not. I have to find a way to forgive myself. Until I can, I'm not care-worthy material." She scooted to a sit and stuffed both pillows behind her back. "Don't you see?"

"I see a lot of things." Aura clasped her hands in her lap. "You're far from the first Shifter to make a mistake and get snared in wicked magic. Hell's bells, woman. I nearly died in the church on Grytviken because I misjudged the strength of my adversary. Juan gave me a raft of crap for it. I still see it in his mind when he looks at me. As if he's trying to reassure himself I'll never do anything quite so stupid again."

"He loves you."

Aura's expression softened. "Yes, he does, but it's not the point."

"Aye. I know. You're trying to normalize what I did. Except you were fighting evil and got in over your head faster than you anticipated. I wasn't doing anything nearly so noble. A pretty bauble caught my eye, and I convinced myself I was the only one who could coax music from it. I believed it needed my skill as a musician to come into its own. How's that for hubris?" A tear escaped and ran down her cheek. Zoe brushed it away.

"Not the word I'd use." Without stopping long enough for Zoe to contradict her, Aura forged ahead. "Hubris means foolish pride or dangerous overconfidence. I've known you for a long time, and I wouldn't use either of those phrases to describe you."

"Ketha and Karin said much the same. It was still a relief when they left."

"Why don't you believe any of us? We're not in the habit of lying to one another to salve our feelings."

Zoe looked away. "I don't know why this feels worse. Maybe because I heard the music for weeks and ignored it. If I'd used magic to follow it to its source, maybe we could have avoided today."

"What does your coyote say?"

"Not much help from that quarter. Its first words afterward were it had failed me."

"Better than blaming you for all the shit you're blaming yourself for."

"Maybe so," Zoe mumbled. There might be a way out of the pit she'd dug herself into. Unfortunately, it wouldn't happen quickly.

Aura angled her head to one side. "Have you heard music or seen the lyre since you got back on *Arkady*?"

"No music. The lyre showed up in a dream I was having when you woke me."

"Do you remember any of it?" Aura's shrewd gaze sharpened another few notches.

"Not much," Zoe admitted. "I had to be back in the U.K. because it was dark and warm and green and rainy. Ireland has a unique smell, and it was all around me. Didn't realize how much I missed that scent until now. Anyway, I'd gone on a ramble in the countryside north of Belfast. A threatening storm was escalating fast. I told myself it didn't matter, and I kept going."

Zoe shut her eyes to recreate the dream's fragments. "The wind tore at me, and I had a sense something harsh and threatening was after me. I was afraid to turn around, but then I remembered the story about shadows following you in dreams and turning around to face your fears. So I did."

Aura crooked two fingers, clearly wanting her to keep going.

Zoe bent forward and wrapped her arms around her upraised knees. "It was the oddest thing. The lyre was suspended in darkness, and it glowed with a fey light. Every gemstone twinkled, inviting me to rescue it." She swallowed back a sour taste coating her tongue. "I turned tail and ran the other way. No hubris there. Just sheer cowardice."

"You are not a coward, and you made the right choice. Interesting comparison, though."

"What do you mean?"

"You mentioned shadow, so I assumed you were talking about the dream Carl Jung had. It was a lot like yours. He was running through dark and fog and wind, sheltering a lit candle—or lantern— with his hands. He had the same sense of doom following him. When he turned to face it, he recognized his fears as groundless, whereas yours were real."

Zoe looked away. "I want to put this whole episode behind me. Am I dreaming about the fucking thing as a way of processing what happened? Or am I dreaming about it because it's not done with me?" A shiver started in her shoulders and tracked all the way to her toes.

"You'll figure it out." Aura stood. "Pull yourself together and come down for dinner before everything's turned cold. Hiding in bed isn't your style."

"I wasn't hiding—" Zoe bit her words off at the source. It had been exactly what she was doing. She felt guilty and ashamed and hadn't wanted to face anyone after Ketha and Karin were done dissecting her actions. Not that they hadn't been kind, but they'd been thorough too. It was why Aura's attempt to draw a parallel with her fight in the church hadn't rung true.

"See you soon." Aura walked across the cabin and let herself out the door.

Zoe tossed her legs over the side of the bunk and planted her stocking-clad feet on the floor. *"We'll find a way through this,"* she told her coyote. It didn't answer. Maybe it was still licking its hurt places too.

"Tincture of time," she muttered as she dragged herself upright.

She felt like she'd been in a fight. All her muscles ached, but they didn't compare to the pain in her soul. She dropped clothing on the floor and stepped into the shower, setting the water as hot as she could stand it.

She hadn't allowed herself to think about Recco before. He blasted into her head as she stood beneath the spray. He'd held onto her. Kept her from making a mistake, one that would have sealed her fate. Eventually, the transformation would have been complete, and she'd have joined the other Sirens, locked in their icy vault at the bottom of the world. Her coyote would have been lost to her forever.

The last of the soap and shampoo sluiced down her body, and she turned off the tap. The shame dogging her earlier returned. Recco was a decent man with a strong sense of who he was. He'd been stronger than she was, and she wasn't certain how she could face him.

"The same way you faced Karin." Her bond animal was back. *"And Ketha. And Aura."*

"It's different."

"How?" the coyote asked.

Zoe quested about for answers as she dried her body and hair and dragged clothing over her still-damp skin. She'd known the women longer, certainly trusted them more. The hard truth was, she wanted Recco to see her as competent and capable.

As partner material.

After today's events, he probably viewed her as vain and weak and pathetic. She sucked in a ragged breath and tugged a comb through her tangled hair. If she didn't sort it out now, it would be much harder to deal with once it dried.

"He helped you because he cares about you," the coyote observed.

"No. He helped because he's a decent man." Zoe waited; her bondmate didn't contradict her. She'd been half hoping it had inside information from Recco's wolf. If it did, it wasn't saying.

She glanced at a clock mounted over the door. Almost an hour had elapsed since Aura announced dinner was in fifteen minutes. Zoe thought about it; her stomach didn't feel up to food. Maybe a shot of whiskey would sit better. After a final glance around her cabin, she left and headed up one flight to the bar. At least she wouldn't have to deal with anyone since they'd all still be at dinner.

Pleased her assessment about not having to see anyone had been accurate, she sat in the bar, hunched over a tumbler of Irish whiskey. Since it was easier not to think about anything, she stared at the amber liquid sloshing around her glass. After the first few sips, her mouth and throat had numbed, and it had become easier to keep intrusive thoughts at bay.

"Mind if I join you?" Recco's deep voice broke into her reverie.

Zoe almost knocked her glass over when she shot to her feet. "I —I didn't hear you."

He reached a hand to steady her. "Sorry. Didn't mean to sneak up on you. I've always had a quiet tread, and it grew quieter once I became a Shifter."

A welter of emotions pummeled her. Happiness. Confusion. Shame. She sat down in a hurry and looked away, the humiliation from earlier fresh enough to make her cheeks heat. "You don't have to babysit me. I'm all right."

The open expression on his face faded. "No one sent me to check up on you, if that's where you're headed." He let go of her arm and stepped back. "Everyone is gathering on the bridge in about half an hour. You need to be there too."

Something about his tone snapped her out of her funk. "Why? What's going on?"

"They can't raise McMurdo on the radio."

Zoe thought about it. "What's so unusual about that? I'm pretty sure Ketha lost contact with the outside world a few years into the Cataclysm."

He balanced from foot to foot with the rocking motion of the ship. "The satellite network is down. Has been for years, but before satellites, ships used shortwave radios to communicate over distances."

"And no one at McMurdo is answering?"

"Exactly."

"It's fine if you want to sit." She stole a glance at him. "I have enough to feel bad about without adding a lack of manners to the list."

Recco didn't wait for a second invitation. He swung by the bar and grabbed a glass before he pulled out the chair across from hers and slid into it. Hefting the bottle she'd placed on the table, he poured a finger into his glass. "What's bothering you? Everyone missed you at dinner. Aura told us she didn't think you'd be down."

Zoe rounded on him. "How can you ask what's bothering me? You were there. Goddammit." She pounded a closed fist on the table and winced when pain lanced up her arm. "You saw what a blithering ninny I turned into."

He closed his fingers around her fist. "Not what I observed at all. The magic from the instrument was powerful. Did you realize part of it was aimed at me?"

Zoe's eyes widened. "Aw shit. Did it hurt you? Or your wolf?"

"No. It made it abundantly clear, though, it expected me to let go of you." He inhaled, a ragged sound that tore at her heart. "You weren't the only casualty. Beyond the lyre's efforts to upset my grip, every man there got hammered with lust."

His cheeks developed a warm hue, but he kept talking. "I haven't had such an instantaneous physical response since I was a teenager. Daide too, and I have no reason to believe Viktor or Juan were immune. Ted and Boris were groping each other, something Boris would never have done in public. Argies aren't as progressive as other cultures, and they tend to keep same-sex activities under wraps."

"Your reaction to them isn't surprising. Sirens lure men to their doom, using sex as bait." Zoe shook her head to clear her thoughts. "What none of us knew was how they made new Sirens."

"Would you have been more careful if you'd known about it?" He took a sip of the whiskey, sighing with pleasure as he swallowed.

Her mouth twisted downward. "Probably not."

He let go of her and spread his hands across the table. "From where I sit, you got snared in one kind of magic. The men and I fell prey to another. What I don't understand is why you're beating yourself up. You wanted the lyre. I wanted one of those Sirens..." he faltered, and then added, "In an up close and personal way. My wolf told me it would have stepped in before anything happened, but its offer to intervene doesn't dilute how much I craved one of those abominations."

"They looked pretty desirable to me." Zoe set her glass down. "Most of us would kill for bodies like theirs. From the waist up, anyway."

"See what you're doing?"

"Not exactly. In truth, I've been trying not to look too hard nor too deep at anything right now."

He focused his liquid dark gaze on her. "You're trying to make me feel better about falling under the Sirens' spell. And you're succeeding by normalizing my reaction to them. The only reason you're chagrined by your response to them is you didn't expect them to recruit you into their ranks."

She wanted to protest her discomfort ran deeper, except maybe it didn't. She'd been quick to offer him latitude for his lust. Perhaps her situation wasn't as unique—or as horrible—as she believed.

"What? I can feel your thoughts churning." He grinned crookedly. "I'm not adept enough to listen in. Not yet, anyway."

"Even if you were, it's not polite to barge into someone else's mind."

"You gals do it to each other often enough."

"Yes, and I blame all those years of close quarters in Ushuaia. We had to fly beneath the Vampires' radar, so we resorted to mind reading and telepathic communication. Kept us safer since Vamps weren't particularly skilled in that regard."

"You didn't answer my question."

"Not sure it has an answer. In the first place, I assumed the Sirens lived on one of the islands off the coast of Greece. Finding them here was a shock, and probably why I never associated the discordant music in my mind with them." She sat straighter in her chair. "It's an excuse. A much bigger item is it never occurred to me mythical beings would tap humans to swell their ranks."

"Aren't there stories about such things happening?"

Zoe rolled her eyes. "Of course there are. I know dozens. For me to put two and two together and come up with fifteen is inexcusable. Maybe part of me never believed the material I taught. All those stories were allegory, kind of like the Bible..." Her words ran down. No matter how she sliced and diced things, she'd made a string of elementary errors, and they'd ended up trapping her.

"This will sort itself out, if you let it. We probably should get up to the bridge."

She nodded and waggled the bottle his way. "Want another shot of fortification?"

"Nah. I'm good. Never was much of a drinker."

"Och, laddie. Sure and ye'd naught survive in Ireland where they take a man's measure by how much booze he can consume and still remain upright." Zoe walked the bottle back to its slot on the far side of the bar. When she returned, Recco was standing.

"Love your brogue."

"'Tis always there. I was laying it on a wee bit thick for emphasis."

They walked out of the bar next to one another, knocking hips as they jockeyed through the doorway. It might be the infusion of whiskey, but she felt more settled, not so sunk in self-pity.

"Thanks for the pep talk," she said as they traipsed up several sets of stairs.

"Thanks for not sending me packing. You came close."

She stopped on the fifth deck's landing. "How'd you know?"

He shrugged. "Try being a vet for a long time. The animals

couldn't talk with me, so I developed other skills to help figure out what was going on with them."

She chuckled. "So now I'm a pony or a wee dog?"

"I don't know. Do you have a totem animal?"

His question surprised her. "Not that I know of. There's my coyote, but I've never thought of it in quite that way. Why? Do you?"

"Yes. They're part of my culture."

Fascinated, she leaned close. "Is it anything like the Shifter bond?"

He drew his dark brows together. "Not really. My wolf is—or will be once I get better with Shifter magic—part of me. Interestingly, my totem animal is also a wolf. I never held conversations with it, though. Young men—and women too—take part in a coming of age ceremony when they reach puberty. Years ago, the ceremony included choosing a mate. You spend three days in the forest on your own. When you return to your people, you've discovered your totem animal and are deemed an adult."

People streamed up the stairs, splitting to move around them. Everyone greeted her as they passed by, telling her they were glad she was still in one piece.

"I'd love to hear more about your traditional ceremonies," Zoe told Recco, "but maybe we should follow everyone else. So Viktor— or whoever is running this meeting—doesn't end up repeating himself."

Recco smiled warmly and hooked a hand beneath her elbow. "I agree. Being late never sets a good precedent."

They polished off the remaining set of stairs and walked into the bridge. Viktor and Juan stood near the helm, both wearing grim expressions. The small island of equanimity Zoe had glommed onto, frittered to nothing. Something had happened. She'd bet her near brush with Siren-hood on it.

Boris, Ted, and Sasha were last to arrive, and they walked to the windows before settling into chairs.

Viktor turned to face everyone. "Good. You're all here. We really didn't need this meeting after all. Someone at McMurdo responded to my radio call. Finally."

Juan elbowed him. "You have to tell them the rest of it."

Something flashed from Viktor's green eyes. It might have been apprehension, except it was gone so fast Zoe couldn't tell.

"Rest of what?" Boris spoke up. Dark hair swept back from a high forehead, and his brown eyes were pinched at the corners.

"Indeed. What is going on at McMurdo?" Sasha asked in his pronounced Russian accent. Bald and with kind, dark eyes, he looked far better than he had when they'd found him living in an ice cave. "We had shortwave radios at Arctowski. Many times, we ping McMurdo, but they never pick up."

"This time, they did," Viktor said. "I'd been trying off and on ever since we left Arctowski, alternating satellites with shortwave."

"Cut to the chase. What's left there?" Karin asked.

"I don't know." Viktor raked curved fingers through his tawny hair. "The conversation was normal enough, except I didn't recognize the man's name. He identified himself as John Anderson. I asked what happened to Jack DeVoe, but he didn't seem to know the last base commander."

"He might have transferred out of there," Boris said. "He'd been talking about retiring for years before the Cataclysm hit."

"Wouldn't one base commander know who preceded him?" Zoe asked.

"I'm not being clear," Viktor said. "This was scarcely a base commander. I got the impression someone wandered by and noticed their shortwave was blinking."

"Did you tell them we were close and planning to stop?" Ted asked. White-blond hair fell across his forehead, and he pushed it out of the way, revealing a pair of keen blue eyes.

Viktor nodded. "John didn't say much. I'd have expected more enthusiasm. They can't have seen anyone beyond whoever's left there for a long time."

"What precisely did he say?" Juan pressed. "You never did tell me."

"It wasn't exactly 'whatever,' but it came close. I asked my raven if it picked up on anything odd, and it hadn't."

"Might bode better than you expect." Aura stood and made her way to Juan's side. "If anyone at McMurdo wanted to trap us or use us for nefarious purposes, they'd have been far more gung ho after you suggested stopping."

"The poles have an unpredictable effect on people," Viktor said. "It's why most of us limit our time here and in the Arctic to the summer months."

"Why would they be any worse off than us?" Tessa spoke up. "We spent a decade in Ushuaia." Her curly black hair had been tamed into braids, and her dark eyes were serious.

"Ushuaia's not nearly this far south. It has trees. Seasons. Some daylight even in June," Juan replied.

"The question is whether we stop at McMurdo." Viktor's statement was devoid of inflection. "I believe we owe it to ourselves to at least take a shot at landing there. If there's too much ice, we'll pass on by and turn the ship north." He sent a pointed glance Juan's way.

The mountain cat shifter sucked in an audible breath. "Most of my reluctance was based on no radio contact. Since you talked with someone, I'm game to see what's left there."

"Discussion?" Viktor's gaze roved through the room. When no one said anything, he nodded. "Done. Who has watch between now and midnight?"

"Me." Boris strode to the front of the room.

Recco stood and waited for Zoe to get to her feet. "Want me to walk you to your cabin?"

"Sure. On one condition."

He eyed her. "I agree."

"You don't even know what it is yet."

"Doesn't matter."

She smiled. "You make it hard not to like you."

"What's the American expression? You used it too."

"Busted?" She furled a brow.

"Yup. That's it. There might be a method to my madness. I'll never tell."

He grinned engagingly and steered her toward the door where they joined the others. No one said much as they filed out of the bridge, and Zoe didn't need her mind-reading ability to know they had to be worried. So far, they were batting three for three. Grytviken and Arctowski had yielded monsters. So had their last toss-up with the Sirens.

No reason to expect McMurdo would ruin their perfect average. She waited for her coyote to pop up with some bit of pithy advice, but it remained silent.

8

ASYLUM?

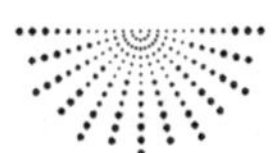

Recco leaned over the rail and peered at McMurdo, a sprawling complex sitting on hills above the Ross Sea. The Ross Ice Shelf Viktor and Juan had been concerned about remained well inland—rather than spilling out into the ocean—so they had a clear shot at getting close enough to launch the Zodiacs.

He took a deep lungful of frigid air, welcoming it after the dry heat of the ship's interior. It hadn't taken long to reach McMurdo, only one more day. He'd wondered about Scott base, a neighboring installation run by New Zealand. According to Boris, they'd temporarily closed it for needed repairs a month before the Cataclysm struck. Leaving Antarctica might have been a stroke of luck for the couple hundred scientists who'd staffed the base—depending on where they ended up sitting out the Cataclysm.

Most of yesterday had been spent working on his fledgling Shifter magic, which meant he'd been with Zoe. She was all business, though. Probably a good thing since it kept him on track. Not that his wolf wouldn't have leapt into the breach if his attention wandered. Becoming more adept as a Shifter wasn't an optional endeavor. It was both serious and mandatory.

He and Zoe sat together at breakfast, mostly continuing the

91

previous day's tutorial on the best uses of his new ability to leverage magic. She'd said she liked him when they left the bridge night before last. It had been the only personal comment from her. He wanted more but was willing to offer her all the emotional space she needed. They had time to get to know one another.

At least the haunted, guilty look had left her eyes. He hoped he'd helped free her conscience from guilt and blame. Once they were done clearing the breakfast things away, he'd invited her to join him out on deck. She'd demurred. The women were having some kind of meeting this morning. No one had offered details, yet Recco felt certain they were planning for contingencies if things went to hell once they landed at McMurdo.

Both Viktor and Juan had tried to reestablish radio contact multiple times, but no one picked up. Recco harbored visions of the hapless soul—the man who'd been dumb enough to respond to the radio—hamstrung in some dungeon. He grimaced. His imagination was probably working overtime.

Just because Arctowski had turned into a snake pit harboring evil didn't mean McMurdo would too.

A dark shadow cut across his field of vision, chopping through the ocean's uneven surface. He shielded his eyes with a hand to cut the glare and scanned the area where he thought he'd seen something unusual, a hollow in the waves that didn't belong there.

Gunmetal gray swells tipped with frothy white rolled past, heading for shore. He was almost ready to decide he hadn't seen anything, when a shiny, black triangular shape slithered across several waves. He kept his gaze glued to it, urging whatever was down there to show more of itself.

Almost as if the creature heard him, a blunt, wedge-shaped head broke the surface. Reptilian in appearance, amber eyes were spaced wide on either side of its head. The creature's mouth was open, displaying double rows of sharp teeth. It twisted until it looked straight at him before angling its head downward. As it dove beneath the surface, long loops of its body created humps before disappearing entirely.

Recco activated his fledgling telepathic skills, one of the many things he'd worked on the previous day. *"Daide. Get out here. I think I saw a sea serpent."*

After a long pause, a garbled, *"Where are you?"* met his request.

"Deck Three. Bow."

Daide must have been on his way while sorting out how to initiate a telepathic query because the sound of boots pounded toward Recco.

"What did it look like?" Daide demanded as he chugged up next to Recco.

Recco moved his gaze from the ocean's surface to his friend. "The Loch Ness monster."

Daide screwed his face into a frown. "Come on. Give me details."

"Blackish-gray. Shiny. Scales. Amber eyes. Head like a trowel. The skull was maybe two feet across with a long snout. Double rows of teeth—sharp, not blunt—and an undulating, snakelike body. I didn't see all of it, but at least six coils flashed past me after it dove. I know how crazy this sounds. The thing looked at me as if it actually saw me."

"Mmph. Where was it?"

Recco pointed a few degrees off the bow. "It was moving pretty fast, so where it is now is anyone's guess. Did my description ring any bells?" Intellectual curiosity sparred with concern. Daide's specialty had been marine life, and Recco silently urged him to come up with a rational explanation. Something beyond sea serpent.

"If anyone except you had seen it," Daide said in a slow, thoughtful tone, "I'd be convinced it was a lungfish, an oarfish, a whale, a shark, or maybe a relict plesiosaur, or a mosasaur, or some other Mesozoic reptile."

"It wasn't a whale or a shark or anything like that."

Daide drew his dark brows together. "I said if it was anyone but you. You never did listen very well."

"Spare me."

"*Amigo.* I don't want to fight with you." Daide scanned the ocean's surface, clearly hoping for a sighting.

Two sets of eyes were always better, so Recco focused on the other side of the bow. "Men have reported sea serpent sightings as far back as we have written records."

"Indeed they have," Daide agreed. "Never in these waters, though. At least not that I'm aware of. Closest they came was off the southern Chilean coast. I always figured they preferred warmer water. Think about it. Reptiles are cold-blooded—"

"Dinosaurs weren't," Recco cut in. "Didn't a 2014 study postulate they were closer to mammals than anything else."

"Yes. Good memory. I was talking about reptiles, not dinosaurs, though. Hey! Is that what you saw?" Daide plastered himself against the rail and stared out to sea.

Recco joined him. Sure enough. The familiar head cut through the waves. This time it didn't look at him. "Yes. That's it."

"Son of a bitch. Not that I don't trust your powers of observation, but I was certain you were wrong."

Recco bit back a tart rejoinder. "Do you know what it is?"

Daide whipped a pair of binoculars out of a pocket and focused on the serpent's head. The creature seemed to be keeping pace with the ship, although it was unlikely.

Recco waited for it to veer off. "Can I look?"

"When I'm done."

"It will be gone by then," Recco protested.

"I don't think so. We've disturbed its hunting grounds, which likely means we're stuck with it until we leave here."

"What is it?" Recco separated the words for emphasis.

Daide handed the binoculars over. "A genuine sea serpent. My guess is it's a leftover from the Mesozoic era. It might have been trapped in ice or stuck in some kind of stasis. The Cataclysm freed it."

Recco dialed in the binoculars to take a more detailed look at the back of the thing's head. It didn't make him feel any better. Barnacles clung to the scales, and it was even more menacing when he had the benefit of a closer view. "I've seen enough." He gave the binoculars back. "Your Cataclysm theory doesn't make sense."

"Why not?" Clearly fascinated, Daide stared at the serpent again.

"I understand beasts entering stasis and their metabolism slowing to nothing, but what's it been eating these last three months since we blew up the Cataclysm?"

"Krill? Plankton? Fish?" Daide shrugged. "It looks healthy enough. If it were starving, it might be up on deck, trying to eat us."

"Very funny."

"I wasn't trying to be. Sea serpents aren't like fish. They can survive out of water. Maybe floating the rafts isn't such a good idea, though. If we sailed *Arkady* in close enough to discourage whatever's out there, we'd risk grounding the hull."

Recco sucked air through his teeth, embarrassed he hadn't connected the dots first. The Zodiacs might have multiple air chambers, even so, they'd scarcely be a deterrent for the three-inch-long teeth he'd seen.

"I'm going to the bridge. Maybe Viktor or Juan know about this thing? They sailed these waters for a long time."

"I'll be right here if you need me."

Daide settled in, leaning his elbows against the rail as he sighted the serpent through the binoculars. Recco recognized his erstwhile partner's body language. He'd shifted to full research mode and would be perfectly happy remaining where he was for hours. Or until he got so cold he had to come inside.

Recco took the outside stairways and worked his way to the bridge. Like as not, whoever had the helm had noticed them staring out to sea with binoculars. They might even have sighted the Mesozoic holdover.

He pushed open the door and unzipped his parka. Juan stood at the helm and nodded Recco's way. "I figured one of you would show up here. Do either of you know what that thing is?"

"Daide thinks it's a prehistoric sea serpent."

Juan looked askance at him. "Really? Didn't most of them die out with one of the last ice ages?"

Recco shrugged out of his coat and hung it over a hook. "I presume your question means you've never seen anything like it before."

"Of course I have. Not here, though."

A tightly wound spot inside Recco relaxed, but only a little. Despite Daide's assessment, he'd been worried the serpent fell into a magical category. "Have they ever caused you problems?"

"No. They've never hung around like this one's doing, either." Juan angled his chin at the windows. Daide was still hanging over the rail, and the sea serpent had moved closer. Rather than swimming ahead, it was definitely keeping pace with *Arkady*.

"Maybe it's lonely," Recco ventured. He knew less than nothing about this variety of ocean dweller, but many animals were happiest in packs.

"Or hungry." Juan's words held a sour note. "The couple of times I've seen them before, they were alone."

"Where's Viktor?"

"Asleep. He had the helm until six this morning."

A glance at the clock told Recco it was ten thirty. "Daide and I were concerned about floating Zodiacs with the predator swimming around. How long before we drop anchor?"

"Maybe half an hour. I'm worried the rafts would be vulnerable too. We could take the Ruger Guide gun and blow the serpent out of our way." He dusted his palms together. "Problem solved. Unless it has a mate hiding in some underwater grotto."

Recco winced. He'd been in the business of saving animals, not murdering ones that hadn't done anyone any harm.

"Didn't care much for my idea, eh?" Juan tapped keys, feeding course adjustments into the ship's computer.

"I'd rather wait until it poses a problem."

Juan shook his head. "We wouldn't have any kind of time to mount a defense. Those snake things are fast. If it rushed a raft, we'd barely have an opportunity to shoulder the rifle. Even if we got off a couple shots— unless we were extraordinarily fortunate and hit something vital—the sea serpent would have plenty of time to sink the raft before it died."

Recco couldn't argue the fact. Most animals took a long time to die. "Besides shooting it outright, do you have other ideas?"

"Damn straight I do. I never wanted to stop here in the first place. I'm going to revisit this whole thing once Vik is—"

A crackling sound snapped Recco's head around. "What was that?"

Juan stared at a bank of instruments, one of which held a blinking red light. "Son of a bitch, it's the shortwave." He trotted to the radio and snatched it out of its cradle. Depressing a switch, he said, *"Arkady."*

"You are the ship, correct?" a woman with a clipped German accent asked.

"We are a ship," Juan replied in a cautious tone.

"Do not play games with me, young man. My name is Etta Achter. I was a general surgeon when this base was still operative. I demand asylum for myself and those remaining here under the terms of the second of the Geneva conventions."

"Geneva what?" Recco murmured.

Juan waved him to silence. "Look. Dr. Achter, there's scarcely enough of the world left for Geneva to come into play. Why are you requesting asylum? What threats do you face? How many of you are there?"

When Juan switched the radio to receive, a long sibilant hiss threaded its way between crackles. "We are ten, including me. Everyone else is either dead or deranged."

Recco exchanged glances with Juan, not liking the sound of *deranged*. Dead was easy enough to understand, but what had driven men and women to madness? Further, what were the deranged doing that made the doctor want to run fast and far from them? The radio fell silent.

"Are you still there?" Juan asked after a couple of minutes slid by.

"*Ja*. I am waiting for your response to my request."

"And I'm waiting for you to answer the rest of my questions. We've had major issues with everything from demons to Vampires to Sirens. You'll forgive me if I don't jump because you snapped your fingers. My ship's safety is my first priority."

Recco grabbed the radio and keyed it. "What he didn't tell you is a sea serpent is keeping track of us. It may not be safe to launch the Zodiacs."

Juan extended his hand and Recco slapped the radio back into his palm, activating its receive function.

"Of course it would not want you to land," the woman muttered, followed by, "If you do not help us, we will all be dead before the next winter is done."

"Maybe they could use their own rafts," Recco suggested. "One trip across the bay is safer than two if we went to pick them up."

"It would address their problems without undue risk to us," Juan replied. "So long as they're human and not some magical monstrosity with ulterior motives that wants to take over the ship."

Recco didn't say anything. Ten was a big enough number, he and the others would never make it through a pitched battle without sustaining casualties.

"*We'd shift.*" His wolf sounded positively feral. "*I'd welcome a good scrap. It's been too long.*"

Juan keyed the radio. "My associate had a good suggestion. Last time I sailed through here, McMurdo had a small fleet of motorboats. They'd do better against an attack from the sea serpent than a rubber raft. I need a list of names of who you're requesting asylum for. And if you coming to us would be acceptable."

"I will get back to you before the night is out."

The radio crackled to silence, and Juan tucked it back into its slot. "She left a whole lot out," he said.

"She certainly did," Recco concurred.

"Who left what out?" A sleepy-looking Viktor with tousled hair trotted into the bridge. "I heard the last bit of your conversation. It didn't make much sense."

"We heard from McMurdo." Juan sketched out what Dr. Achter had said.

Viktor dropped onto a stool and dragged his hair into a sloppy queue, securing it with a length of leather cord. "She really quoted the Geneva Convention?" At Recco's nod, Viktor shook his head. "She must be old as Croesus, or a good historian."

"She wouldn't have to be either," Recco said. "She's had years with not much to do except troll through the library I figure they have at the base." He directed his next words at Juan. "What do you suppose she meant by 'Of course it would not want you to land'?"

Viktor looked from one to the other of them. "What wouldn't want us to land? Would one of you back up so I understand what's going on?"

"Remember the beached sea serpent we found above the Arctic Circle in Norway?" Juan asked.

"Sure. It had been dead for a long time. Why?"

"There's a live one, and it took a fancy to the ship." Juan waved an arm at the windows. "See Daide out there with his binoculars trained on the water? He's keeping an eye on it."

"Nah," Recco cut in. "It fascinates him. He'll watch it until he's skirting hypothermia."

Viktor got to his feet and strode to the radio, staring at it as if it had grown two heads. "Crap. Why can't anything ever be straightforward? We can't launch rafts with something as likely to eat us as bid us good day, patrolling the bay. It's good you asked them to show up in their own boats. At least they have metal hulls."

"Won't matter," Juan cut in, "if the thing swims beneath their boat and upends it."

"The good doctor said she'd get back to us before the night is out," Recco said. "We can't sail past until we hear from her. What if her story is true? She sounded afraid. I could be off by a few hundred, but this base used to hold something like fifteen hundred people. It's hard to wrap my mind around their numbers being reduced to ten."

"She never did say how many were deranged." Juan blew out a tired breath. "It could be part of the problem. Maybe they're contained in some way, and require constant oversight. I've been at McMurdo, and it's far from a secure facility."

"She might not have wanted to say much because she was afraid of being overheard," Recco suggested.

Viktor made a fist and pounded it into his other hand. "Too many mights and maybes for my taste. We need their list of names, and I need more information before even one of them sets foot on my ship. I'll be goddamned if I bring someone on board who morphs into those hybrid animal nightmares we faced at Arctowski.

"Gosh, I kind of liked the Gila monster with the sea serpent's head." Recco tried for humor to lighten the mood, but Viktor glared at him.

"Yeah, you liked it so well you killed it." Juan stalked to the windows and stared out, clearly thinking.

Recco joined him and eyeballed Daide. His posture hadn't altered by so much as a finger twitch since Recco left him. Something didn't seem quite right. He wasn't sure what was bothering him since Daide frequently spent long hours observing marine life. Why did this feel different?

Zoe, Karin, Ketha, and Aura walked out a side door and joined Daide. Recco couldn't hear, but it appeared the women were talking to him. Worried looks bloomed on all their faces, and they each grabbed a part of Daide and dragged him away from the rail. He flailed against their hold, shouting something, except it was unintelligible from so far away.

The area around the five developed the iridescent aspect Recco associated with Shifter magic as spells bubbled around them.

"What the fuck?" Juan splayed his palms against the glass.

Recco didn't wait around to answer. He grabbed his parka and ran out of the bridge, taking the outer stairs since they provided a direct line to the broad open deck below. The cold snatched breath from his lungs; he zipped up to his chin and buried his head in the insulated hood.

Worry warred with guilt. Recco moved as fast as he could and not fall ass over teakettle down the metal risers. He never should have left. Not with the thing in the water.

Yeah. Twenty-twenty hindsight is always a boot in the backside.

By the time he got to where the women had Daide spread faceup on the deck, he was moaning and thrashing from side to side. At least he wasn't trying to get away.

"What's wrong?" Recco fell to his knees next to his friend and grasped a gloved hand. "Talk to me, *amigo*."

"He'll be fine," Karin said in her best doctor voice.

"If he's not in immediate danger, let's at least move him inside." Recco started to heft Daide into his arms.

"I can walk," Daide said in a gravelly voice that sounded like he'd been asleep for a hundred years.

Recco rocked back on his heels and pulled Daide to his knees. From there, he helped him to his feet. The women hovered, talking to one another in hushed tones, but Recco wasn't paying any attention.

"What happened to you?" he asked as he half dragged Daide through the closest door before letting go of him.

Daide's drained expression developed rueful edges. "No one to blame except myself. My coyote did its damnedest to dissuade me. You know how I am once I fall into observation mode."

"Yeah. I know. You still haven't told us what happened."

"The sea serpent—and I was correct, it's a plesiosaur—has ways of communicating. I was talking with it. Or rather, listening while it recounted its life story."

"How is talking with a sea serpent even possible?" Recco fell back a pace, dumbfounded.

"And why not?" Zoe demanded, her brogue in full bloom. "Ye talk with the bond animals. Why would conversation with any magical animal be so surprising? I'd take the whole *life story* presentation with a few grains of salt, though."

"Daide isn't bonded to the plesiosaur," Recco protested. "Why would it talk with him?"

"Not for lack of effort on the serpent's fault," Zoe retorted. "Hence my grain of salt cautionary note."

Understanding kicked Recco full in the guts, and he grabbed Daide's arm. "Christ. I never should have left you alone."

Daide rolled his eyes. "Since when did you turn into my parent? It's been bad enough playing the other half of the *Odd Couple* with you for twenty plus years. Besides, even if you'd been standing guard, it wouldn't have mattered. You wouldn't have had any better luck pounding sense into me than my coyote." Daide slumped against the wall, looking cowed. "I was fascinated. When I realized it was talking with me, I got sucked in. I'm still not sure how it happened."

The area around Daide grew taut with pulsing magic until a shadowy coyote with russet fur formed. Its paw flashed out, and four bloody streaks formed on Daide's cheek. The magic dissipated as quickly as it had risen.

Karin rushed toward him; he waved her back. Blood welled down the right side of his face, but he didn't try to staunch its flow. "I deserved that. My bond animal marked me. It's a warning to any others who would seek to disrupt our bond."

"Thank the goddess it didn't decide you're more trouble than you're worth," Aura muttered.

"You may not believe me, I'm grateful for its loyalty as well."

Daide staggered slightly and turned toward his cabin. "I'm going to throw cold water on my face and pull myself together. Nothing like coffee and humiliation for breakfast."

Recco watched him go. "Don't take too long," he called after his retreating form. "We have other problems."

Daide didn't even turn around. "'Fraid my problem cache is full up, *amigo*. Solve whatever this one is without me."

9

ONLY ONE WEE PROBLEM

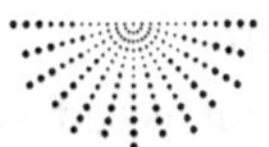

Zoe swallowed hard. At least Daide was safe. If they hadn't shown up when they did, it was anyone's guess what might have happened. Daide had been deep in the creature's thrall. If it hadn't been trying to woo him, gain his trust, he'd have moved back inside. As it was, they were damn lucky he hadn't vaulted over the rail when the four of them stormed him. If he had, they'd never have pried him from the monster's clutches.

"What is that thing?" Recco asked in a strangled-sounding voice.

"Sea dragon," Ketha said. "It might look the same, but it's in a whole different universe than sea serpents."

"When did you come to that conclusion?" Zoe's voice cracked, and she cleared her throat. It didn't get rid of the thick places, though.

"Between the outside deck and here," Ketha replied. "It's not like there are a whole lot of choices. If it was a plesiosaur, like it told Daide, it wouldn't have magic, now would it?"

"Daide needs to know." Recco turned to follow his friend.

"No, he doesn't," Karin said. "At least not right away. He feels bad enough about what happened. No rush to add information. It's not like he's going to sneak back out on deck and give in to the thing."

"This pretty much kills stopping at McMurdo, huh?" Aura moved closer to Recco.

"There's another wrinkle," he muttered.

"Only a single wee problem? Sure and we can uncover more than one." Zoe tossed her hood back and unzipped her red, insulated parka.

"Your sarcasm isn't useful." Ketha sent a pointed glance scudding across the space between them.

"What's the wrinkle?" Karin asked.

"A doctor at McMurdo requested asylum for herself and nine others."

"Asylum from what?" Karin set her mouth in a harsh line.

"I have no idea."

"How is it only ten people are left at such a huge research station?" Aura asked.

"Don't have that answer, either," Recco replied. "Some died, but the doc gave Juan and me the impression the others had lost their minds. Deranged was the term she used."

"Deranged, eh." Zoe shifted from one booted foot to the next, not liking the sound of any of this.

"Anyway"—Recco hurried on before they could pester him to death with questions—"Juan asked for a list of names of the asylum-seekers. Viktor wants a whole lot more than names. He wants to know their positions at the base. The doctor is supposed to get back to us sometime before midnight."

"I don't see how we can motor across the bay, pick up a bunch of refugees, and motor back without the sea dragon raising hell," Karin muttered.

"Sorry. Left that part out." Recco gazed at them out of worried dark eyes. "Apparently McMurdo has several aluminum boats with outboard motors. Juan told the doc she'd have to find her own way out to us. She knew about the serpent…er, the dragon. Didn't seem surprised it was patrolling their inlet."

"Unless she commands magic," Zoe spoke slowly, "she'd have no idea *dragon* was even in the running for what the thing really is."

Ketha made a sour face. "There go all those plans we hatched up."

"Don't be so quick to toss them out." Zoe felt protective of their earlier strategy session. The creak and clank of the anchor chain blasted her.

"It appears we've arrived," Recco muttered.

"We'll be here for a few hours," Aura said. "I'm going up to the bridge to see if there have been any new developments. Like further radio contact from McMurdo."

"I'll join you," Ketha said. "Viktor will want a full report on Daide."

"What are you going to tell him?" Recco seemed to have moved past his shock and accompanying disbelief about the sea serpent being a sentient dragon.

"Everything." Ketha trotted up a nearby set of stairs with Aura right behind her.

He rubbed a hand across his stubble-covered chin. "I'm still trying to absorb dragons being real, although I'm not certain why they're any harder to accept than Vampires."

"Or Shifters?" Zoe couldn't rein in her sarcasm, and she kicked herself for being a bitch. Her cheeks heated, and she mumbled, "Sorry. It came out wrong."

He moved closer to her. "You hail from the British Isles, traditional home of dragons. How about telling me what you know about them?"

Still in a foul mood, she twisted to face him. "Och, ye mean the fire-breathing bastards that swoop down and scoop up unsuspecting virgins."

"The same." His grin was infectious. "Although I imagine they spent more time filching sheep, goats, and cattle than virgins. Easier to find."

"Pfft." Karin shook her head. "I can skip the mythology refresher.

I'm going to check on Daide. Make sure he's not beating himself up too badly."

"Might be a good call," Recco said. "He tends to be harder on himself—less tolerant of mistakes—than anyone else would be. Whenever one of his patients died, he'd spend days—sometimes weeks—doing a post-mortem to determine if he'd missed something critical."

"An endeavor he and I have in common," Karin muttered and walked down Deck Three's main corridor, her tread heavy and purposeful.

Zoe felt Recco's gaze on her. It pleased her and made her self-conscious at the same time. He was a damned attractive man, but he'd seen her at her worst. Daide's words about humiliation being served up with breakfast skirted close to what she'd felt like when she'd given in to the lyre and its hypnotic pull.

"Shall we stop by the kitchen?" Recco angled his head to make better eye contact. "We could get a nice cup of something hot, and then you can teach me about dragons."

A small shiver that had nothing to do with being cold slid down her spine. At least he hadn't suggested holding their tutorial in a cabin. Tongue-tied and awkward as a sixteen-year-old on her first date, Zoe turned and almost ran down the nearby stairwell. To cover her confused feelings, and push past her attraction for the man behind her, she said, "The first dragons actually hailed from China. At least I believe they did."

Zoe shouldered into the galley and plucked two mugs off hooks, handing one to Recco. He stuck his beneath the coffeemaker's spigot and nodded approvingly when dark, fragrant liquid dribbled into his cup. "Not much left. Enough for one cup, though." He tilted the machine to encourage what was inside to trickle out.

Zoe poured hot water over tea leaves and stirred in a small spoonful of sugar. "Ready?" She glanced his way.

"Lead out."

She walked through the swinging door and made her way to one of the corner tables. Recco sat across from her.

"How come you're not tossing questions at me?" she asked and took a sip of tea. The hot liquid tracked down her throat, its taste and scent reminding her of the home she'd never see again.

He shrugged. "Not sure what to ask. I figure there are two distinct lines of logic here. Dragon myths and real dragons. They must be related."

"Aye, they are. Men have reported dragon sightings forever. In truth, I have no idea whether the Asian or European variety came first. When the world grew smaller and explorers from the Orient discovered Europe—and vice versa—they uncovered common mythologies. Dragons were an element in many folktales."

"Have you ever seen one? Before today, that is." Recco set his cup down.

"Nay. If we had access to any of the Shifters' archives, though, we could research when the last dragon sightings were. I also have no idea what percentage are the seagoing variety."

"Mind if I run something by you?" He arched a dark brow.

"Not at all. I apologize for how short I was with you earlier. The women and I were finishing up with plans to deal with anything unusual at McMurdo when my coyote howled a warning. Before I could question it, a huge wave of power splatted against us. Ketha was first to react. She pounded out of the bar at a dead run with us strung out behind her."

"The magic left a trail, huh?"

"Aye, one I'd have been able to follow even after death."

A troubled look washed over his face. "Why didn't I feel it?"

"You must have. 'Twas only a few moments afore you showed up."

"I was on the bridge. I saw the four of you drag Daide away from the rail and came as fast as I could. No magic in play at all."

He looked so chagrined, she laid a hand over his where it rested on the table. "Magic has physical properties. If you weren't in its direct path, you wouldn't have sensed it."

"Or maybe I'll never be any good at this." He dragged his hand from beneath hers. "I never cared about developing competence as a Vampire. Bare bones ability was plenty to satisfy me." Something naked and raw ran beneath his words.

Her heart hurt for him. "Viktor and Juan were on the bridge with you. Right?" At his nod, she went on. "They didn't feel the magical barrage, either. Believe me, if they had, they'd have reacted to it."

A corner of his mouth turned down. "Just because I'm not the only inadequate one doesn't make me feel better. Don't mind me. I'm worried about Daide, and it's sent me into a funk."

"Och, and I know all about ill moods. Mine erupted all over you earlier. Back to dragons?"

"Sure. When you're starting with nothing, any information is valuable."

"Insofar as I know, no one's reported a dragon sighting—real or otherwise—since the early 1800s." She took a measured breath and smiled ruefully. "Modern life spelled the death of magic, or at least sent it underground. Each new scientific discovery made it harder to justify the existence of anything science couldn't dissect or explain.

"Along with the rise of science came far less tolerance for incidents eventually labeled as mental illness. Trances, predictions, even channeling psychic energies to heal illness became suspect occurrences."

"It was true in Argentina too," Recco murmured, looking thoughtful. "Shamans were common in my grandfather's time. They'd vanished—or gone underground—by the time I was old enough to understand such things."

"Aye, and so we killed all the mysteries. Bully for us, eh?" She closed her teeth over her lower lip feeling sad—and angry. "Along the way, we cut ourselves off from our most valuable resource: belief in the unseen world."

"My mother's father said much the same."

"How old were you when he died?"

"Ten. He left very specific instructions for what he wanted done with his body."

Zoe tilted her head to one side. "Let me guess. He wanted his remains cremated."

"How'd you know?"

She shrugged. "'Tis the only reliable way to be certain your enemies can't nab a bit of your essence, take it into themselves, and block your entry to the next world. My area of specialization as an archaeologist was native and indigenous peoples."

"Any particular reason you picked them?"

"Of course. They still believed in magic." Zoe tamped back a shy smile.

He narrowed his eyes. "Is there a link between dragons and death rituals?"

"Because dragons command fire? It's a tantalizing connection, except they didn't normally dabble in human affairs—unless they wanted something."

Drawn in by Recco's sincere expression and dark, liquid gaze, Zoe felt safe enough to lower her guard. Not only was he so stunning she'd never get tired of looking at him, he had a razor-sharp intellect, and the ability to approach problems from many sides—

"Why was that?"

"Why was what?"

"Dragons. Why'd they avoid human affairs?"

His question redirected her to the last thing she'd said. "The closest I can come is it would be like a king paying heed to the lowest commoner toiling in his field. If dragons considered humans at all, I suspect they saw them as a pesky inconvenience or something to amuse them. Shifters didn't fare much better."

Recco spread his hands in front of him. "If it's true, then why was the one out there"—he jerked his chin toward the windows lining one side of the dining room—"trying to lure Daide?"

Zoe shot to attention in her chair. "Holy godhead, 'tis a most excellent point."

"Thanks. What does it mean? Is fell magic powering it? Hell, is it even real or only a collection of cells, like those monsters the sorcerer at Arctowski constructed?"

Karin strode through the door at the far end of the room. "There you are," she called. "After talking with Daide, I'm convinced the serpent or dragon or whatever's out there isn't any more real than anything else we've come across."

Zoe pushed to her feet. "Och we've dealt with plenty that's real. Demons. Sirens. Vampires in stasis. It's beside the point. What did Daide say that made you question the dragon?"

"It was trying to convince Daide to leave the ship and remain at McMurdo. Dragons fly or swim. Neither variety would have the slightest use for a scientific research base."

"Aw crap." Recco stood too. "Did you stop by the bridge first to let them know?"

"Uh-uh. You were closer, and"—she turned her copper eyes on Recco—"I thought you might want to talk with Daide. He's still really morose."

"Doesn't surprise me. He expects a lot from himself. Always has. It made him a very good diagnostician because he was careful, went the extra mile for the tough cases, but his level of perfectionism cuts both ways. So did his control-freak inclinations."

Zoe watched him walk away. Despite the uneven start, she'd been enjoying their conversation. And his company. Probably far more than she should.

"He's a good man," Karin said without preamble as soon as the dining room door shut behind him. "You could do far worse."

Zoe's face warmed, and she looked away. "We're just getting to know one another," she protested. "Rowana was the matchmaker among us." The memory of her friend trickled through her like a sad, slow tide.

"Yeah. I miss her too, but not for her matchmaking skills. Something isn't right about this place," Karin muttered. "My magic is activated. My wolf is growling in the background. Hasn't said much, though."

Zoe snapped her fingers. "Daide's coyote. It wouldn't have been so upset it felt the need to show itself and mark him if the scaled fucker paddling around out there weren't real."

Karin's eyes widened. "Goddess's teats. You're correct. Then why the hell would the dragon bother with subliminal suggestion about the research base? On the rare occasions dragons went to the trouble to co-opt humans to their will, they took them flying."

"Just before they unseated them, ensuring they fell to their deaths," Zoe muttered. "Dragons were never our friends. If Daide's as quick to heap blame on himself as Recco suggested, maybe you didn't get the whole story from him."

Karin stood and headed out the door. "Why titrate it?"

"Because he'd have felt like a selfish ass—and a prime idiot—if he'd told you he'd always wanted to live in the ocean with a dragon." Zoe hustled out of the dining room, keeping pace with Karin. "I presume we're headed for Daide's cabin?"

"Where else? We need more information."

The sound of raised voices reached Zoe a few doors away from Daide's cabin. She knocked but didn't wait for a response before pushing the door open. None of the cabins had locks. She'd thought it odd, at first. When she'd asked why, Juan quoted some regulation for ships in *Arkady's* class.

The argument bouncing between the men cut off abruptly when she knocked. After she crowded inside with Karin, there wasn't much more floor space. "What was the fight about?" Zoe crossed her arms beneath her breasts and dropped an obvious truth spell over Recco and Daide.

"What the fuck is that?" Daide batted at white-gold netting settling over him.

"To make certain both of us tell the truth." Recco angled a hurt look Zoe's way.

"I could have made it invisible." Zoe battled impatience. "We have to figure out what's going on here. No room for half of anything."

Daide glared at her from haggard eyes. He'd never appeared worried about much of anything when he was a Vampire. Of course, Zoe hadn't known him very well then, either. An inch or so shorter than Recco, he had a more compact build with broad shoulders and a square jaw. Same dark hair and eyes, though. And same Native features.

Karin sidled between Zoe and the men. She stabbed an index finger into Daide's chest. "Your bond animal is convinced the sea creature is real. I trust it way more than I trust you."

"Thanks." Daide looked away.

"Did the dragon tell you how it got here?" Karin urged. "Was it another casualty of the Cataclysm?"

"Go on, *amigo*." Recco elbowed Daide. "Tell them what you were in the middle of telling me."

Daide's face turned ruddy, and he stared at his boots before curling his big hands into fists. "It chose to go to ground here. I'm not sure when. It never mentioned the Cataclysm. Someone at the base discovered its presence and freed it from ice where it had been frozen for god only knows how long."

"How long ago?" Zoe kept her voice soft, her question nonconfrontational.

"I'm not certain, some years after the Cataclysm was in full swing. I don't understand why the poisoned ocean water didn't kill it."

"Maybe it wasn't as toxic here," Karin muttered.

"What exactly did it want from you?" Zoe tweaked her spell. Daide flinched, so it must have zapped him.

"Is that really necessary? Christ. You have me cornered."

"Maybe it was overkill." Zoe reeled in her magic. "Will you answer my question now?"

Daide nodded. "It wanted me to seal it back into its crypt or tomb or wherever it chose to wait out Armageddon." His deep voice vibrated with emotion. "The fish are only now returning, but whoever released him has been force-feeding him humans for years. He's disgusted and appalled. He wants out, except he can't break free."

"What would happen if he swam away?" Recco asked.

"He said he's tried, gets confused, and ends up treading in circles in the Ross Sea."

Truth pinged cleanly off Daide's words. "Why'd you craft a batch of half-truths for Karin?" Zoe asked.

He raised his chin and met her gaze squarely. "Because I hadn't given up on finding a way to help the dragon. I made peace with my coyote after it marked me. My bondmate didn't understand, and it was jealous."

"Is your coyote willing to help now?" Karin spoke up.

"Yes. Frankly, I could give a fuck less about whoever's left at McMurdo. I want to honor the poor beast out there. We're the first people who've been here since the Cataclysm. The way things are going, it could be years before another ship stops."

The PA system crackled. "To the bridge, pronto," Viktor said. "Boats are headed our way."

Recco and Daide stared at each other. "The gangway," Recco muttered. "It's got to be up."

"I'll check it," Daide said. "The rest of you get to the bridge and tell them not to let anyone board."

"On my way." Karin bolted from the cabin.

"I'll pull up the rope ladder on the other side of the ship," Zoe said, leaving the room at a run before she was even done speaking.

She burst through a side door, not bothering to bundle her clothing close. She wouldn't be outside long enough to worry about freezing to death. Skidding to a halt in front of the handles that raised and lowered the thick ropes, she gave them a solid twist. They were coated with rime ice and didn't budge. Zoe grabbed the grips with both hands and really put her back into it. Grunting, sweating, swearing, she forced them to move a quarter turn at a time.

Before she was done, the drone of outboard motors reached her, but she was on the wrong side of the boat to see them. Damn. How many were there? She bent over the rail and assessed the rope. It was winding in easier now, so she raised it another three feet. Satisfied she'd done all she could, she ducked back inside and hastened to the bridge.

1 0

SKIN IN THE GAME

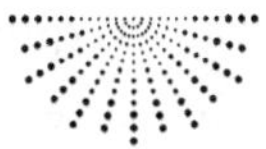

ecco ran to the gangway and breathed a little easier when he saw the ladder fully retracted and parallel with the waterline. A staunch breeze was picking up speed under gray skies, and visibility was still decent. Three small outboard crafts skimmed across the bay, fighting two-foot swells. At least it slowed them down. Zodiacs were better equipped to deal with rough water since their rubber bodies flexed.

"Don't trust me by myself, huh?" Daide sent a sour look his way. Before Recco could come up with something to soften the truth in his friend's words—it wasn't about trust so much as making certain the dragon didn't interfere—Daide clapped him on one shoulder. "I wouldn't trust me, either. Come on."

Recco raced up the stairs after him. The bridge was crowded when they got there. He scanned the crowd for Zoe but didn't see her. Maybe he should run back down and offer to help with the rope ladder. He crossed the bridge, intent on the door to access *Arkady's* port side, when Zoe blew through it. Her cheeks were white from cold, and she'd stuffed her hands in the pockets of her parka.

117

"I was headed your way," he said, aiming for a tone that didn't suggest a lack of faith in her competency.

"No need. 'Tis done." Skirting around him, she half ran to the windows, looking out.

"Most of us are here," Viktor said. "There's been no further communication from McMurdo, and those boats launched a few minutes ago. One is definitely in the lead. I have no fucking idea why those people disregarded my requests."

"My guess," Juan cut in, "is someone made a break for it, and those others have some skin in the game. Either they don't want the first batch to reach us at all, or they decided if the getting was good, they were jumping on the last train out of Dodge."

Aura snorted. "You've watched way too much American television."

Daide surged toward the door, but Recco caught him up before he got outside. "What is it?"

"Watch." Daide jerked his chin at the tableau playing itself out in the cove between them and the research base.

"If you know something"—Viktor raised his voice for emphasis —"let's hear it."

"The sea dragon is furious. It's bugling in my head when it's not cursing."

"What does it have to do with whoever's in those boats?" Juan asked.

"The quick and dirty version"—Daide turned away from the windows—"is someone at the base forced it from its lair, and then imprisoned it."

"It approached Daide, requesting assistance," Karin spoke up, aiming her words at Viktor. "Which is close to what I told you, except you were too wrapped up in watching the motorboats to pay much attention."

"The sea dragon wasn't part of the equation, then," Viktor muttered. Annoyance turned his eyes a darker green, and he said,

"Sorry, I'll try to do better. Feel free to clunk me over the head if I'm not as present as you need me to be."

"The dragon's out there. I see it." Zoe slapped a palm on the glass.

Recco hustled to her side, staring in the direction she indicated. Sure enough, the creature's dark, triangular head had broken the waterline. Opening its mouth, it screeched an unmistakable challenge, audible through the bridge's thick windows.

Four people were in the lead boat. One of them rose to his feet, a rifle balanced over one shoulder.

"Nooooo," Daide screeched.

The sea dragon dove beneath the choppy waves just before the rifle's report blasted, loud and lethal.

"Where's the polar bear gun?" Daide planted himself in front of Viktor.

"In the locker nearest the gangway on Deck Three," Viktor said. "You'll never retrieve it and get it loaded in time. Besides, the sea dragon seems like it can hold its own."

"I'm getting it anyway." Daide ran out of the bridge.

"Ted. Boris. Man the anchor." Viktor's command was terse.

"Do you mean pull anchor?" Ted asked, seeking clarification.

After a short pause, Viktor said, "Yes. Originally, I'd planned to have you standing ready. My raven is squawking up a storm. If things turn to shit, it'll happen fast. Hauling up the anchor takes time. We may not have any to spare if we need to power out of here."

"Got it." Boris faded through a side door, pulling on a jacket as he went. Ted followed him.

"Makes it more dangerous for the folk in those boats to use the gangway," Juan observed.

"You think I don't know that, mate?" Viktor's nostrils flared. "I'd be more inclined to put their safety first if they'd followed through on their end. Given us the information we need, rather than just showing up."

"Agreed. This feels a whole lot like Arctowski. I'm trying to argue myself out of it," Juan muttered.

"Makes two of us." Viktor turned away, studying the bank of instrumentation next to the helm.

Recco's brain churned as he sorted through possibilities. He tapped Zoe's arm. "If whoever trapped the dragon is in one of those boats, wouldn't they be able to control it?"

"Not necessarily." She creased her forehead into a worried expression. "It's not easy to corral something with magic. You have to keep changing the spell or it will discover a way to elude you."

"Like bacteria and antibiotics," he muttered. "Creative little bastards develop immunities, and it forces us to develop stronger drugs."

"Exactly." Approval flashed from her brown eyes.

"If the dragon hasn't found a way out, it must mean a powerful sorcerer is behind this." Recco's stomach tightened as adrenaline surged. He wanted to launch a raft and challenge the son of a bitch. The sea dragon was a magnificent creature. It deserved freedom.

Zoe nodded. "To force a dragon to his will, he'd have to be strong."

"Might be a her. Your prejudices are bleeding through."

Zoe snorted. "Aye, sure and no woman could be quite so wicked. Look."

He followed the line of her extended finger. Sure enough, the dragon was back. Farther out this time, but clearly with its own agenda. The figure in the boat had shifted to a kneeling position, rifle raised and ready.

"Can anything as prosaic as a bullet penetrate those scales?" Recco asked.

She glanced his way. "Dragons are immortal. It's how this one survived encased in ice or wherever it hid itself."

Daide ran out onto the broad deck he'd stood on earlier, the Ruger Guide gun tucked beneath one arm. Ted and Boris emerged a moment later and veered hard right to hunker over the anchor housing.

"Crap. Got to stop Daide before he shoots someone by mistake. He's developed a real savior complex around the sea dragon." Juan zipped into a parka, snapped on mitts, and pelted from the bridge after grabbing a bullhorn from its charging cradle.

"I'm going down there too," Recco said. Worry for Daide filled him. Maybe the sea dragon's motives had been pure, but he wouldn't bank on it. If it could use Daide in some way to buy its freedom, it would.

Zoe followed him outside, working her zipper up to her chin and flipping her hood over her bright hair. "Damn near froze my ass off working on the rope ladder," she muttered. "Not making the same mistake again."

He hooked an arm through hers, steadying her as they ran down several flights of stairs after Juan's retreating form. Recco had picked the outside staircases so he could keep an eye on Daide, the dragon, and the boats. Apparently, Juan was reading from the same script.

Once they reached the large, open deck, Juan strode to the rail and raised the bullhorn, aiming its cone at the lead boat. "Identify yourselves." His voice boomed, amplified by electronics. "Stow the rifle. If you fire one more shot, *Arkady* will exit these waters and leave you here."

Daide sent a pointed glance at Juan. "We're not leaving until the dragon is free."

Recco recognized the stubborn set of Daide's shoulders. The only way he'd abandon his post was if the dragon that had thrown itself on his kindheartedness was no longer imprisoned.

The driver of the lead raft picked up their own bullhorn. "You do not understand. The gun is for the serpent. You must let us board," a woman with a strong German accent cried.

Recco recognized the surgeon from earlier.

"Negative. You're not in command of this ship," Juan

countered. "You ignored my orders. I require a list of names, and my captain wants to know the role each person played at McMurdo."

"There is no time." The driver pointed behind her at the two other motorboats quickly gaining on them.

"Who's in them?" Juan asked.

"You will never believe me. The serpent controls them, and it ordered them to follow us. Probably to make certain we never reached your ship."

"What the hell? I thought it was a victim. How could it have minions?" Recco muttered.

"An excellent question," Zoe said. "One I'm asking my coyote right now."

Daide ran lightly to Juan. "Can I use the horn?"

Juan took the rifle, keeping it trained on the lead boat, and gave Daide the bullhorn. The small craft was almost to Arkady's shadow, but the surf was loud enough to make shouting back and forth unpleasant without an electronic assist.

Zoe leaned closer to Recco. "My magic is activated, and not in a good way."

Recco turned his attention inward to his wolf. *"Do you know anything that might help us?"*

"No. Leaving is the wisest course."

"What about the sea dragon?" Recco waited through several long breaths. His wolf didn't answer.

Meanwhile, Daide raised the horn to his mouth, fiddling with buttons with mitten-clad fingers. "Which of you controls the sea serpent?"

"No one controls that thing." The German doctor's retort was instantaneous. "We have been trying to make it go away for years."

"Not all of you," Daide countered. "Someone has been feeding it."

"You're mad. We scarcely have food for ourselves."

"It's eating humans."

"*Ja.* Because it sneaks close to shore after dark and grabs us."

"Give the horn back," Juan said. "Someone is lying. We have to figure out who."

Daide settled the rifle back into firing position.

Loops of chain clicked and clanked behind Recco. At least *Arkady* would be able to beat a retreat if needed. "Hey, *amigo*." He poked Daide. "Ask the dragon which of them is holding it against its will."

"I already did. It doesn't know."

The words rang sourly off Recco's magic. Daide wouldn't lie—not about something he'd adopted as a cause he was willing to go to the mat for.

"Och, but I think it does," Zoe said. Gaelic flowed from her, and she wove her hands into a complicated pattern. Magic rose. Multihued with an iridescent shimmery quality, it formed a path from her out into the dark-gray waters roiling around *Arkady*.

Her words became a chant, and the sea dragon swam along the path she'd created until its head was even with *Arkady's* hull. The shooter in the boat sighted down the barrel of his rifle. Juan raised the bullhorn. "If you pull the trigger, you'll be next."

"Thanks for permission." Daide's mouth split into a snarl so feral he barely looked human anymore, but his gaze remained glued on the dinghy.

"You will not fire until I say you can. Unless that bastard fires first." Juan shifted his gaze to the lead boat.

The sea dragon dragged scaled lips back from its double rows of teeth and spoke directly to Zoe. "I am not anxious to trade one master for another." Steam hissed through its open mouth.

"Who is your first master?" Zoe sang the words, dripping with a truth spell so potent Recco hunted through his memory banks for someone—anyone—who would fit the description of master, so he could confess his sins.

"Dragons are a free people. We answer to no one."

A spate of Gaelic was followed by, "Aye, yet ye related a tale of woe to one of our own for a purpose. What was it?" The pitch and timbre of Zoe's magic changed, adding compulsion to her truth spell.

The fine hairs on the back of Recco's neck quivered unpleasantly. Evil was near. He'd bet his last peso on it. *"Can we help Zoe?"* he asked his wolf.

"Maybe. This could go many different ways."

Ketha and Karin burst through one of the ship's inner doors and beat a track to either side of Zoe. Both women wore such troubled expressions, Recco inhaled sharply. His wolf had said *many different ways.* What did it mean? Ketha and Karin must have come on a dead run from the bridge as soon as Zoe lured the dragon with her spell.

"What's going on?" he blurted out, harsh and strident.

Ketha made a chopping motion and harmonized with Zoe's song. Karin joined in too, and the dragon pushed another couple of feet of coils above the waterline. The occupants of the first boat stared gape-mouthed. Maybe Zoe's spell had snared them too—or at least immobilized them. Recco had no idea what impact words spewing from a bullhorn would have on the magic cascading around them, and he didn't want to find out.

"Who is your master?" Zoe repeated. "Tell me, and I will release you."

Standing on the sidelines ate at Recco like acid. He readied magic intent on joining the women's spell.

"Do not do anything rash," his wolf said. *"Zoe took a huge chance. She merged her energy with the dragon's to gain knowledge."*

Recco made a fist, but stopped shy of pounding it against the rail. *"What's the downside?"*

"You mean the risk?"

"Yes." Impatience rattled through him like slot cars hurtling around a toy speedway.

A low, rumbling snarl filled his belly. Recco kept the sound inside. *"Dragons never form a bond with anyone unless it will work to their benefit. That one picked Daide—"*

"I already know," Recco cut in. *"What I don't understand is why."*

"Why else? It saw him as a weak link who'd do his bidding and not ask questions."

Recco winced. *"Was the dragon actually trapped here and unable to leave?"*

"Maybe. It might have been caught up in one of its own spells gone bad. Maybe it tried something, and the Cataclysm perverted its magic."

"Why pick on Daide?" Recco asked again, seeking a deeper knowledge.

The wolf hesitated. *"My first guess is no one living here had magic, and the dragon required an infusion of power beyond its own."* Another growl shook Recco from the inside out. *"If I'm correct, it would have sucked Daide dry, tossed him aside, and moved on."*

"What about his coyote?"

"The dragon's magic is superior to ours. It did something to lull the coyote into believing it."

"Could the dragon have hurt Daide's bondmate?" Recco persisted.

"No, but I know that coyote. Regardless of the outcome, it will blame itself for years for falling under the dragon's enchantment."

Recco wanted to run to Daide, shout the truth at him, and shake him into believing it, but the women's chanting had escalated in volume until the serpent's head was only about a foot below the level of the rail. Judging from the part of its body above the water, it must be better than thirty feet long. Recco sucked air through his teeth, fascinated and repelled at the same time. To have a specimen like this to observe would be any zoologist's dream.

Magic slithered around him, the air alive and electric with it. The sea dragon breathed power in as fast as the women produced it. It puffed steam between breaths. Realization kicked him in the guts. The dragon was becoming stronger, feeding itself from the women's magic.

Did they know?

Could they stop their spell, or had it developed a life of its own, nurtured by connivery on the part of the dragon?

Daide still had the rifle trained on the small boat. Juan's gaze darted from the women to the sea dragon, his expression drawn and worried. Recco focused his magic into what he hoped was a private message for Juan. *"Amigo. We have to intervene."*

"Are you sure?" Juan stared at him.

"Hell no, but this isn't right. The dragon's running this show. Don't ask how I know. I just do."

"Mmph. My cat agrees."

"Does it have any suggestions for how to proceed?"

Juan edged toward Recco, trading telepathy for speech. "Pull all the power you can. Once it's within you, balanced, do the best you can to ward yourself. Then we get between the dragon and the women. It won't be pleasant, but it's the only way to sever the magic's flow."

Recco cut his gaze to Daide. "Can he help us?"

Juan shook his head. "No. The dragon deceived him. If he thinks we're going to hurt it, he's as likely to blow us to hell as see reason. On my count of three, *amigo,* or there won't be anything left to salvage."

A sidelong glance at the women confirmed Juan's words. They'd developed an insubstantial aspect, a glowing nimbus that merged with a similar corona around the dragon. Soon, they'd be one and the same.

Fury filled Recco, burning like a beacon, and he dug deep. He felt the wolf helping, and he dredged power into as strong a shield as he could muster. As if from a great distance, he heard Juan.

"Uno. Dos. Tres."

Recco leapt in front of the women from the left. Juan did the same from the right. A scream ripped from him, followed by another from Juan. He tried shaking himself. It only made things worse. Breath caught in his throat until it felt as if he'd inhaled ground glass. If he'd jumped into a high voltage electrical field, it wouldn't have hurt this bad. Pain attacked him from all sides. Invisible knives, pickaxes, sabers. All with burning points that sloughed flesh from bone.

The dragon screamed its outrage and plunged back into the water, but not before the man in the boat recovered enough to squeeze off a shot. Daide sighted down the Ruger's barrel.

"No," Juan shrieked. "Do not shoot those people." At least he was still on his feet, face etched into agonized fissures as he dealt with the same pain punching through Recco.

Daide swung the rifle wide at the last minute, and his bullet arrowed toward the choppy sea. An outraged howl ripped from him, followed by another. If Recco hadn't felt like his entire body had dropped into a vat of scalding grease, he'd have hurried to his friend's side.

His vision hazed red then gray then red again. Breathing was a struggle since his lungs were seared by the same fire attacking him from without. He forced himself to move. He had to get to Zoe. She lay facedown on the deck with Ketha and Karin huddled over her. Half crawling, he dragged himself to the women.

"Zoe? Be okay?" came out as a croak. Goddammit. Why wouldn't his mouth cooperate and form words?

"Yes. She's unconscious because the primary spell was hers, and it boomeranged back at her when you severed it," Ketha explained. Magic flashed blue-white from her fingertips, forming a protective canopy around Zoe.

Karin hissed like an overheated teakettle. "Not that spell. Christ, woman. She's not dying, and she'll have a hell of a fright when she comes to and sees a shroud hanging over her."

"Picky, picky." Ketha made some adjustments, and the canopy faded into something less substantial.

"Not dying?" Recco forced the words out. His heart thumped hard in his chest, and he hoped to hell he'd heard right.

Karin peered at him, copper eyes sharp with concern. "Zoe will recover. So will you, but you took the brunt of this. You and Juan. Thank you, by the way. Goddess damn dragons. Self-centered fuckers. It would have drained us and then romped on back to the base where it's been eating its way through the scientists and other staff for years."

"Slowly. Savoring them, enjoying the hell out of their fear," Ketha added. Her mouth twisted as if she'd bitten into something bitter. "Vampires weren't the only ones who rejoiced about the Cataclysm. That dragon could finally embrace his inner beast, the one he stuffed under wraps after the Middle Ages ended."

Daide slid to his knees next to Recco. "Let me help you up, and then we'll go inside so I can work on your wounds."

"Good plan." Recco's tongue still felt thick, like it belonged to someone else. He caught Daide's worried gaze on him. "Do I look bad?"

"Worse than bad."

"Go ahead." Karin made shooing motions. "I'll see to Zoe and Juan."

Recco twisted his head toward Karin. The motion set off a barrage of new pain, and he bit back a howl. "You're sure Zoe is—?"

"Yes. You have my personal guarantee. She'll be fine. Get going."

Daide hauled him to his feet, and Recco leaned heavily on him as they made their way inside the ship. "You okay?" he asked Daide.

"Better than you."

"Not what I meant. You were howling."

Daide pushed the door to Recco's cabin open and followed him inside. "Let's peel these clothes off you and get you under the shower. Once there's no more debris in your abrasions, I'll figure out where you need stitches."

Recco let Daide undress him, helping as much as he could. His clothes were shredded down to skin level. They needed either a marathon session with a sewing machine—or a trash bin. The intense pain had yielded to a dull ache.

"Howling? Why?" he repeated.

Daide shucked his own clothes and followed Recco into the shower. He snatched the shower head from its cradle and adjusted the flow, aiming a gentle spray at Recco's abraded flesh.

"I shot the dragon. Not sure how it happened. All the magic batting against itself snatched the bullet. When you and Juan severed the women's magic, and it bounced back into the dragon, the bullet went with it."

"Zoe said they're immortal." Recco arched his back as warm water sluiced down his body. It hurt, but the tight places all through his body started to unwind.

"Immortality couldn't have saved the sea dragon. Not this time. The bullet went straight into its brain."

"How do you know?" Recco's head was clearing, and he welcomed a return of lucidity.

"I felt it. Zoe wasn't the only one linked to the creature." Daide's face darkened. "It lied to me. I have no bloody idea what its plans were, except I'm certain it would have played me for a sucker and then killed me."

"Yeah. Even your coyote was deceived. Bet it's fit to be tied."

"It's not overly pleased." Daide made a face. "Its initial take on the dragon was right on. Should have listened to it."

"Yeah. My wolf is damned wise too. Aw crap."

"What? Is the pain worse?" Daide moved the spray away from Recco, regarding him through worried eyes.

"No. All those people in the boats? What happened to them?"

"Boris and Ted were talking with them, and Viktor showed up about the time we left. Aura too. She said something about the dragon's enchantment breaking or ending or something, which fits in with you believing it's dead. Anyway, between all of them I'm sure they've taken care of everything."

Recco twisted the taps and turned off the water. "You can't know, not for certain. We have to get dressed and get back out there. What if—"

Daide plastered a towel over Recco's mouth before draping it around his dripping shoulders. "The only thing you'll be doing is sitting in the chair once you're dry. I'm going to come back with suture material. Two of those gashes need stitches. Once they're done, you can decide what happens next."

Recco draped a terry cloth robe around himself and staggered to the chair. It was easier than drying himself. His head sagged toward his chest, and his eyes closed. What if he hadn't realized what the dragon was doing?

The thought snapped his eyes open, but not for long. "Thanks for your help," he told his bondmate.

"Thanks for yours." The wolf's praise was warm, genuine. *"Your instincts were solid. They averted disaster."*

Recco blew out a tense breath. Maybe, just maybe, he'd end up worthy of his bondmate. It was a good goal, one that felt more achievable than it had a few weeks back.

Daide pushed into the room, medical kit dangling from one hand. "I'm surprised you're still awake."

"So am I, *amigo*. So am I."

11

MISUNDERSTANDINGS

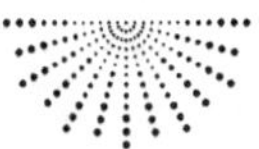

Zoe had the mother of all headaches. Her temples pounded and throbbed and boomed, and her eyes were squinched shut. She'd opened them when Karin and Ketha had carried her to her cabin, and her head spun so viciously, she'd thrown up. The vomit stink clinging to her clothing didn't help matters.

Someone pressed something to her lips. "Drink this." Karin was back in doctor mode.

"She'll need to sit up," Ketha muttered from the other side of the room.

Zoe flailed, working to push herself up on her elbows. "Can't you use magic?" she gritted out.

"Don't have a whole hell of a lot left right now," Karin retorted. "Besides, I have been. I'm hedging my bets."

"I'll help. Hang on." Ketha crossed the room, her tread slow and heavy. She wrapped an arm around Zoe, stabilizing her so she could drink from the glass.

Bitter, chalky liquid flowed down her throat, so astringent it made her mouth pucker. "Geez," she sputtered. "What the fuck was in the potion?"

"Things you need." Karin set the glass down with a clank. "Take a few deep breaths to center yourself, and then open your eyes. Don't flirt around with it. Take charge and open them."

Zoe wanted to protest her stomach wasn't feeling settled, particularly not with Karin's recent addition. Instead, she inhaled. It was surprisingly difficult to haul the breath to the bottom of her lungs, so she repeated the gesture, sucking air like a bellows.

"That's it," Karin said encouragingly. "A few more exactly like the last couple. Your color's finally improving."

Zoe paused between breaths. "What color was I?"

"You matched the sheet beneath you to a T." Ketha chuckled.

"Too much magic," Zoe mumbled and went back to breathing. She felt the coyote inside her, but it wasn't chiding her—for once. Maybe it recognized her intentions had been good. Besides, once she'd understood what had to happen, she'd moved fast. Before the evil she assumed had imprisoned the dragon could intuit her objective and block her.

If she'd had any inkling the dragon was her enemy, she'd never have left herself open to its power.

"Eyes," Karin reminded her.

Zoe took one more deep breath and blew it out. Ready as she figured she'd ever be, she dragged her lids upward. The room swam into focus. At least she wasn't too queasy.

Karin directed a smug look her way and dusted her hands together. "Easy as pie."

"Yeah well, it wasn't earlier." A surly note threaded beneath Zoe's words. She cut her churlish attitude off at its roots. "Thanks for sticking this out with me."

Karin's mouth curved into a smile. "It's what we doctor types do. Thanks for not dying on me."

Shock ratcheted Zoe to a sit, and she stuffed a pillow behind her back. "Jesus, God, and all the bluidy saints. Was it close?"

Karin patted her hand. "Not really, but the bastard dragon was well on its way to absorbing your essence, along with Ketha's and mine by default." She rolled her eyes. "We were the value-added bits. If the men hadn't severed your spell, the dragon would have succeeded. Nothing I launched as a countermeasure touched it. I still can't fathom how strong it was."

"Nor can I." Ketha perched on the edge of the bed. "Did you have a plan?" Her words were cautious and devoid of inflection.

"Of course I had a plan." Defensiveness raced through Zoe in a blistering tide. "At the time, I thought the poor, wee dragon was a prisoner, and I was going to free it." Bitter laughter slithered out. "Sure and I was a right bloody fool. Zoe Seisyll, patron of the downtrodden, savior of animals, children, and idiots."

She stretched out her fingers from where she'd curled them into fists. "I played straight into its hand."

"I didn't sense the trap, either," her coyote spoke up. *"Not until it snapped shut around us. I tried to force a shift, except I was powerless."*

"I heard your coyote," Ketha said. "None of our animals recognized how malevolent the sea dragon was—until it was too late."

"Daide's did," Zoe said, "but then it changed its mind after the dragon seduced it." Breath hissed through her teeth. "I'm glad it's gone." She bit her lower lip. "It is gone. Right? I thought I felt it die, but—"

"It's dead," Karin said. "When power ricocheted back into it, one of those two bullets plunged into its brainstem. I kept waiting for it to resurrect itself."

"It never did," Ketha cut in.

A knock sounded at the door just before it opened, admitting Viktor. "How are you?" he asked Zoe.

"Thanks for asking. I'll live. The men—Juan and Recco—are they recovered?" She latched her gaze onto Viktor to make certain he told her the truth.

"Yes. They'll be fine." He shifted his attention to Ketha. "Can they spare you here?"

She stood. "I suppose so. Why?"

"Most of the McMurdo crew are in the dining room. I told them to hold off with their story until all of us could listen. Meanwhile, we're sharing a meal with them."

Zoe took stock of her body and swung her legs over the side of the bed. "I want to be there. I'll clean up and be down."

Karin narrowed her eyes and jabbed her with magic. Zoe swung her head aside. "I'm fine. Have a smidgeon of faith in your healing ability, why don't you?"

Karin snorted. "Sure and ye caught me flat-footed with that one." She aped Zoe's brogue.

Ketha walked to Viktor's side. "See you soon," she told Zoe, and left hanging onto her husband's arm.

Karin stood. "If you're sure…"

"I am. I can even feel my magical reservoir starting to replenish itself. Go get some dinner. You and Ketha may have been peripheral to my casting, yet you still sustained a fair amount of collateral damage."

Karin nodded once. "It could have been worse. If you need me, use telepathy. And if you're not in the dining room in half an hour, I'll trot right back here to find out why."

"Fair enough."

Gratitude for Karin's skill and unflappable nature filled Zoe as she watched the other woman walk out of her cabin. Pushing to her feet, she stripped off her clothes to skin level. Only her outermost layer had vomit on it, so she dragged the jacket into the shower, intent on washing it.

Her head still spun, but only a little, and the vertigo receded as she stood under the water. Soap and shampoo had a revitalizing effect, still she didn't linger. Everyone would be waiting for her, and she didn't want to hold them up any longer than absolutely necessary.

Dried and dressed, she unwound a towel from her hair and let the damp curls trail down her shoulders. She'd brush it out later.

Her jacket hung dripping in the shower where it would dry eventually.

Surprised she felt as good as she did, she left her cabin and headed for the dining room. Everyone else was, indeed, waiting for her, but no one seemed upset. A chorus of greetings rang out, and Recco strode toward her.

"Glad to see you up and about." He broke into a broad grin and grabbed one of her hands.

She thought she should pull away, except she couldn't quite make herself follow through. "Sorry, folks," she called out and glanced at all the unfamiliar faces. "Apologies you had to wait on me."

Recco squeezed her hand and murmured, "We'll talk later." Releasing her, he returned to a table he shared with Daide, Tessa, Moira, and Karin.

"No apologies needed." A rangy, broad-shouldered woman came to her feet and walked toward Zoe before extending her hand. "Etta Achter." Steel-gray hair framed her face like a helmet. A pair of shrewd dark eyes crinkled at the corners. She looked around fifty and projected the same no-nonsense aspect as Karin. A beige, insulated garment rather like a flight suit covered her from shoulder to ankle. McMurdo Antarctic Station was embroidered in faded red across its left side.

Zoe grasped the woman's outstretched hand and shook it. "'Tis a pleasure. I'm Zoe Seisyll. You must be the doctor from McMurdo."

Etta nodded, and a shadow crossed her face. "Once I was one of half a dozen, but now I am the only one left." She let go of Zoe and swung to face the groups of people sitting over cups, glasses, and half-eaten plates of food. "If none of my associates have any objections, I will begin. If I miss something important, please correct me."

A murmur of assents swept through the room.

Etta stood straighter and clasped her fingers in front of her. "Before I begin, I speak for all of us at McMurdo when I offer our heartfelt thanks for destroying the serpent. I never understood quite how, but the creature had to be sentient. It saw through every one of our attempts to stymie its raids on our people."

A huge sigh rattled from her chest. "I still cannot quite believe it is gone. It was far worse than the atmospheric storm track that trapped us here for so many years."

Zoe stood off to one side. Catching Ketha's eye, she raised one brow and employed telepathy. *"Should we tell her what it was?"*

"Not yet. Let's wait to see how this shakes out," Ketha replied. *"If they want to throw in their lot with us, we'll have to tell them we're Shifters. If they'd rather remain at McMurdo, no reason to disclose more than we have to."*

Aura sent a pointed glance at both of them and shook her head, the gesture barely there.

"Permission to speak?" A man sitting toward the rear of the room pushed his chair back and stood. He wore the same one-piece, insulated suit as the doctor. Medium height, he had thinning brown hair, dark eyes, and a fireplug build.

Etta crooked two fingers at him. "You do not require my permission, Ron. I am greatly relieved whatever had you in its clutches let you go. I suppose it had something to do with the deuced serpent. You are free, and it is gone. This cannot be a coincidence."

"I'm not quite sure what happened." Ron screwed his gaunt features into a frown. "It's like I've been asleep for a really long time. Can't remember anything. Neither can the rest of us in those two outboards chasing after you." He looked down. "No one was more surprised than us when we…"

His voice ran down and he tried again. "Last thing any of us remember is being herded into one of the storage buildings, but it feels like it happened a really long time ago. Maybe years. My mind didn't click on again until we were in the bay, heading for this ship." He scrubbed the heels of his hands down his face, distorting his features. "I conferred with the others, and we all had a similar experience, with a few minor variations, none of which appear significant. They agreed I should be our spokesperson."

"It will be all right." Etta smiled with more warmth than Zoe would have suspected her capable of. "I knew all of you had returned from wherever you'd been, or I'd never have let you onto this ship."

"I don't get it," Ron stared at her. "How'd you know?"

She shrugged. "You felt human again. Not like something out of *The Walking Dead*."

"Mmph. Thanks. I think." Ron tipped his head at the doctor and sank into his seat.

Etta rolled her shoulders back. "I will not bother to describe the vicious storms that pinned us here. From what your captain told me"—she glanced at Viktor—"you experienced the same weather phenomenon in Ushuaia. We lost several hundred researchers during the first two years, mostly because they insisted on leaving. I suspect they died before reaching safety, but I have no way to verify anything. None of them ever returned. Aside from their ill-conceived exodus, we were fine for many years. Maybe half a dozen, and we would have continued to survive adequately. We have a greenhouse, full desalinization equipment, everything we required to be self-sufficient."

"How are your stocks presently?" Viktor asked.

"We have enough. It was never a major problem." Etta pressed her mouth into a harsh line. "The serpent arrived one day, swimming merrily as you please into the bay. Its presence was noteworthy since most sea creatures, certainly ones of its size, had died off, leaving only krill and such. Small marine life with rapid metabolisms."

She scrunched her features into a thoughtful expression. "At first, the sea serpent was sneaky. We began losing men and women. One here. Another there. I made a mistake back then. A big one. I assumed the enforced isolation had rattled their sanity, and they'd marched off into the cold to die. It is an easy death, and a relatively quick one. By then, most of us were certain we would never leave McMurdo. Some adjusted more easily than others."

Etta returned to where she'd been sitting and scooped up her glass, taking a deep swallow. "Over time, the serpent grew bold. When one of the nurses shook me awake early one morning with the news over two dozen of us were missing, I knew I had to adopt drastic measures."

"What happened to Jack DeVoe?" Juan asked. "He was your base commander, wasn't he?"

Etta nodded slowly. "Indeed he was. A good man and a most excellent friend. He was one of the two dozen shanghaied. I had no idea what happened to any of them until today."

Zoe did some quick calculations. There'd only been twelve people in the outboards chasing after the one with Etta in it, which meant the dragon had done away with the others.

"It tortured and killed them," her coyote growled. *"Kept them alive, feeding off them as long as it could. You know. You were joined to its mind long enough to see."*

Zoe did know, and the imagery filled her with fury the dragon's death hadn't been more drawn out and painful.

Etta's gaze tracked through the McMurdo folk. "Do any of you know what happened to Jack?"

"Wish we did," a slightly built blonde woman said. Like the others, she wore what appeared to be a regulation-issue beige flight suit. "I have no memory of anything until I woke up in the outboard dinghy today, and frankly it's damned unnerving."

Zoe opened her mouth to tell the woman to pick up the threads of her life and move on. It wasn't her place to butt in. Those were memories best left under wraps, though. She hoped to hell this motley band of survivors never picked enough scabs off their minds to open a channel for those lost years to surface.

Etta tilted her chin at a resolute angle. "Not much more to tell. We barricaded ourselves into the two primary buildings. No one went anywhere alone. It was nerve-racking, but we lived that way for a long time. When we picked up radio transmissions from your ship, I was certain it was some trick. I presumed the serpent had found a way to force one of the missing people to dupe us, draw us out into the open."

A tall, redheaded man sitting in the middle of the dining room pushed to his feet. "I'm John. John Anderson. Etta told us not to answer the radio. I'm not certain why I did. It's why I pretended not to recognize Jack's name. Figured the less I said, the better." He laced his fingers together in front of him. "I wanted you to be real, not some stupid hallucination, with such desperation it was all I could think about. After a while, you kind of lose track of what's tangible and what isn't, and it's not a good place to be stuck."

Color crept up Etta's pale cheeks. "I gave him hell for insubordination, but I grilled him too. The conversation he'd had with *Arkady* appeared normal enough, I took a chance and rang you back to request aid. We had held the serpent off for a long time. Sooner or later one of us would make a mistake..."

She didn't finish her sentence. She didn't have to. Zoe's heart went out to all of them. What a strong, courageous bunch of men and women. Tears pricked behind her eyelids; she blinked them back.

"Thank you." Viktor stood and walked to her side. "I'm guessing you number twenty-two or thereabouts."

Etta nodded. "Yes."

Zoe was grateful Viktor didn't inquire how many they'd started with.

"Do you still want to join us on *Arkady*?"

"It is not my decision." Etta spoke slowly. "I need to confer with everyone. Since we no longer have to creep around fearing for our lives, I would rather remain at McMurdo Station. It has been my home for almost twenty years. Still, not everyone will feel the same way. At least I do not believe they will."

"Take whatever time you need," Viktor said.

"We shall have an answer for you by midday tomorrow," Etta

said and gestured to the others. They stood and moved toward the dining room doors amid a chorus of thank-yous.

Viktor extended a hand, and Etta clasped it. "We owe you a lot."

"Nonsense. You would have helped us if the situation were reversed."

"*Ja*, I would have." She narrowed her eyes. "You're German. From Heidelberg?"

Viktor grinned. "Yup. Damned accent gives me away, but only to another German. Berlin, correct?"

Etta smiled. "Right, but so long ago the memory grows dim. Once upon a time, I thought I might like to visit some of my old haunts. It isn't likely to happen. Not the end of the world if I never return there." She switched to German, and she and Viktor walked out of the dining room, chattering away."

Zoe straightened from where she'd been leaning against a wall. The day had more than caught up with her, and she felt like sleeping for hours.

Recco joined her. "How're you holding up?"

Zoe focused on him. A purple-and-green bruise covered one cheek, and a line of stitches held a long gash over one eyebrow closed. What other damage had he sustained protecting her after her spell slipped away from her control?

"I could ask you the same question," she retorted. "The maneuver you and Juan finessed earlier was incredibly stupid. You risked yourselves in ways you didn't even realize. Things could have gone so much worse." Her voice had risen in intensity, and she tempered it, but she was upset. If he'd lost his life during his Sir Galahad act, she'd have had a damned hard time living with herself.

He drew back as if she'd slapped him. "You're lecturing me for saving you from falling into the dragon's clutches?" Before she could respond, he plowed on. "You're the one who miscalculated, Miss Magic Expert. If you hadn't, Juan and I wouldn't have been forced to jump in and save you from your folly." He narrowed his eyes. "Two sides to every story."

Heated words crowded into the back of her throat. Telling him he was an arrogant prick wouldn't help. She shoved away from the wall and stalked out of the dining room before she said something she truly regretted.

"That was ill-conceived," her coyote said, not bothering to mask its annoyance.

"Stuff it. I've had all the lectures I care to hear for one night."

She headed straight for her cabin, intent on barricading herself in before she burst into tears. Last thing she needed was any of the women cooing over her or Karin mixing her a tonic for nerves.

What she needed was Recco, and she'd just pushed him away with both hands. Or maybe he'd never been as interested in her as she thought. He'd been damned quick to jump down her throat.

Yeah, right after I told him he was stupid.

Zoe groaned and dragged herself into her cabin, kicking off her boots once she was inside. Not bothering with the lights, she dove into her bunk and yanked the blanket over her head. In addition to the battered places from the dragon's onslaught, her heart felt empty. She tried to tell herself it was impossible to lose something she'd never had to begin with. The dull ache behind her breastbone didn't cede to reason and go away, though.

She might have been exhausted and heartsick, but hours passed before her racing thoughts stilled enough for her to fall asleep.

12

IT'S A TOSS-UP

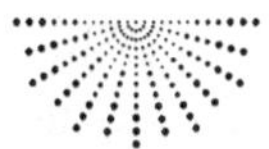

Recco watched Zoe march out of the dining room. How dare she bitch him out for what he'd done and then walk away? Maybe it hadn't been the most elegant move, but everyone was still alive. So, his half-baked scheme, concocted on the fly with Juan, had worked, goddammit.

Startlingly well from his perspective. Why the hell couldn't she see—or appreciate—it? Or him?

Anger simmered, flaring to painful brightness when Juan and Aura strolled by, arms wrapped around one another. She might not have been part of today's confrontation, but she appreciated Juan, was grateful he was still alive. It showed in the way she leaned into him.

Before a few minutes ago, Recco thought Zoe cared about him. Obviously, he'd read the signs all wrong.

"Looking pretty bleak there, *amigo.*" Daide joined him. "What's wrong? Are those sutures hurting?"

Wouldn't it be lovely if it were so simple?

Recco gritted his teeth. "They're okay. You did a good job."

"Quite a story from the McMurdo staff, eh?"

"No shit." Recco dragged his thoughts out of the drain they'd

143

been circling around, surprised it was so difficult. "Poor sods. It's a wonder any of them have a scrap of sanity left."

Daide was still regarding him intently. "Maybe you should lie down for a while."

"For Christ's fucking sake. I'm not one of your patients."

"Really?" Daide narrowed his eyes. "Not so many differences. They didn't talk to me, either."

"Where you off to next?" Recco changed the subject. No point falling farther down that particular rabbit hole.

Daide shrugged. "Not sure. It's a tossup between the lab or the bar."

"I vote for the bar. In fact, I'll see you up there."

Without waiting for Daide to tell him alcohol was a really bad idea after any kind of head injury, Recco hurried out of the dining room and up the nearest staircase. His head hurt, and his skin still felt raw, but he'd live. He didn't hear the distinctive tread of Daide's boots behind him. Relief mingled with disappointment in a puzzling shitstorm of emotions.

On the one hand, he didn't want Daide probing. On the other, spilling his pain and confusion might help square things so he could occupy the same space with Zoe. *Arkady* wasn't particularly large. No matter how he choreographed his shipboard life, he was bound to run into her.

He strode into the empty bar, crossing to where the liquor lived in slatted shelves, and picked up several bottles of wine before settling on blended whiskey. He wanted oblivion as fast as he could manage it. Wine didn't have enough alcohol content. He'd poured a tumbler half-full of fragrant, amber liquid when a thought blasted him. He didn't have to remain on *Arkady*. Assuming some of the McMurdo group opted to remain at the base, he could stay there. Surely, with the resurgence of marine life, they could use a veterinarian. Never mind Daide was the one who'd specialized in marine mammals and birds.

He rolled the idea around as whiskey slid down his gullet,

creating a warm glow in his midsection. The only real downside was leaving Daide. They'd been friends and partners for a long time. Guilt flickered. Viktor and Juan had been nothing but kind, and they'd invested time and energy training him to be a crew member. The infusion of new blood from McMurdo would give them plenty of raw material to shape to their liking.

Recco stared at his empty glass. He hadn't even sat down, and he'd finished the generous drink he'd poured. The whiskey hadn't hit him yet, so he poured another tumbler and made his way to a table. The thought of leaving was heady. A new adventure. He'd visited McMurdo twice and been impressed by the sophistication of their lab equipment and the array of talent stationed there.

"Won't be anything like that now," he muttered. "Most of them are dead."

All the more reason he could do some good. If communications ever resurfaced worldwide, they'd have a way to report their findings. Effects of the Cataclysm on pinnipeds and—

"A man should never drink alone," Daide announced. After transiting the bar, he slid into a chair across the table from Recco.

"Jesus. You're worse than a wife," Recco mumbled.

Daide cast another speculative look his way. "Don't know about the wife part. We managed to remain friends through ten years of being Vampires. Surely, it counts for something since Vamps don't form friendships."

"We didn't have to form one. It was already there."

"Yeah, but we could have let it die. We didn't," Daide said.

"You're relentless. What the fuck do you want?"

"Told you down in the dining room. Something's eating at you. What is it?"

Recco splayed his hands across the table. Cuts and bruises covered the backs of both. "What are you worried about?" He tossed the ball back at Daide.

"I'm concerned you're dealing with some residual magic from

the sea dragon. Something I missed when I worked you over for injuries."

Daide looked so sincere, and so worried, Recco pushed his half-empty glass aside. "Can't even let me get drunk, huh?"

"No. Not if being drunk means some leftover bits of dark power gain ascendency. Goddammit, Recco. None of us understand how this magic crap operates. I work with what I can see and fix, not with invisible manifestations of evil."

Recco sucked in a deep breath, blew it out, and did it once more. No reason not to float his McMurdo idea. It was a hell of a lot easier than talking about Zoe. "I've been thinking about something."

Daide furled a brow. "You'll have to say more, *amigo*. My mind-reading skills are rusty."

"And here I thought you were the original animal whisperer."

Daide crooked two fingers. "All right. If leftover magic isn't in play, your sarcasm clinched things. You're using your rapier-sharp wit to avoid talking about something. What is it?"

"No wonder you're not married. You'd have driven your wife into an early grave."

"And now you're doing it again. I know you. Don't make me drag whatever this is out of you."

Recco looked his old friend square in the eyes. "I'm considering staying here."

Daide's mouth dropped open. "Of all the things running through my mind, that is about the last possibility. Here? As in at McMurdo?"

"Why not? You and I visited there. They had vets on staff." Recco batted back defensiveness. It was a pretty outrageous idea. Besides, he might not be welcome at the research base even if a few scientists opted to remain.

"We did, except it was mostly you coming along for the ride. Since when did you develop an interest in seals and penguins?"

"I've worked on them."

"True, but not necessarily by choice." Daide leaned closer. "What about Viktor and Juan and this ship? They've made it clear they could use double our numbers, particularly after we head into blue water north of here."

"They just recruited over twenty—"

"You don't know if any of them will leave McMurdo," Daide cut in without letting Recco finish talking. He made a grab for Recco's glass and drained what was left in it. "Were you going to discuss this with me? Or were you just going to say, '*Sayonara*, pal'?"

Recco cut his gaze away from Daide's direct stare. "Not sure what I was going to do. Hadn't thought it through. It's only an idea so far." He pushed back from where he'd been leaning his hands on the table and balled them into fists in his lap.

"You hadn't thought it through, huh?" Daide's eyes darkened with anger, and he blasted to his feet. "Do what you want, bud. Those years you were a Vampire left a huge mark. I'm sorry I didn't notice it sooner. If I had, I'd have run the other way." He turned on his heel and stormed out of the bar. Fury and disappointment spilled from him.

"*You're doing a great job,*" Recco's wolf piped up. "*Keep going and you'll have alienated everyone.*"

"Aw crap. You too?" Recco muttered.

"*Why not? Did you think I'd gone somewhere? Or that I'd quietly leave you to your idiocy?*"

Afraid someone might wander into the bar, Recco switched to telepathy. "*What idiocy? Zoe has no use for me, and Daide is pissed.*" Recco's hands hurt, so he unclenched his fingers. "*Of the two, I understand Daide's position. I'd be annoyed too, if he dropped something monumental in my lap as a done deal.*"

A low growl filled Recco's chest, and he let it rumble out. Easier than holding it inside. "*Loyalty is where wolves live,*" his bondmate noted. "*Pack is everything.*"

"*I already admitted Daide has every right to be furious. If I have a pack —beyond you and me—Zoe isn't part of it.*"

"*You'd like her to be.*" The wolf was implacable.

"I've wanted a whole lot of things from the time the Cataclysm locked us in Ushuaia. Not many of them happened."

"Do you want to know what I think?"

Recco sucked air through his teeth. He curled his fingers around his glass, intent on returning to the bar for a refill. *"I have a feeling you're going to tell me no matter what I answer."*

"You're a coward. Not how I had you pegged, or I'd never have bonded with you."

"Fine." This time the snarl blowing past his lips came from him, not the wolf. *"Everyone else is deserting me. You may as well leave too. Don't fuck around about it. Just go."*

A tight place burned deep in his chest; Recco built walls around it. It was good to cut the dead weight, get down to bedrock once he found out who was on his side—and who wasn't. His family had sent him out into the countryside when he turned thirteen. It was an old-time ritual followed by his tribe, one of the few they still adhered to.

His task was to discover his totem animal and to stay alive for three days. Being hungry wasn't what would do him in. Jaguars roamed the wilds. So did poisonous snakes. He still remembered how scared he'd been, but he'd pretended he was on top of the challenge, that he had it nailed. He'd swaggered out of the Buenos Aires slum he'd been raised in and gotten into his uncle's rattletrap Jeep. An hour later, the Jeep rolled to a halt, and his uncle poked him in the side.

"Get moving." Uncle Carlos hadn't even looked at him, and his tone left no space for disagreement.

Recco had scrambled out of the car, jumping back so it didn't spray him with gravel as it sped away up the rutted dirt track. His chest had felt tight then too. So had his throat. He didn't know what he'd been expecting. Some parting words of wisdom, or maybe encouragement. His uncle acted as if he couldn't wait to be rid of him.

He'd moved to the side of the road, hunkering in the dirt and feeling very sorry for himself. The sun beat heavily on him, and sweat rolled down his body. A slithering hiss drove him to his feet, heart pounding against his ribs. The jararacussu—although he hadn't had a name for it then—struck and missed, and it marked the beginning of his trial. No more squatting in the dirt, wallowing in self-pity.

Recco pushed to his feet and walked the glass back to the bar sink, rinsing and drying it. No more booze. Not today. His three days in Argentina's bush had changed him. He hadn't been a man afterward, not yet, but he'd taken the first steps toward independence. Though he'd had no way of knowing it at the time, those seventy-two hours shaped the adult he'd become. Fed his determination not to need anyone.

Daide had spent years drilling holes in Recco's barriers. He understood them because he'd undergone a similar coming-of-age ritual, except his included a dozen young men. Their interdependency was what pulled them through.

Insights spilled through Recco as he hustled out of the bar. Things he should have known all along but had ignored. Daide welcomed others. Recco never had. There'd been no need since Daide handled that end of their professional lives. He'd been the one who set up their field trips, their lectures, even their required continuing education.

"What the fuck did I do all those years?" He winced. He'd kept the lab and their shared living quarters clean, managed the accounts, and ordered supplies. Basically, he'd done all the things a confirmed loner would do. The items not requiring him to tip his hand and disclose anything about himself. He'd never had to tell anyone anything personal.

Probably why the transition to Vampire had been marginally tolerable. Emotional isolation was already a comfort zone for him. The blood part had been distasteful, but he'd had an easier time pretending it wasn't happening than Daide, who'd puked his way through the first several months of feedings.

So long as he was on a roll, he forced himself to examine the wasteland his life had been. How he'd said what he needed to entice women into his bed, moving on the moment one made any noises about wanting something more permanent. His confirmed bachelor status had been his fault, not Daide's.

"It's a start." The wolf was back. *"Still don't care if I leave?"*

Recco ducked out a door onto one of *Arkady's* many walkways. Cold air blasted through his clothing. He welcomed the brisk breeze. *"I never said I didn't care. All I said was if you were going to leave, you should get on with it."*

"Not what I asked," the wolf persisted. *"Do you care about being a Shifter?"*

Recco bit back a sarcastic comeback. Something about the wolf's tone demanded honesty, not flippant commentary. *"Yes. I care."* He swallowed around tight jaw muscles.

"How do you feel about me?"

The question caught him off guard, and Recco stammered, *"What do you mean?"*

"It's clear enough. You care about being a Shifter. Do you care about me, specifically? Your bondmate?"

"Of course I do." Recco curled his fingers around the cold metal railing but let go fast before his flesh adhered to the chilly surface.

"You never asked me what I think about your McMurdo idea."

Recco was starting to shiver. It was far too cold to be outside for long without his jacket and insulated pants. He wasn't sure how to phrase things, so he blurted, *"Is it a requirement?"* and winced. *"Sorry. Didn't come out right. Do we make decisions as a team about where I live?"*

"Under normal circumstances, no. The post-Cataclysm world is far from normal. If we remained at McMurdo, we'd be the only Shifter there. It would be lonely, difficult. Worse, if you changed your mind, there'd be no way to leave. You can't count on another ship wandering by. Even if one did, they might not want a Shifter aboard."

The wolf hurried on before Recco could craft a reply. *"The answer is twofold. I wouldn't offer an opinion unless I felt you were making a mistake. One we'd both have to live with."*

Even trying to hold his jaws shut didn't keep his teeth from chattering. Recco made for a nearby door and went back inside.

Juan charged down the corridor. "There you are. What the fuck, *amigo*? Daide told Viktor and me you're jumping ship. He's pretty spun out about it. So am I. And Vik is livid."

Recco wrapped his arms around himself to conserve what body heat he had left. "Daide has a big mouth. I was only floating possibilities."

"What does that mean?" Juan crossed his arms over his chest. "Are you leaving or not?" Without waiting for Recco's reply, he kept bellowing. "I thought Viktor made it abundantly clear how short we are on crew. It's only going to grow worse when we leave Antarctic waters. The roaring forties and fifties got their name for a reason. We may have a hell of a rough passage and—" He shut his mouth with an audible *clack*.

"First off," Recco began through teeth that still chattered, although not as badly, "I assumed you'd pick up a bunch of folk from McMurdo."

"You have no bloody way of knowing," Juan countered. "If the doctor remains, I bet most of her people will too. Their main nemesis was the dragon, and it's dead. Besides, this isn't about them, it's about you."

"Mind if we move this into my cabin where it's more private?"

"All I need is a yes or a no. One word scarcely requires privacy. There's not any combination of reasons you could gin up to justify—"

"Justify what?" Recco latched onto anger of his own. "Since when did this ship turn into the *Bounty*, Captain Bligh?"

Though the corners of Juan's mouth twitched, he didn't come close to smiling. "This is serious business, *amigo*. Either we're a team. Or we're not. We have a goal that's bigger than any one of us. It's closing the primary gateway Ketha and Aura discovered on

Wrangel Island. Our goal is ten thousand nautical miles from here, give or take a few hundred. It will require all of us—and we still might not manage to transit the globe."

Recco flinched. He hadn't forgotten about the portal forged by the Cataclysm, an entry point for evil from other worlds, but it hadn't been in the front of his mind, either. He felt petty and small, a coward precisely like his bondmate had pointed out. At least the worst of the shudders racking his body had calmed. He set his mouth in a tight line.

"No. I'm not leaving *Arkady*. It was only a thought, probably not a viable one. Daide had no business—"

"He had every business. We're a family. No secrets." Juan stuck out a hand.

After a slight hesitation, Recco shook it. "Signed and sealed, eh?"

"About the size of it." The expression on Juan's face could have curdled milk. "Be grateful it's not the 1800s where once you signed on, you crewed for life—or until the ship sank, whichever came first."

"You don't understand."

"And I don't need to. I'm still pissed, but I'll get over it. I'm glad you've reconsidered. What you need to understand is *Arkady* is a stand-in for the children Vik and I never had. We feel protective of her. We lost one ship, and it cut deep. We don't aim to lose another. Every single crew member is a hedge against disaster. Plus, it will take every magic-wielder we can come up with to take on whatever's waiting for us on Wrangel Island. Assuming we even get that far."

The PA system crackled, and Viktor's voice blasted from a speaker sitting right above them. "Everyone to the bridge, pronto."

Breath whistled through Juan's teeth. "Goddammit. What now?" Spinning, he took off up a nearby set of stairs.

The last thing Recco wanted to do was face Viktor. Presumably, he was as put out as Juan had been. Better to give things time to settle. *Everyone* included him, though, so he trudged up the same stairs Juan had taken, albeit more slowly. He wasn't in any hurry for a public dressing down.

"The beginning of wisdom is recognizing your limitations," the wolf observed.

"Or my foolhardiness?"

"That too."

"You were correct about me being a coward. I didn't want to deal with Zoe's rejection. Leaving seemed easier."

A howl was followed by, *"I'm always right. Get used to it."*

Recco bit back a comment about Daide's coyote being wrong about the sea dragon, except it hadn't been. Not really. So far today, he'd managed to alienate Zoe, Daide, Juan, and Viktor. And his bondmate. It was time to eat humble pie, not make any more enemies. His insight from earlier slapped him hard. He might see himself as a self-sufficient island, but the hard truth was he couldn't go it alone in a world scoured by the Cataclysm.

And he would have had a far harder time running a veterinary clinic by himself even before the Cataclysm, if it hadn't been for Daide taking care of the things he preferred to ignore.

"Next time you see him, you might thank him," the wolf said, sounding smug.

"Next time I see him, I will."

He'd apologize too, without any prodding from the wolf.

The sound of footsteps running up the stairs behind him was accompanied by the distinctive feel of Zoe's energy. Recco moved to the side of the staircase to let her run past.

Except she didn't. Closing her fingers around his arm, she said, "I heard you're leaving the ship. You can't go. I'm sorry about earlier. It's just..." Her words vanished in a volley of pants as she caught her breath.

Before he had a chance to tell her she didn't owe him any explanations, she threw herself into his arms and kissed him. It shocked him so much, moments passed before he gathered her close and kissed her back.

13

OLD SECRETS

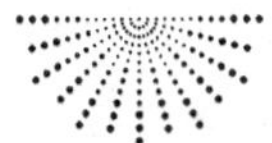

Half an Hour Before

Zoe bolted awake when her cabin door crashed against its stops and Daide rushed inside. "Good," he gritted out. "You're up."

"I wasn't until right now." Zoe rubbed her hot, gritty eyes. Her vision blurred, so she gave it up for a lost cause. It felt like she'd just fallen asleep, or else she'd been out for hours. Her brain was fuzzy, uncooperative.

Daide stomped next to her bunk, and she scooted to a sitting position, noticing she still had all her clothes on. Sometimes being a sloth paid off.

"What happened?" She peered up at him, still marshaling her resources. If she'd had any adrenaline left, it would have kicked in by now. As things stood, she slogged through thick, sticky mud that slowed everything to a fraction of normal speed.

He closed a hand around her upper arm and narrowed his eyes to slits. "You have to get up. Recco wants to stay here, and I suspect it has something to do with you. Whatever you did, woman, undo it. I will not have my partner and my closest friend stranded at the southern pole forever."

155

Defensiveness ran hot and swift. Zoe tempered it fast and aimed for a modicum of dignity. "He's a grown-up. He can make his own choices. Besides, I'm sure I have no idea what you're talking about." Daide might be Recco's male equivalent of a best friend forever, but it didn't give him the right to insert himself quite this far into Recco's business—or their argument.

"The hell you don't." Daide shook her. Not hard. It still annoyed the crap out of her, and she wrenched out of his grasp.

"Now look here, you great bluidy bloke—"

"Ye dinna hear me." He copied her brogue so badly, she'd have laughed under any other circumstances.

Daide bent so his face—its harsh expression carved in stone— was even with hers. "Recco is leaving *Arkady*. Because of you. If you don't fix whatever you broke, I'll make your life so miserable, you'll wish you'd jumped ship with him." Spinning on his heel, he stalked out of her room, slamming the door behind him.

Zoe stared after him, the dregs of sleep fading as his words hit her like a doubled-up punch to the stomach. She shook her head hard. When it didn't help fast enough, she staggered to the basin and ran icy-cold water. Bending over the sink, she dropped her face into her cupped hands. The water was cold enough to hurt, but it brought consciousness roaring back.

Everything throbbed, from her headache, which had never truly left, to muscles she hadn't thought about in years. Pain brought Daide's words into finely honed focus, and she choked on panic. Surely, he had to be wrong. Recco was loyal. He'd never desert *Arkady*.

"*Don't be so certain.*" Her coyote yipped deep inside her, a desolate howl. The one coyotes reserved for losing pack members.

Zoe snapped her attention inward. "*Tis true, then?*" She inhaled raggedly, urging her bond animal to refute Daide's prediction.

"*He's not gone yet.*" The coyote didn't add to its words, and she felt it within, watchful and waiting.

Zoe dried her hands and stuffed her feet into her boots, the one item of clothing she'd taken off before diving headlong into her bunk, mostly so she wouldn't get grit and seawater on her sheets.

The PA system crackled, followed by Viktor's voice. "Everyone to the bridge, pronto."

"Awk. Christ and all the bluidy, fecking saints," she muttered and fled into the corridor feeling torn. She had to find Recco, but Viktor had ordered them to the bridge. Did it mean Recco would be there too? Or was she too late and he'd already launched a Zodiac? The coyote had suggested otherwise. When she asked it again, it didn't reply.

The adrenaline she figured she'd run dry pounded through her, leaving a bitter, metallic taste on her tongue. She sent a thread of magic outward, seeking Recco. He had to still be on the ship. For Daide to burst into her room, and shed all semblance of his usual mild-mannered presence, told her how frantic he must be.

She realized she'd missed the closest stairwell and doubled back. All the ship's metal made her magic ping back crazily. First, she was certain she felt Recco's distinct energy, but then it frittered to nothing. She missed a step and stumbled, barking her shin. A shot of magic kept her upright. Why couldn't anything ever be easy?

Get over yourself. Her inner voice held a sharp rebuke.

Focus.

Zoe reeled in her guilt, her responsibility, her agitation. They could be why her seeking spell was bouncing around like an overly enthusiastic Ping-Pong ball. Sure enough, once she forged a calm center out of the chaos her mind had become, she felt Recco dead ahead and one floor up.

Perfect. She could catch him before they reached the bridge. She didn't have much she wanted to say, but she'd prefer not to have an audience. Zoe pushed her sore muscles to greater speed. White-hot darts shot up both legs; she ignored them.

The next corner yielded a set of stairs with Recco partway up them. He must sense her. It wasn't as if she was being the least bit stealthy. Her boots slapped the linoleum risers, and she must sound like a wee bellows as she forced air through her lungs in hopes it would yield more speed.

He moved to the side, not bothering to turn around. Goddammit it. He wasn't going to make this easy. Couldn't a lass have a meltdown because she was worried? About him, for chrissakes? He'd misinterpreted her concern as criticism and overreacted.

She sought words to convey everything welling inside her. The task was daunting, too hard, especially in her current state. Plus, she didn't much care for the blaming part. It might be his fault, but she'd tossed out incendiary comments first.

No one's fault. It's not the way to approach this problem.

Two more steps and she'd be even with him. No time to plan anything elegant. Closing her fingers around his arm, she blurted, "Daide said you're leaving the ship. You can't go. I'm sorry about earlier. It's just..." Her words vanished in a volley of pants as she caught her breath.

A startled look flitted across his face, but he didn't appear particularly relieved—or welcoming. Zoe took a chance and flung herself into his arms, slashing her mouth over his. At first, he didn't react, and she felt like a fool. Determined not to give up, she wound her arms around him and upped the ante on her kiss, licking, sucking, biting, hoping he'd open his mouth to welcome her tongue.

Humiliation heated her from the chest up. She'd thrown herself at a man who'd never wanted her, and her ill-timed seduction scheme was only making things worse. He stood stiffly against her, but he'd stopped shy of unwinding her arms from around his neck, probably to avoid hurting her feelings.

His lips felt amazing. Firm and velvety, and he tasted of Irish whiskey. She wanted to sink her fingers into his thick, dark hair, except she really needed to detach herself from the one-sided kiss. She would. Very soon. This would be the only kiss she'd ever share with Recco, and she hated to let him go. No matter what happened now, her embarrassment couldn't grow any worse. The deed was done, and she'd have to live with it.

She started to pull away. Should she apologize? Or blunder through reasons he had to rethink his decision about McMurdo. Had he already talked with the German doctor? Did they roll out the welcome mat for him? She wouldn't resolve any of those questions with her mouth glued to his.

The stiffness left his body, and he threaded his arms around her. Splaying his hands across her shoulders, he kneaded her sore muscles and ran his fingertips down her spine. He kissed her back, not only opening his mouth but sparring with her tongue, and the hot length of him pressing into her belly sent sensation spilling through her.

Time ground to a halt as they grappled with one another in the narrow stairway. Her breath quickened, and her heart thumped hard against her rib cage. This time it had nothing to do with running to catch up with Recco, and everything to do with a growing desperation to drag the man in her arms off to the nearest place they could lie down and divest themselves of enough clothing to make love.

He ripped his mouth from hers, dark eyes burning with intensity and need. "Zoe. Darling. I've dreamed of holding you like this, but I thought—"

She placed a hand over his mouth. "We can hash everything out later. Tell me you're not leaving."

His face split into a smile, and it set her world alight. "No. Juan already dredged that commitment out of me." He rolled his eyes. "Christ, Daide has a big mouth. I passed an idea by him, and he raced out of the bar like a madman with a mission."

Zoe angled her head to one side. "He loves you like a brother. He made it abundantly clear if you left, he'd pin my hide to the wall. I had no idea he was anything other than mild-mannered. It was quite a shock to be on the receiving end of his wrath."

Recco made a sound somewhere between a grunt and an amused snort. "Daide's mild-mannered, Clark Kent persona is a front. He can get amazingly spun out, but he corrals his temper well—most of the time."

"What part of *bridge* or *pronto* didn't sink in?" Viktor inquired dryly from the top of the stairwell.

"Oops. Got diverted." Zoe tried for a smile. It faded when she saw the grave cast to Viktor's features. He was angry. Annoyance jetted from him in choppy little spurts. When she tuned in with magic, she heard his raven shrieking curses.

"Get up here. Both of you." Viktor stepped backward into the space between the top of the stairs and the door into the bridge. Once they stood in front of him, he said, "The lecture will be brief. I have a roomful of people in there"—he jerked his chin over one shoulder—"waiting for you."

"We are sorry—" Recco began.

Viktor made a chopping motion. "While I'm glad the two of you got over whatever snit made Recco believe McMurdo would be preferable to this ship, when Juan or I give an order, you comply as fast as possible. What if there'd been an emergency? What if I hadn't had the luxury of time to hunt you down?"

"Got it. I truly am sorry," Zoe said.

"I don't give a rat's ass if you're sorry. What I need is for this to not happen again. That's it. Get moving." He pointed at the bridge.

Zoe bit back an acid question about keelhauling and if it was still the preferred method of dealing with unruly ship's crew. Viktor took his job seriously, and the job included keeping all of them alive. She should get down on her knees and thank him, but her Irish temper had always been her undoing. She felt like a ten-year-old who'd been reprimanded for leaving the barn door open, after the family's prize pig escaped and was run down by a tractor.

Guilty and responsible seemed to be her theme songs today. The emotional balance point she'd had before the Sirens and their lyre was elusive, slipping beyond her grasp time and again. She needed to reclaim it—and damned fast. Her big mouth had already gotten her in hot water with Recco. This wasn't Belfast, where everyone was a firebrand, and she had more latitude to spout off.

Recco held the door to the bridge and gestured her through. His nearness was intoxicating, but she couldn't think about him. Being fixated on him was why they were late to this mandatory gathering —because she'd hoped the kiss would last forever. She wanted to talk with him—and hold him and explore his body—far more than she wanted to hear whatever Viktor had in mind. Apparently, Recco had felt the same because he hadn't been in any hurry to join the others, either.

She nodded at him and made her way to where Karin and Ketha stood off to one side. "What in the goddess's name happened to you?" Karin hissed.

"Long story," she whispered back.

Viktor clapped his hands together once. It had the desired effect because side conversations died.

"Etta got back to me on the radio," he informed the group. "Most of them will remain at McMurdo. A handful want to join us." A muscle twitched beneath one eye. "Who wants to break the news to them about all but five of us being Shifters? I didn't figure it should be me or Juan, since we're new at this magic stuff. While I'm at it, do we fess up about being Vamps for ten years?" His gaze roved over the group.

"What about the Cataclysm?" Juan cut in. "Do we tell them why it receded?"

"What about the sea dragon?" Tessa asked. "If we tell them the truth about everything else…"

Zoe arched her brows Karin's way and said, "Seems to me, we'd have to disclose everything. Nothing quite like being stuck on a ship with a bigger mouthful of dead sea fruit and arcane practices than you ever believed existed."

"Yeah. Did you notice how they explained away the sea dragon's more unusual abilities under the veil of science?" Ketha asked.

"Why wouldn't they?" Daide retorted. "Science is where they live."

"Anyone else?" Viktor scanned the room.

"I agree with Zoe. It's all or none." Aura spoke with conviction.

"And it canna be none," Zoe muttered, not bothering to moderate her brogue. "Because then, none of us would be able to shift. *Arkady's* not big enough to hide something like that."

"Even worse," Karin cut in, standing straighter, "we wouldn't be able to use magic to fight. If what we've run into so far is any indication, we'll need every scrap of our paranormal abilities. We can't be hindered by having to mask who and what we are."

Conversation ebbed and flowed. Consensus fell on the side of full disclosure.

"Who's going to tell them?" Moira demanded, her dark eyes radiating worry. "And will it be in person or over the radio?"

Zoe pinched the bridge of her nose between a thumb and forefinger. "Aye, 'tis the sixty-four-thousand-dollar question. News like this is oft best delivered in person. If it scares the bejesus out of them, sends them scrambling for the Zodiacs—"

"Or their rifles to shoot us," Karin added sourly.

"Aye, that too." Zoe turned her hands palms upward. "Mayhap the radio is safest. If they have a meltdown, we can pull anchor and be gone afore they decide we have no right to live."

Boris cleared his throat and caught Juan's eye. "Accepting your magic was quite an adjustment, but I knew you before either of us suspected anything arcane existed. It helped because I'd already carved out a relationship with you and trusted your intentions."

"You helped us," Sasha said in his gravelly Russian-accented English. "You also help people from McMurdo. It may assist them to tolerate you being...different."

"It's a good point. Are we certain none of them are magical?" Recco asked. He'd staked out a corner of the bridge with Daide, and it appeared they'd found a way to shelve their differences. Maybe they'd been conversing telepathically while the rest of them debated the pros and cons of revealing what they were.

Zoe rolled the question around. "I dinna check." She sent pointed glances at the ten other Shifter women. Everyone shook their heads.

"I might not have checked, but I doubt it," Ketha said. "If any of them possessed magic, they'd have recognized the sea dragon for what it was."

"Are you certain?" Viktor asked.

"Not a hundred percent," she admitted. "Damn close to it, though."

Motion flagged the corner of Zoe's eyes, and she snapped her head up to stare out the windows. "So much for using the radio." She extended an arm. "A raft is headed our way."

Juan hustled to the bridge's glass wall. A low growl rose from his throat. "How many wanted to leave McMurdo?" he asked without turning around.

"Four, I believe," Viktor said. "Let's do our best not to alienate them. We need crew."

"I have an idea." Boris joined Juan at the windows. "How about if Ted, Sasha, and I deliver the information. We're human. They're human. We clearly haven't been co-opted by the devil, so they might believe us when we assure them they'll be safe."

"Might work." Ted drew his thick, blond brows together.

"I want to help." Diana detached herself from a shadowy corner. A brown-eyed thirty-something with longish brown hair, she'd been one of the survivors from Arctowski.

"Me too." Nora, still painfully thin, limped to Diana's side. Her red hair hung in braids to her waist, and her blue eyes shone with determination. "So far, I've been dead weight around here."

"You've been recovering from losing your son and almost dying yourself." Karin strode to her side. "Give it time."

Nora nodded. "You've been more than kind to me, Doc, but I need purpose now James is dead."

"All right, people. We have a plan." Viktor raised his voice to be heard over multiple conversations. "I'll lower the gangway and herd whoever's on the raft into the second dining room."

"We'll be there," Boris said, and trotted out of the bridge with Ted, Sasha, Diana, and Nora behind him.

"I'll remain after I shepherd the folks to Boris," Viktor said. "Not front and center, but in the back of the room in case things go badly and I need to organize a quick exit for our guests."

"Do you want me with you?" Ketha asked.

He shook his head. "Probably best if you're not."

"If they don't run out of here screaming their heads off like a bunch of ninnies, do you suppose there'd be any chance of us going ashore and culling through some of the lab equipment they're not using?" Recco asked. A hopeful note rode beneath his words.

"Phenomenal idea," Karin crowed.

"No shit. I'm ashamed I didn't come up with it," Ketha muttered.

"One thing at a time," Viktor said. "Let's get through this next part. If we're still playing on the same team afterward, I'll ask about spare lab materials." Grabbing his parka, he slipped into it and left the bridge.

Zoe blew out a tired breath. Everything still hurt despite focusing healing magic on her injuries. Food and sleep were her best antidotes. A glance at the clock told her she hadn't eaten much in hours. Determined to take care of herself so she got past feeling like warmed-over haggis, she decided to swing by the galley. There'd be food from the last couple of meals, and it was as good a place as any to start.

Recco and Daide were deep in conversation. She didn't want to intrude, so she turned to leave. Besides, it seemed premature for her to report her comings and goings to Recco. She craved more one-on-one time with him. It could wait until she was in better shape. She'd barely cleared the door when the men caught up with her.

"Sorry I was harsh," Daide said.

Zoe twisted to face them. Too trashed for subtlety, she blurted, "Are you? I bet Recco told you to apologize."

Color heightened the copper tones of Daide's skin. "I do a few things on my own."

She winced at the dour undernote in his words. "I should keep my mouth shut until I've had something to eat and about ten more hours sleep."

"I could make you a plate and bring it to your cabin," Recco suggested. When he trained his dark eyes on her, they brimmed with concern.

Her heart did a funny little flip-flop. "'Twould be lovely. The spectacle playing itself out in dining room two won't take very long, though. If things go south, we'll be moving along. If things go well, you'll want to visit the research station to see if they have anything we could use."

Her gaze swung from Recco to Daide and back again. Recco looked disappointed. Daide appeared pleased—and relieved. She understood Recco's emotions because she wanted more time with him too, but Daide's simmering satisfaction confused her. What did it mean?

"I'll check in with you later," Recco said, and gave her a quick hug.

"I'd like that." Zoe trotted down a nearby stairway, her thoughts a muddle. Neither man had married. Was it because no woman could compete with the bond they'd forged over twenty plus years? She'd find a delicate way of asking about it when she wasn't so tired.

Aye and if I do, 'twill have to be a quid pro quo.

She wasn't exactly ready to kick the lid off her sordid love life. She'd left Ireland for good reasons. A year away would have been perfect to let the hoopla die down from the trio of married men she'd been spending time with. No one knew about anyone else— until one of their wives caught wind her husband was cheating and sicced a detective agency on Zoe.

The results hadn't been pretty. At least she'd avoided lurid headlines shouting, "Nympho College Professor Can't Keep Her Knickers On."

She hip-butted the galley door and trudged inside. Her appetite had fled, but she stuffed an assortment of food into her mouth, chewing and swallowing so fast it was a miracle she didn't choke. Or puke it all back up. Pouring a glass of herbal tea, she doubled back for her cabin.

She'd been outspoken about full disclosure with the folk from McMurdo. The same rules applied for any human interaction. She had to tell Recco about her fall from grace before they shared any more kisses. Or much of anything else.

"What do you think?" she asked her coyote, hoping for a reprieve. For it to reassure her she didn't have to bare her soul. It wasn't as if any of her lovers had been Shifters. Only men with a hankering to score a wee bit of no-strings-attached tail.

"Such decisions are above my pay grade," her bondmate replied archly.

"Damn it. I hate it when you do that." She didn't bother with telepathy. No reason to since she was inside her cabin.

"Do what?"

"Use modern phraseology."

A spate of almost unintelligible Old Gaelic rattled from the coyote, followed by, *"Did ye like that better, lass?"*

"Never mind. Forget I asked anything."

Feeling glum and achy, she downed three ibuprofen, set the tea in a metal holder in case the ship set sail, and huddled in her bunk. The descent into blackness was almost immediate.

14

WHEN VIGILANCE ISN'T ENOUGH

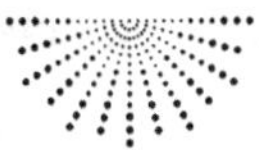

Darkness had long since fallen when Recco clambered up the gangway, laden with chemicals and instrumentation. McMurdo's lab facilities were extensive, and what was left of the staff been generous. The only price had been an intriguing question-and-answer session. Dr. Achter and her colleagues had probed first about vampirism, and then about Shifter abilities. Rather than being shocked or horrified, scientific curiosity rose to the fore, with every question forging a path for several more.

According to Viktor, the researchers who wanted to sign on as crew for *Arkady* had been equally fascinated when Boris and his companions threw down the gauntlet in the second dining room. A paleontologist, a biochemist, a zoologist, and a physicist, they'd been full of questions too. So many, Viktor encouraged them to settle in with Moira, Tessa, and Becca once they'd selected cabins.

Recco reached the top of the gangway and made his way inside, intent on dropping his loot in the lab and calling it a night. He replayed the questions from earlier. They'd held depth and enough sophistication, he'd learned a lot about Shifter history and abilities. Toward the end, the conversation moved to other types of magical beings. Viktor, Ketha, and Karin were still at the base. From the looks of things, they might not return until dawn.

Even though he could have remained, Recco was weary. The aftereffects from taking on the sea dragon dragged at him. When he'd suggested returning to *Arkady*, Juan jumped on it, which told him the other man probably wasn't in much better shape. Daide and Aura opted to join them. The night crossing in a Zodiac had been bitterly cold, but the sky was crystal clear and richly decorated with constellations.

"Feel like a nightcap?" Daide called from behind him.

Recco jumped. He'd been so wrapped up in his thoughts, he hadn't even noticed Daide's presence. Kicking the lab door open, he made for the cabinets at one end of the room. Lights flared, so Daide must have hit the switch. Not concerned with arranging anything, Recco slotted materials into bins that would protect them from the ship's movement and turned to face his friend.

"Maybe not tonight. I'm done in."

"One drink? You'd save me from drinking alone." Daide unloaded the backpack filled with chemical reagents, a darkfield scope, and assorted other instrumentation.

"Nah. I'll see you in the morning. Vik and them will be back by then, and I bet we leave soon thereafter."

Daide set his jaw in a tight line and narrowed his eyes. "You're going to Zoe's cabin, aren't you?"

Recco was so surprised, he fell back a step. Defensiveness vied with anger, and his sore muscles tightened into rocks. "No. I'm doing exactly what I said. Going to bed. My own. Since when do I report to you?"

"You don't." Daide looked at his boots. "It's just that—"

"Just what?" Recco rounded on him. "Look, Mr. Big Mouth. You stirred up a whole kettle of shit when you ran to Juan and Viktor and Zoe about a few offhand comments I made." Without waiting for Daide to reply, he kept on rolling. "Furthermore, I like Zoe. It's the first time I've felt like this about a woman in a really long time, and I am not going to push my feelings under a blanket because it might trample on some kind of holy ground between us. What is it with you? Every single, fucking time I even consider getting involved with someone, you do your damnedest to sabotage it. It's hard enough for me to connect with other people, but you made it all but impossible."

"That's not true. I had relationships too." Daide's words were strained. His shoulders squared off at an unnatural angle as if he'd rather be anywhere except here.

"Yeah, but they never lasted long, and"—Recco doubled up a fist and brought it down on a desk—"I never cared who you saw, what you did with them, or anything else about your personal life. It was yours."

"We operate differently. I always watched out for you." Accusation pinged sourly off Daide's words.

"Because I didn't insert myself into your love life didn't mean I didn't have your back in case something went wrong. You're not my parent. Nor am I yours. Christ. Do we have to do this now?"

Recco rubbed his temples, snagged his fingertips on a row of sutures, and bit back a curse. Breath whistled through his teeth, and he made a grab for his temper, which had lurched outside its sandbox. The space between himself and Daide sharpened into painfully clear focus, and his hand was still fisted. He squeezed his arm against his side. It took effort not to punch Daide square in his face.

Try as he might, Recco couldn't keep quiet. He drew his lips back from his teeth and snarled, "Everything's always been fine so long as you called the shots. I rarely argued, to keep peace between us, but by God, you will not harass me about Zoe. Do I make myself clear?"

"Sorry I brought it up," Daide said, tightlipped. His words didn't match his body language. Every aspect from his rigid posture and clenched jaw to his flaring nostrils screamed frustration and annoyance.

Recco teetered on the edge of a point of no return. He could blow up at Daide—something he'd come close to doing many, many times—and blast their long friendship to smithereens, or he could tread a customary path and back down. He breathed deep, the scents of the lab familiar and soothing in an odd way, and forced himself to be rational.

This wasn't like the other times he'd swallowed outrage. He and Daide would have to hash this out. Now wasn't the time. "Look," he said. "We're both tired. Not the best occasion to talk about anything." Walking to Daide, he dropped a hand on his shoulder, hoping to make peace.

Eyes still hooded, Daide shook him off and all but raced out of the lab.

Recco stared after him. A headache pounded behind one eye. Had the sea dragon done something to Daide? He'd always had an obsessive need to control things, but his actions today were way over-the-top. Plodding to the door, Recco dowsed the lights and headed for his cabin. Where before he'd been tired, now his brain spun in feverish circles.

He needed to think clearly. It didn't seem to be in the cards. Moving on autopilot, he entered his cabin and switched on the reading light over the bunk. He washed his hands carefully in case some of the lab equipment held any stray bacteria, and then undressed, thoughts still whirling.

He'd joked with Daide they were like the original *Odd Couple*. It was closer to the truth than a witticism. They complemented one another, and Recco had never minded Daide's fixation on running things his way. So long as the veterinary clinic turned a profit and patients kept flowing, Recco was happy. Daide's control-freak inclinations had proven to be a hindrance after Raphael turned them, but Recco hadn't paid much attention to his stream of bellyaching.

Maybe because he hadn't offered grist for the mill, Daide eventually settled down. Recco sluiced water over his face and gave his teeth a cursory brushing before slumping onto his bunk. Daide was a good friend. The best. But he'd be damned if he'd let him drive a wedge between him and Zoe.

Hell, the relationship had barely gotten off the ground. Daide would have to find a way to live with it, assuming today's beginnings blossomed into something bigger. Even if they didn't, the episode that had unfolded in the lab—coupled with Daide's frantic call to arms when Recco said he was considering leaving—convinced him a major restructuring of their relationship was long overdue.

"Yeah," he muttered. "Friends doesn't mean we own one another. More specifically, he doesn't get to make my decisions. I've never tried to make his."

He flicked out the light and shut his eyes. It helped the throbbing in his head a little. The first thing to figure out was if the sea dragon had contaminated Daide's mind in some way.

"Can you or Daide's coyote help sort through it?" he asked his wolf.

"Possibly."

"Thanks for being there so I didn't have to explain everything."

"I said possibly. Dragons are ancient and powerful."

"This one's dead."

"Maybe. Even if it is, its magic didn't necessarily die with it."

"Keep talking. Please."

A whuffling growl, maybe lupine laughter, rumbled through his chest, activating more sore places. Recco groaned and rolled over, trying to find some body part that didn't hurt to lie on.

"The dragon may be dead. It might have left for another world to heal its wounds. For us, the important part is it's no longer in these waters. I don't believe it's likely to return."

"Should be a great relief to the folk at McMurdo," Recco mumbled.

"I still sense traces of its magic," the wolf went on. *"Whether they're linked to Daide or only to this area is beyond my ability to discern."*

"Can his bond animal determine the source?" Recco inhaled

sharply, wanting the answer to be yes but suspecting it couldn't be so simple.

"I don't know," the wolf answered flatly. *"The coyote was first right, and then wrong, about the dragon. I wasn't at all comfortable how easily it was fooled by the dragon's victim illusion."*

"Maybe the women can figure something out."

"Or their bond animals."

"I hadn't forgotten them."

Recco fell silent. He wasn't going to unravel anything tonight, and if he didn't get some sleep, he wouldn't be worth crap for much of anything. Part of him wanted to blame the dragon. That was dangerous territory—and an easy way out. If its magic wasn't mucking with Daide's mind, the only explanation left was his friend was a selfish bastard. Recco had been making excuses for him for years, but he was done.

"Maybe it's both," the wolf piped up. *"Or maybe his brief connection to the dragon scared the guts out of him and amplified his tendency to be over-vigilant."*

A snort blew past Recco's lips. Over-vigilant didn't come close to Daide's compulsive need to micromanage everything. After he rolled onto his other side, his trashed body caught up with him and he was asleep in moments.

THE CRACKLE of the PA system barged into the latest in a string of Fellini-esque dreams, and Recco pried his eyes open. Daylight flooded through the porthole, so much light it had to be midday.

"We're pulling anchor in thirty minutes," Juan announced. "Seas outside this bay will be rough, so batten down your cabins. If you're hungry, grab something now."

Recco swung to a sitting position and planted his feet on the floor, taking stock of his battered body. The two long gashes where Daide had stitched him up burned, and his muscles were still sore.

Beyond those items, he felt miles better than he had when sleep hammered him into oblivion.

A quick tap on the door was followed by it opening a crack. Zoe's bright hair came into view. "Are ye decent, laddie?"

Pleasure ran through him in a warm tide, and he chuckled. "A full retreat to your Celtic roots, eh? Come on in. You're safe enough. Never did take my long johns off."

She sidled into the room, hair done up in multiple braids that fell to mid-chest. Her brown eyes sparkled with humor. "Wouldn't want to offend my maidenly modesty. Feel like grabbing coffee and something quick to eat? The rest of us had breakfast over an hour ago. There's plenty left."

Recco slid trousers over his legs and zipped into a light jacket. "No one announced a meal. I'd have heard it."

"Several of us were still asleep, including Vik and Ketha. Juan didn't want to wake anyone before he absolutely had to."

"You were up." He tugged on his boots and straightened. "Ready."

"Aye. I'm an early riser. Doesn't matter what time I went to bed." Tilting her head to one side, she regarded him and crossed to the sink where she wetted a washcloth. "Come close. There's a wee bit of blood on your face. It leaked from the gash across your forehead."

He stepped next to her and bent his head, so she could reach the abrasion easily. He could have taken the cloth from her, but he liked the idea of her touching him. She smelled of cinnamon and amber; he inhaled hungrily as she dabbed gently at the dried blood.

"Better." She bent around him and rinsed the square of terrycloth, hanging it over the sink's edge.

Recco circled her shoulders with his arms and held onto her from behind. "I can't imagine a more welcome visitor."

She leaned against him, all lean muscle and tight curves. "Och, you Latin types were born with silver tongues."

"Maybe so, except in this case, I truly meant it. When I heard someone knock, I was afraid it was Daide. We had a blowup last night."

She turned in his arms, brows drawn into a worried line with a small fissure between them. "I hope it wasn't over me. He seemed way too pleased when I left the two of you to troll through McMurdo's lab yesterday afternoon."

"Wasn't your imagination. He'll get over his snit. I hope."

"So it was about me. Damn." She pursed her lips into a thin line. "I'm sorry. Is there anything I can do? Do you know why he doesn't like me?"

Recco smoothed stray hairs that had escaped her braids over her shoulders and cupped the side of her face in one hand. "It's not you. He hasn't approved of any woman I've ever taken up with."

A speculative expression crossed her face, and her eyes shaded to amber. Spots of color splashed across her high cheekbones. "Is it because… Er, does he maybe want you for himself?" She glanced down, long lashes brushing both cheeks as the tint shading her freckled face deepened.

He grazed a thumb across her full lower lip, loving the silky feel of her skin. "No. He's not gay. Believe me, he wouldn't have been able to hide something so monumental from me. Not for as long as we've been together."

"What, then?" She tilted her head into his touch and met his gaze, eyes liquid with concern.

"He likes to control things. Way more than anyone else I've ever run across." Recco took a measured breath. "Don't get me wrong. He's more than competent, and his instincts are usually decent— unless he's gotten spun out about some detail that escaped his iron hand." He hadn't meant to dive straight into the sea dragon question, but this was a perfect opportunity.

"What about the sea dragon?" Her gaze never wavered.

His eyes widened, and he stammered, "You're inside my mind."

She shrugged slightly. "Aye. Saves time. I apologize, though. 'Twasn't my intention to pry."

"Can you and some of the other women find out if the sea dragon still has Daide in some kind of thrall?"

"Maybe. Why do you suspect it might?"

"Because his actions yesterday were over-the-top—even for him. I have no idea what he said to you about me and McMurdo. Did he come off as heavy-handed? I realize you don't know him, but apply the same standards you'd use for anyone."

"Och aye, he was more than heavy-handed. Draconian comes closer to describing it. He grabbed me, and none too gently, mind you. Told me he'd make my life so miserable I'd wish I'd jumped ship with you."

A spurt of anger bubbled from Recco's guts. "He threatened you?"

"Aye." She hurried on. "Mayhap you're onto something about the dragon. I'll round up Ketha and maybe Karin and Aura once we're underway and see if we can't figure things out. Did you ask your wolf?"

"Yeah. It wasn't any help with this particular problem."

He cradled her against him, wanting to hang onto her forever. Her body nestled close, fitting perfectly. As if they'd been born to be together.

"Breakfast." Her words were muffled against his chest. "'Tis far harder to eat when we hit rough water. Besides"—she tilted her head back and smiled—"you need food and sleep so your magic can fully recover."

Evidence of her concern flooded him with feelings he'd forgotten existed. He wanted her to care. Further, he wanted to protect her from every wicked thing in the world.

She untangled her arms from where they'd been wrapped around him. "Come on, *a chara.*"

He raised a brow. "I can learn Gaelic."

"It means friend."

The pleasure warming him rose in a thick tide, and he kissed her forehead. "I'm honored to be your friend." He laced his fingers in with hers. "You'll have to teach me words for darling and lover. Afraid the only word I know is Sassenach."

Zoe laughed. "From *Outlander*. I loved those books."

"I did too. Read them on the sly."

"Too much on the chick lit side? Worried they'd tarnish your manly image?"

"No, I was more afraid Daide would find them and give me a hard time. About all he ever read were scientific journals. I needed a break from time to time."

Recco pulled the door of his cabin open and stopped dead. Daide stood in front of the door, a hand raised to knock. When he saw Zoe, his smile faded. "Thought I'd see if you felt like breakfast. It appears you already have company."

"Always room for one more." Zoe extended a hand. Daide didn't clasp it. She dropped it to her side, adding in a pointed tone, "No hard feelings on my side."

Karin bustled down the hall. "Did I hear the word breakfast? I was a total sloth this morning, and I'm starving. I'd love to join you."

"We should hurry," Zoe said. "From Juan's announcement, we'll be underway soon."

Recco brought up the rear as the four of them trotted across the hall and down one flight to the galley and kitchen. Questions charged from one side of his mind to the other. Had he happened to open the door precisely when Daide was poised to knock, or had the other man been listening through the door? It wasn't the kind of thing he could ask outright without creating a scene. Distrust tightened his stomach into a knot.

The specter of his oldest friend spying on him was so distasteful, he chopped off his line of thought at its roots. He had to be overreacting. Still feeling the aftereffects from the previous day. He tried probing Daide's mind but found an unyielding wall. Maybe it reflected his lack of magical skill. Presumably Daide was just as magically naïve, and he'd managed to erect an impenetrable ward.

"Oops. I forgot something," Daide muttered and doubled back about the time they reached the dining room's swinging doors.

"I'll lay you a place," Karin called after his retreating back. Daide didn't even turn around. She frowned. "What's up with him?"

Zoe herded them into an otherwise-empty dining room. "Hate to drop another bomb. Is it possible the dragon isn't dead?"

Karin closed her teeth over her lower lip. "I see where you're going, and I don't much care for it. Do you have reason to believe it's using Daide for a conduit, much as it did before? Is that why he felt so…odd?"

"I don't know what to think," Recco said. "All I know is he's really different than he was when he patched me up after we fought the dragon."

They moved into the galley and stood over pans of eggs and biscuits. He and Karin shoveled food into their mouths, any semblance of sitting down forgotten. Recco got it. They needed sustenance, not gracious dining.

Zoe picked at a biscuit, but her brow was crinkled into concerned lines, and she didn't offer any ideas.

Karin spun her fork in a circle. "Makes sense the dragon hunted for a weak link, assuming it recovered somehow. Goddammit. I was certain it was dead."

"Daide said it was," Recco countered.

"Aye, and look who the messenger was." Zoe sent a pointed look his way. "It wanted us to believe it was dead."

Recco slopped down a cup of tepid coffee, not bothering to add powdered milk. "We can't leave. Not if the dragon's going to continue to prey on who's left at McMurdo."

"Let's not overplay this," Karin said. "If the sea dragon was functioning at anywhere near a hundred percent, it would be swimming around out there. We injured it. Perhaps made it impossible for its serpent form to cross the veil from wherever it went to ground."

"Which doesn't mean it can't still sow mischief," Zoe muttered. "By playing mind games and setting us against one another.

Dragons in the old tales were famous for pitting one king against his neighbor. Once they killed one another, it swooped in and ate all their sheep and cattle."

Recco finished his biscuit and decided he'd had enough. A nagging wrongness pricked him, making the small hairs on the back of his neck stand on end. He pushed to his feet. "I'm going to find Daide and figure out what's going on."

"We'll come with you," Karin said.

"I'll tell Ketha via telepathy that we might have a problem. She can alert everyone else." Zoe gathered their forks, spoons, and knives and dropped them into a nearby sink.

Recco marched out of the galley and then through the dining room doors, flanked by the women. No matter how much of a pain in the ass Daide had been these last few hours, they went back over twenty years. He'd hold up his end of their friendship not only because it was the proper thing to do, but because he cared about Daide.

The uncomfortable sensations intensified as they climbed the stairs to Deck Three. "Do you feel that?" he asked, worried the pins and needles poking him from odd angles weren't real.

"Of course," Karin snapped. "I'm trying to determine what the hell it is."

"Not the sea dragon." Zoe's words held conviction. "My mind was joined to it long enough for me to take its measure."

He grabbed her arm. "If it isn't the dragon, then what the hell is going on?"

Zoe didn't answer. She squared her shoulders in a resolute gesture that tugged at his soul. He should be protecting her, not the other way around. Employing magic to interpret the world was far from his strong suit, though.

A few more steps and they'd be at Daide's cabin.

Karin pushed in front of him, hands raised and blue-white light crackling from her fingertips. Zoe mirrored her posture and said, "May as well go in with all our guns blazing."

Recco bristled. No matter how much of a neophyte he was in terms of being a Shifter, he'd be goddamned if he'd hide behind two women. He slid in from the side and opened the door to Daide's cabin in one fluid movement. A putrid stench rolled out—rotten eggs raised to the hundredth power—and shadowy figures flew every which way. They had to be illusion, so he batted at them.

Behind him, the women crowded in and he heard the cabin door slam shut.

One of the flying things drove a sharp beak into his shoulder. Recco did look then, appalled the apparitions were real. He seized the crow-like creature that had attacked him, threw it to the floor, and stomped on it. Bones crunched beneath his feet. His orderly, scientifically trained mind demanded explanations, but they'd have to wait. Breaking bones were real enough to tell him they had a big problem.

Magic sizzled from the women, along with a brilliant flare illuminating the gloom shrouding the cabin. Daide lay on the floor, his spine bent at an unnatural angle and his face drawn into a rictus of pain and horror. His eyes were closed, and he'd thrown an arm across his face. Whatever used his body had discarded it, but not before it poked multiple holes where blood flowed freely, adding a metallic reek to the rest of the noxious smells in the cabin.

Recco dove for his friend, cradling him in his arms as he did a fast assessment. He found a heartbeat, rapid and thready but present. Respiration clocked in at double normal.

"Get him out of here," Zoe cried. Furred and feathered shapes— mostly black, but a few rust-colored ones—fell like rain as she bombarded them with blasts of power.

Karin knelt next to Recco. "We have to seal off this cabin. Once it's done, we'll have a prayer of containing this influx."

"Where's it coming from?" The words tore from Recco, and he followed them with, "Never mind. If I leave, who's going to help you and Zoe?"

"Ketha and Aura are on their way, along with Moira and Tessa and Becca and the rest. We'll be fine."

Something looking like a cross between a marmot and an armadillo exploded, showering them with viscous red goo that smelled like a slaughterhouse. Recco gagged. He staggered upright with Daide slung across his shoulder in a fireman's carry. Karin dragged the door open, and Recco stumbled outside.

Ketha, Aura, and the other women raced around him and into the cabin infested with hell-spawned denizens, slamming the door behind them.

Daide groaned, and Recco carted him across the hall to an empty cabin. Shouldering the door open, he laid him on the floor and took stock of what he'd need. Bandages, suture material, antiseptic, antibiotics, injection equipment. Blood flowed from numerous wounds, and Daide thrashed weakly.

"It will be all right." Recco infused a confidence he wasn't feeling into his words.

Daide's dark eyes flashed open. "No, it won't." He clawed at his midsection. "Things are inside. Eating me from the inside out. Get a scalpel. Cut them out. Or let me." A fey light shimmered around his prone form, but at least his spine had straightened.

"He has to shift," Recco's wolf sounded frantic.

"How do I make him do that?"

"Encourage him."

"Daide. *Amigo.* You have to shift. It's the only way to fight this."

He shook his head. "Can't. Nothing real is left. Can't find my coyote. It abandoned me."

"No. It didn't," the wolf insisted. *"Evil things are blocking it."*

"Tell me what to do," Recco begged. He hated feeling helpless, and he was afraid if he left Daide for long enough to gather medical supplies, he'd claw his own belly open.

"Shift. I'll take over."

Amid ripping fabric, he ceded his form to the wolf. As soon as it took shape, it bent and closed its jaws around Daide's neck.

"What are you doing?" Frantic, he'd been snared in some bizarre manifestation of evil, Recco tried to shift back, but the wolf clung to its form.

"Do. Not. Fight. Me." A growl punctuated every word.

It went against everything Recco believed in. His heart pounded, and sweat dripped down his metaphorical body, the one waiting in the wings. He reeled in horror and disbelief as the wolf nipped Daide's neck, adding more blood to what he'd already lost. *"Don't kill him."*

"I'm saving him. Believe in me, or this won't work."

His bondmate's words were like a pitcher of ice-cold water. Whatever maneuver it was executing had to work. Had to. Daide couldn't die while Recco stood by and did nothing.

I'm not doing nothing. His thoughts didn't reassure him, though.

As he watched through the wolf's eyes, a coyote tried to form in the air above Daide. Tried and frittered to nothing. After it happened three times, Recco dug deeper and funneled every scrap of magic he had into the wolf, frightened to his bones it might not be enough. He felt desperation in the wolf's heart; it added to his helplessness and his panic.

They were close, so close. He felt it. Could taste it on the wolf's tongue.

Close doesn't cut it. We have to break through.

Behind him, the cabin door ripped open, and waves of magic blasted him, weaving with his own and strengthening it. The additional power from Zoe and Ketha turned the tide. Daide morphed into his animal form, a bloody, battered coyote that yipped and howled.

A second coyote—Zoe—ran to its side, also yipping and yowling. In between, it licked Daide's muzzle, face, and flanks, its tongue sealing the hurt places. Recco's wolf joined in, laving wounds with its tongue.

"Thank you," Recco told his bondmate.

"We're not out of the woods yet. This runs deeper than healing his body.

If we can't seal the conduit evil came through, once and for all, we'll have to kill him."

15

OVERDUE TRUTHS

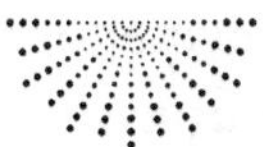

oe heard Recco's wolf. While she agreed with its assessment, her heart hurt for Daide and his coyote bondmate. The coyote would return to the animals' private world, but she bet it would never bond with anyone again. Filled with self-castigation, it was convinced it had failed Daide. First by not recognizing the sea dragon's duplicity, and now by not warning him he was ripe for the plucking from any evil thing hunting for access to the human world.

"You had no way of knowing." She tried to soothe its agitation and continued licking its hurt places.

"I did. I didn't try hard enough." It hesitated. *"I was still angry with my bondmate for not making more of an effort after we first joined our lives. It clouded my judgment."*

"Fine. Now pull your head out of your ass and behave like a bond animal, not a prima donna." Ketha's wolf's voice cut like a whip.

Zoe cheered it on and moved over so Ketha's wolf could join the healing lick-fest. A black-and-gray timber wolf, its fur sported more dark tones than Recco's wolf, and in a slightly different pattern.

Daide's coyote laid its ears back and started to flip onto its back to show its belly as a sign of defeat and submission.

"None of that." Zoe nipped it. *"You will stand proud until we are done."*

Ketha's wolf skinned its muzzle back, baring its teeth.

Karin stalked into the cabin with the other women crowding behind her. Blood and something black streaked her face, hands, and clothing. "The cabin across the way is clear and sealed from darkness. Do you need help with Daide?"

"Aye." Zoe bypassed her coyote to talk with Karin. *"Can ye repair the weakness within him? The magnet drawing demon spawn?"*

Karin pushed between the wolves and hunkered next to Daide's coyote, running her hands along its lush, gray-brown fur. Its flanks shuddered beneath her touch, and it whined softly. A desolate sound compared with its earlier yips.

Karin drew her white brows together and used a hand to help herself upright. "For now, we'll establish a twofold approach. We'll draw wards around the ship, and I'll do what I can to help Daide acquire faith in himself and locate his inner strength. Once he decides he's worthy, he'll be far more vigilant."

Recco's ears pricked forward, and he left off his ministrations to plant his wolf body in front of Karin. *"What do you mean inner strength?"* he demanded. *"Daide has always been one of the strongest men I know."*

A tired smile formed on Karin's face. "He did a pretty good job if he fooled even you. When I culled through his memories just now, I found hurt places that run deep. His family abandoned him when he was quite young. The distant relatives who raised him took him in out of pity and obligation. He never felt he was worth anyone's consideration—including his own."

Surprise rippled over the wolf's face, more subtle than it would have been if Recco had been in his human body, but apparent nonetheless.

"Ye dinna know?" Zoe aimed her words at Recco.

The wolf shook itself from ears to tail, and she took it as a no.

"Do not go picking through the bones of my past." Daide's words held a harsh, warning note.

Ketha's wolf nipped his haunch. *"We'll do what we need to,"* she informed him. *"And you will cooperate. I'll not have you putting the rest of us at risk."*

"Leave me at McMurdo."

Recco leapt back to the coyote and swatted him with a paw. *"I don't think so. You pitched a fit when I—"*

"Enough." Karin didn't raise her voice, but it vibrated with command and annoyance. *"Arkady* is underway. We're not turning around. For anyone."

Zoe had been so focused on crushing the hell-spawned creatures in Daide's cabin, she'd never noticed the drone of the ship's turbines humming from below decks. She sent a thread of magic outward to assess if the coyote was healed enough for Daide to shift back. Having him shift to drive wickedness out had been brilliant. The animal nature was purer than the human one, and far more amenable to shaking off the dregs of evil things.

Ketha and Recco worked on a few last wounds. The coyote's body was mostly patched up. Certainly, healed enough to allow a shift. She reached for Daide's coyote. *"Can you move past blaming yourself? Hard work lies ahead. Your bondmate will require the best you have to offer him."* Without waiting for a reply, she went on. *"The two of you got off to a rocky start. Nowhere is it written you can't use the knowledge you gained to strengthen what's to come."*

The coyote shook itself and fluffed out its tail. Turning slowly, it faced Zoe and touched her nose with its own. *"I'm one of the younger animals. Not confident in my own skin yet. It might be why I was attracted to Daide. We share insecurities—"*

"Speak for yourself," Daide blustered around his bond animal.

To its credit, it spoke over him. *"The benefit of a shared weakness is I understand him. And if he allows it to happen, he will develop compassion and an accord with me. This is one instance where the bond will make us stronger together than either of us are as individuals."*

"Well-spoken." Karin nodded solemnly. "I'll fetch a robe. It's time for you to shift."

"Time for the rest of us too," Ketha said and nudged Karin with her snout. *"Are you planning to fetch robes for us all?"*

"Oh hell no. You can get your own." She skewered Ketha with her astute copper gaze. "Once you're decent, see to some type of warding that won't drain us down to bedrock but will at least serve as an early warning system if we're attacked again."

A howling snort rose from Ketha. Magic shimmered around her in a glistening cascade. Zoe picked up the cue and found her human form. She felt Recco's gaze, hot and curious, as she hustled out of the cabin to snatch up a robe. She could take the time to dress later. The ship had begun pitching and rolling, which meant they'd left the protected waters around McMurdo station.

By the time she got back to the cabin across from Daide's original one, he and Recco were human. Both men stood swathed in belted white terrycloth robes, and Daide had a mulish look on his face. They'd been conversing in Spanish, but fell silent when she padded into the room.

"Where's Karin?"

"She'll be back soon," Recco said. "She went to get herbs or a wand or tarot cards or something similar."

"Nah. She went after her broom." Daide's words might have been a joke in a different context, but they held an unmistakable bitter undertone.

Zoe rounded on him, bristling. "She doesn't have to do anything for you. Show a wee bit of respect."

The other man's brittle aspect crumpled before her eyes. He turned away to hide the defeated expression in his eyes, and she wished she hadn't been so harsh.

"Amigo. There's no shame in something that happened when you were a child," Recco said softly, his words brimming with kindness.

"You weren't there." Daide still faced the porthole. "I was

uncontrollable, stole food I had no right to. My family was well within their rights to abandon me."

"You didn't have enough to eat?" Zoe moved close but stopped shy of touching him.

He turned slowly; raw pain had dug trenches in his cheeks and forehead. "You grew up in the U.K. You have no idea what it's like in rural South America. I was born into a tribe of what you'd consider hunter-gatherers." He hissed derisively. "Sounds romantic. Pah. It was dirty, grubby, a hardscrabble existence where diseases that could have been cured if we'd been anywhere near a modern hospital, killed people. Half the babies never made it to their second birthday."

"How come you never told me any of this?" Recco broke in.

"It's not like I lied." Daide tilted his chin at a defiant angle. "I let you believe the life you saw when we met was the one I'd always led. It wasn't all that great, either, but it was a big step up from the starving seven-year-old urchin who staggered into Buenos Aires, more dead than alive. The authorities found me and delivered me to a cousin's house."

"At least they took you in." Zoe tried for a positive spin.

"The government gave him and his wife money." Daide screwed his face into a grimace. "It was one of BA's slums where dozens of neighbors crowded close after an official car pulled up. My cousin couldn't have said no in front of such a big audience without looking like a selfish asshole."

Recco nodded his understanding. "Family is important in Argentine society."

"Not in the bush, it's not," Daide mumbled. "I still remember being so hungry my gut was distended. It hurt all the time."

Recco touched Daide's arm. "What did you think would happen if you'd told me the truth?"

He hooded his eyes, looking away. "I did my damnedest to pretend those first seven years of my life never happened. Buried them so deep, I thought I'd succeeded. Raphael knew, though. He taunted me. Made certain I remembered being hungry, so I'd be more enthusiastic about blood and embrace being a Vampire."

Zoe shuddered. Compassion cut a path through her, but it wasn't what Daide needed. She could tell him nine different ways that stealing food when he was a child wasn't his fault. He had to believe it. Belief would spring from self-acceptance, a path each man had to walk on his own.

A blast of magic pushed the door open, and Karin strode through, arms full of bags. The pungent smell of herbs tickled Zoe's nose as Karin started to stack things on the small desk. A rapid-fire pitch and yaw altered her plans, and she moved everything to one of two bunks set at right angles to one another.

"What can I do?" Zoe asked, thinking she'd cast a tarot spread or add complementary magic.

"Nothing." Karin strung the bags' handles over a hook. "The two of you need to clear out of here. Help Ketha with the ward. Go work on supper. Get to know our new crew members." She made shooing motions. "Sooner you get moving, the sooner Daide and I can get to work."

Daide sank to a sit on the end of the empty bunk, a resigned set to his shoulders. When Zoe looked closer, though, a ray of hope flickered in the backs of his dark eyes.

"You good with this, *amigo?*" Recco asked.

Karin's copper gaze shot darts at him, but he wasn't paying any attention to her.

Daide nodded. "You don't have to watch over me." A flash of the old Daide surfaced, and he added, "Not that I don't appreciate the attention after all the effort I poured into you over—"

"I get the drift. We're out of here." Recco laughed and held the door for Zoe.

She turned to him once the door was closed, feet spread wide to compensate for the ship's rocking motion. "I'm going to grab some clothes. Good thing this ship had plenty of them."

He turned a smile her way. "I'll dress too. Is there a short version to describe what Karin's doing?"

"Yeah. She's making Daide whole, so evil things can't sneak past his boundaries. He made decent progress on his own before she arrived, though."

"I don't understand." He grabbed the railing running along every corridor to stabilize himself.

"This isn't rational. When parts of who you are cause you shame, it creates weak places in your psyche. Normally, they aren't problematic, but we don't live in normal times. The Cataclysm activated evil. Think of it as omnipresent, always knocking about the edges, looking for a way in."

"Which would be why the dragon picked on Daide?"

"Aye, exactly."

"And why once it was gone, something else saw opportunity and dove into the breach."

Zoe nodded, pleased he understood. "The magical world has rules too. Exactly like the Vampire world or the one you lived in before the Cataclysm. 'Tis a matter of acknowledging and respecting them." She inhaled, nostrils flaring. "Even though I was born a Shifter, I spent most of my life living in a non-magical world. I'm not as quick as I should be when it comes to recognizing these types of things."

"Do you mean we should have dug deeper after the sea dragon episode?"

"'Tis precisely what I mean."

Karin dragged the cabin door open. "Take the conversation elsewhere. Now." Before Zoe could apologize, Karin slammed it in her face.

She gestured to Recco and walked to the end of the corridor. "Sorry about Karin. She's always had a shorter fuse than mine, which says a great deal."

"No need to apologize." He wrapped his arms around her, breath warm against her forehead. "Let's continue this conversation once we're dressed."

Recco's nearness was enticing, and breath caught in her throat. He still smelled like his wolf, fresh and wild; the combination sang to her blood. She threaded her fingers through his thick, unevenly cut hair and tilted her mouth up.

Recco closed his lips over hers in a slow, lazy, exploratory kiss. He nibbled her lips, and she bit back, sliding her tongue inside his mouth. He sparred with it and licked his way over to her earlobe taking it into his mouth. Heat spooled in her belly, and her nipples hardened where they pressed against his chest. He rubbed his palms over her tight shoulder muscles, kneading away tension, and she melted into his embrace.

His hair felt like silk where she tugged it through her fingers. Stubble from his beard left trails of sensation wherever he moved his mouth. Her heart thudded against her ribs. Breath clotted, narrowing her throat. She hadn't made love with anyone since leaving Ireland, a self-imposed penance for the insatiability that landed her in hot water with her three lovers.

Awk. I have to tell him. First. Before anything else happens.

Zoe ripped her mouth from his. "Sure and we have to talk."

His dark eyes had deepened to midnight; banked fires flared to life in their depths. This man held passion. Every detail from the way he clung to her, to his hungry gaze, screamed once they made love, he'd stake a claim to her. One that would last forever.

Part of it was the Shifter bond. They mated for life. No exceptions. No excuses. Recco's intensity predated both Vampirism and becoming a Shifter. Why had he never married? Any woman would welcome a man like him, one who'd put her above everything else in his life. Who'd worship and cherish any woman he labeled as his.

"I'm listening." He dipped his hands to the curve of her ass, settling them there.

She cut her gaze to her cabin door. "Inside, where 'tis a wee bit more private."

"Is it only talking ye have in mind?" He mimicked her brogue.

Zoe chuckled and sent a jot of magic to open the door, walking through. Once she was inside, she perched on the edge of the berth she didn't sleep in. It was littered with books and papers, all of which had shifted into untidy piles. Too late, she recalled Juan's exhortation to batten down their living spaces.

"Aye. Talking for now." She tucked her robe more tightly around herself, body still humming from his touch and kisses.

He sat catty-corner from her and placed a hand on her thigh. "What is it that can't wait?"

She glanced upward, organizing her thoughts. There wasn't any way to put a positive spin on her indulgence. Besides, he didn't need the gritty details, merely the gist of things. She tucked a pillow behind her back and leaned against the wall.

"Shifters marry other Shifters for obvious reasons. Unless we wish to live a lie in our intimate lives, we can't disclose what we are. Humans, most of them anyway, wouldn't understand. There aren't many choices of mates, so most of us remained unattached."

Zoe exhaled raggedly. So far so good. Recco regarded her, an interested expression on his face. "Although we don't marry," she went on, "we still enjoy, erm, carnal pursuits."

He broke into a grin. "What an old-fashioned term." He squeezed her thigh. "Zoe, if this is a long-winded lead-in to you explaining why you're not a virgin, I don't care. I wouldn't expect you to be, and I'm certainly not."

Heat rose to her face. "Nay, I fear 'tis worse. I didn't set out to have several lovers, but it happened. All of them were married, which was my hedge against them becoming overly intrigued by me." She licked dry lips. "One of their wives found out and hired a detective. He uncovered not only her husband but the other two as well."

"Other than the poor sod whose wife likely told him to hit the bricks, I'm not seeing the problem, or why you felt the need to confess. It's certainly not something I'd hold against you." He made a noise midway between a laugh and a snort. "I do admit to being jealous, though. I'd love to have three women warm my bed."

"'Tisn't as if 'twas at the same time. Those men may have been into cheating. Beyond infidelity, they were a stodgy lot." Zoe smothered a laugh, and wondered why she'd worried about letting her secret out.

He winked broadly. "Too bad. Ménage is far more interesting than—"

Understanding he was teasing her, she lunged at him and mock punched his upper arm.

He pulled her across his lap, hanging on tight, and she wriggled to get closer. "Why'd you want me to know?" he persisted.

"Och, Belfast isn't as modern as all that. I lived in fear the tabloids would get hold of the story and ruin me. 'Twas when I decided I should leave for a span of time and how I ended up gracing the University of Wyoming's archaeology department."

"Would the university in Ireland truly have sacked you?"

"Och, aye, and in a heartbeat. They'd have seen me as a bad influence on Ireland's best and brightest."

Recco cradled her head against his chest. "They'd have lost a damn fine professor."

Pleasure at the compliment kindled a warm glow in her midsection that had nothing to do with the fires igniting from his closeness. The ship lurched from side to side, suggesting they were in for a stretch of rough water, probably days of it.

"I don't have anything nearly as interesting to trade in return." Recco's deep voice rumbled against her hair. "I had the odd lover. So did Daide. Never at the same time, or some of those relationships might have worked out better."

"Why do you think so?"

He tilted his head so he could look at her. "After college and vet school and practicing together for a long time, Daide and I were close. Not in the way gay men are, but in every other way. We worked together, studied together, shopped together, took turns cooking and cleaning. I can't speak for his women. The few of mine who gave me a reason before they stopped dating me said they couldn't compete."

Recco raked a hand through his hair and kept talking. "At first, I blamed Daide. He did give my female friends the cold shoulder, but I ignored his women and they left too. Once they got to know him, his need to micromanage everything drove them away. He always seemed content when it was only him and me. I wasn't, but I also wasn't willing to take an otherwise satisfying life and turn it upside down."

"You never met the right woman." Zoe sent a knowing look skittering between them.

"You'd be correct about that. I took a stand with Daide the night we returned from McMurdo. Told him in no uncertain terms if he tried to get between you and me, it wouldn't be pretty."

Delight churned through her. "You did that? For me? When we were nothing more than friends?"

He looked down, lashes grazing his cheeks, and nodded. "I had hopes for more than *friends*. Still do."

Zoe threw her arms around him and held on. "It may be the sweetest thing anyone's ever said to me."

The PA speaker jumped to life. "Things are rough up here," Viktor said. "Other than Karin and Daide, everyone else to the bridge. Now. And I mean everyone. New. Old. Dress fully to travel around the ship, and that includes life preservers. Avoid the outer walkways."

Zoe peered around Recco. All she could see out the porthole was impenetrable gray.

He let go of her and got to his feet, hanging onto the desk to remain upright. "Damn. Sounds serious."

She stood too. "See you upstairs as soon as I can get there. Viktor's last lecture still stings."

Recco's expression turned serious, his eyes pinched at their corners. "Yeah. For me too. Wonder what new monstrosity is out there?"

She crooked two fingers into the sign against evil. "Pray 'tis only unruly water."

Recco lurched out of her cabin, and she pulled on clothes as fast as she could. Big waves could sink them. It was self-serving on her part, but she'd finally met a man she could love. She'd be damned if she'd let bad luck screw her out of a mate. There'd never been enough Shifter men to go around. Coupled with a low birthrate and their long lives, the problem had done nothing except grow worse over time.

She turned her attention inward. Her coyote was silent. "What do you think? She demanded.

"Get moving. Recco will make you a good mate, but it's not why Viktor wants everyone front and center."

Zoe buckled her life vest into place and bolted out the door. The ship bucked and heaved beneath her, and she hung onto railings to get up each set of stairs. Though she waited, biting back anxiety, the coyote was done talking with her.

She replayed the last few hours, searching for what she might have done to piss it off, but couldn't come up with a thing. Maybe the episode with Daide's coyote had upset it. The more she thought about it, the more she decided she was on the right track.

Zoe pushed into the bridge and dove into a chair before the boat's motion, which was even more pronounced on the upper decks, tumbled her onto her ass.

Viktor stood next to the wheel, not hanging onto anything. He offered her a curt nod. She nodded back and scanned the room. Recco was already here; so were the newcomers and the group they'd picked up on Arctowski.

"The reason I convened this meeting," Viktor said, "is we have decisions to make, and I can't leave the helm. Not in seas this big.

We've posted a duty roster—two-hour shifts to spell Juan and me—on the white board over the chart table. You're all included."

"The main question we have to answer now"—Juan took over—"is whether we continue on our current course, which is due north. Or if we double back and try to transit the Drake Passage. It's a much smaller stretch in terms of distance. Notorious for rough water, though."

Discussion ebbed and flowed around Zoe as she fanned magic beyond the bridge walls, hunting for something unnatural that might be driving the big seas. Ketha had overseen constructing a partial ward, but it didn't extend to the water surrounding the ship. In truth, they didn't have enough power among all of them to create a bulletproof shield encompassing anything as big as *Arkady*.

Zoe poured more magic into her seeking spell, but didn't come up with a clear answer. Not sure what would come out of her mouth, she raised her hand. When Juan called her name, she said, "I don't have hard evidence. My gut tells me dark things are out there." She waved an arm toward the windows speckled with sea spray and went on. "If I'm correct, no matter where we sail, the weather will be perfectly rotten."

Viktor caught Ketha's eye. "If Zoe's right, is there a counter spell to keep us floating?"

Ketha scrunched her forehead in concentration. "If there's a way, we'll damn well find it." She lurched upright. "Come on, women. Meet me in the presentation room on Deck One."

"What about Karin?" Aura asked.

"I'll stop by and let her know where we'll be," Zoe said.

"I'll tell her," Recco said. "I planned to check on Daide when I left here, anyway."

"Look at the roster before you leave," Viktor reminded everyone. "Whoever doesn't have bridge duty, get something simple going for supper."

Zoe rose from her chair and wished she hadn't. Racing for a railing, she caught hold of it. Magic would help, but she didn't want to waste any. As she moved through the ship, she reached for her coyote.

"Are you all right?"

"Fine. Listen and listen well. I've been talking with Ketha's wolf. There's a spell in that book of hers—"

"Which spell?" Zoe interrupted. "The book is enormous."

"You'll know it when you find it." The coyote shut up.

Zoe understood. Conversations between the animals were private. That her bondmate shared as much as it had reflected how precarious their situation was. "Why wouldn't Ketha's wolf point her in the same direction?"

"It's not sure, and after everything else today, it doesn't want to upset her."

Maybe to avoid the temptation to say even more, her coyote left. The place it lived inside her felt hollow, empty. Zoe made a note to thank it later and hustled down the last flight of stairs into the bowels of the ship. The lower she'd gotten, the easier it was to walk.

"Oberon's balls"—Tessa sidled up to her—"my people were a seafaring lot. You'd think I'd warm to this, but all I want is off the ship."

"Don't wish too hard." Zoe angled a pointed glance her way and pulled on the door to the cavernous presentation room where tourists had gawked at slideshows.

"No kidding." Tessa pressed her mouth into a thin line and scuttled through the open door. "Off as in down the gangway to a dock, not off as in sinking to the bottom."

Zoe patted her arm.

"Hurry," Ketha called from the front of the room. "I ran an idea past my grimoire"—she tapped a fat, black book with an index finger—"and for once it agreed with me."

16

CHALLENGES AND CURES

Recco walked as fast as he could back to Deck Three and the cabin where he'd left Daide and Karin. As long as he didn't fight the ship's motion and made a point of flowing with it, he had an easier time. It reminded him of martial arts training where he'd tapped into a subconscious wavelength, letting it guide his movements.

The door was still shut. He hesitated. Should he knock? If he did, would he undo any of Karin's work? Recco marshaled his clumsy grasp of magic into an attempt at telepathy. Before he got any words out, the door swung open. Karin's white hair had escaped its bun, and untidy strands framed her face. Her copper eyes glowed warmly.

"We're almost done," she informed him.

Recco didn't want to pry, but he couldn't stop himself from asking, "How is he?"

"Better than he was."

The reply was so like Karin—dry and barbed—Recco grinned. "How soon can I talk with him?"

"Give us five more minutes," Daide called from inside the room.

The strained note had left his voice, and he almost sounded like himself.

"More like fifteen." Karin scrunched her eyes into slits. "You stopped here for a reason. What?"

"The women are in the auditorium on the first deck working out a strategy. They want you to join them as soon as you can."

"Already know about it."

"How? Did someone else use telepathy?"

Karin grunted derisively. "When you've lived as long as I have, not much gets by you." She cocked her head to the side as if she were listening to something. "It's getting interesting down there. You and Daide might want to join them."

Her comment about age was too good a lead-in to bypass, so Recco stared her down and asked, "How old are you?"

"And here I thought you Latin men were more mannerly than to ask a woman her age." She sniffed audibly. "What you want to know is how long Shifters live. We're not like Vampires, but we can hang on for a few centuries if nothing interrupts the connection to our power."

"What kinds of things might do that?"

She made shooing motions. "Daide and I need to finish this. Come back in a quarter hour."

The door closed in his face. At least she didn't slam it.

Recco had never been fond of downtime, and he didn't have bridge duty until tomorrow. He'd checked the roster on his way out. The schedule actually worked out nicely. They were an even twenty-four, so each of them had drawn a two-hour slot every other day. He glanced at Daide's cabin right across the hall. Karin had pronounced it clear, but he bet it hadn't been cleaned up. Might be a good way to kill the few minutes stretching before him.

A distinctive antiseptic scent met him when he opened the door, but the pervasive wrong feeling was totally gone. Beyond that, the small space was a mess. Cut off from whatever magic powered them, the piles of feathered, furred, and scaled bodies had transformed into a gooey mass. He traipsed down the corridor to a closet with janitorial supplies and grabbed a broom, dustpan, garbage bags, and a bucket. Back in Daide's room, he swept, scraped, and tossed debris into plastic bags that he hefted into a nearby rubbish chute. Once the floor was cleared of fallout from the confrontation, he ran water into the bucket and went to find a mop.

The floor was almost clean when Daide poked his head around the corner. "Christ, *amigo*. You didn't have to do all this."

Recco eyed him. "*Gracias* will do. You never did like to clean."

"*Muchas gracias*. And you're right about my housework allergy. Only got motivated when I couldn't find shit."

"Hang on a moment." Recco scrubbed the last square foot of linoleum, rinsed the mop in the shower, and returned everything to the supply closet.

When he got back, Daide was sitting in the room's only chair, so Recco perched on a bunk and scanned him from head to toe. "Not looking much worse for the wear, buddy."

A crooked smile split Daide's face. "Karin's magic is powerful juju. I went from feeling like warmed-over penguin crap to better than I've been in a long time."

"Did you, um, rather are you...?" Recco hunted for supportive words.

"You want to know what happened." Daide steepled his fingers together in front of him.

"Of course I do," Recco sputtered. "Wouldn't you?"

"Yes and no." A thoughtful expression creased Daide's forehead into a mass of tiny lines. "One of my problems was I was convinced if I didn't stay on top of every single detail, things would get away from me. I must have been a dick to live with, and I apologize."

Recco started to object, say apologies weren't necessary, except they were, and he appreciated them. "Thanks. You weren't always awful. Just sometimes. Besides, your obsessiveness meant we ran a successful business."

Daide rested his chin on his fingertips. "The clinic is a long way behind us. I'm done hiding my less-than-stellar beginnings. Establishing détente with my shame should lessen my neurotic need to control everything. If I fall off the wagon, feel free to punch me. My coyote and I found common ground, and we've started over. Hopefully with more faith on both sides this time."

Recco slumped against the wall as relief washed through him, and he exhaled in a whoosh. "Better news than I expected. I'm happy for you."

"Hell, it's far better than I expected too. I owe Zoe a huge apology, and I'll let her know how sorry I am for being an asshole. I didn't realize how close her coyote and mine are. Hers was frantic once it discovered how despondent mine had become."

"Close as in?" Once again, Recco was reminded how little he knew about Shifters despite the string of lessons he'd received.

"Blood kin. Cousins or something. Maybe second or third since my bondmate is far younger than hers."

"What does *younger* translate to? Decades? Centuries?"

Daide chuckled. "Damn, I miss sourcebooks and the Internet. Best I can tell, mine might be somewhere in its second century. Zoe's could be as much as a thousand years old. They never die."

Curiosity burned a path through Recco. "Cousins suggests the animals reproduce. Do you know anything about that?"

"'Fraid not. Karin mentioned young Shifters spend untold hours learning about their heritage—and their magic. By my count, it will take us a long time to catch up."

"Yeah. Years. In the meantime, trouble's brewing."

"What else is new?" Daide rolled his dark, expressive eyes. "The worst part about both the sea dragon and the incident a few hours ago is how close I came to dragging everyone else down with me. Karin didn't stop hammering me until I let her know I not only understood, but I felt like shit about it."

The ship pitched to starboard, and Recco made a grab for a book that was about to turn into a projectile. "We're all rotating through bridge duty. You and I are up starting tomorrow morning. I drew the ten to noon slot; you're noon to fourteen hundred. Vik and Juan will be there all the time. The purpose of adding another person is to spell them so they can catnap."

"How long does Juan believe this storm will last?"

"He didn't say. The women are of the opinion it's not a natural storm, but one driven by evil."

Daide whistled long and low. "Which means it could dog us all the way to Siberia."

"Yup. Feel up to joining them down in the auditorium? Karin invited us."

"Sure." Daide pushed to his feet. An uncomfortable expression distorted the pleasant mask he usually wore. "No easy way to say this. I wish you all the best with Zoe. She's a beautiful woman, and she has mettle. I saw it when her bond animal raked mine over the coals."

Recco stood too. "It sounds like you really mean it."

"I do. I admit to engaging in passive crap with your other women. I liked our life exactly the way it was. A wife—on either side—would have altered the status quo, and my grasp on making it from day to day was too brittle to let that happen." Daide looked away. "When you grow up the way I did, anything anyone else got meant less for you. I was afraid if you hooked up with a woman, there'd be nothing left for me. My fear wasn't rational, but it drove the way I acted, and I'm not proud of any of it."

"It wasn't only you." Recco squared his shoulders. "I could have pushed back way harder than I did. Truth was I could have moved out and seen you during work hours. The life we carved out was a comfort zone for me too. So if we were broken, we were broken in complementary ways."

Daide screwed his face into a grimace. "You were so easygoing, though. I took advantage of your good nature."

Recco sliced one hand through the air in front of him. "When we walk out of here, this conversation is over. So is ruminating about it. This isn't a matter of who was more at fault. We each made decisions and acted on them. Now we have an opportunity to restructure our friendship. Not many people get a chance for do-overs."

"Thanks."

"*De nada. Andale.*" Recco tugged the door open and walked into a sharply tipping corridor.

"Damn. Way more noticeable out here." Daide followed him to a set of stairs. "Gives you a whole new appreciation for the men who left Europe in those rickety, wooden ships."

"Doesn't it, though." The ship pitched, rolled, and yawed as they stumbled down two floors. The motion eased somewhat the lower they went. "Must be an absolute bitch on the bridge," Recco muttered.

"No shit. Vik mentioned he lashed himself into his bunk when the water was rough. I was in his cabin one day for something or other, saw lengths of leather attached to the wall near the bed, and made a bondage joke. He laughed and said BDSM would be way more fun than how he used those straps."

They reached the auditorium doors. Recco pulled one open just far enough for them to slip inside. A heated conversation was in progress, and he listened, trying to pick up the gist of it without adding fuel to a volatile mix by asking questions.

Daide tilted his chin at seats toward the back. Recco followed him and sat on a small couch with one leg shorter than the others. It rocked along with the motion of the ship.

"No way of determining if 'twill do aught except court disaster." Zoe was on her feet, holding onto the back of the chair in front of her. Judging from how thick her brogue was, she was upset, but not willing to back down.

"Let me walk through this since I arrived late." Karin sat at the front of the room next to Ketha.

Magic pulsed in blue-white sheets from the old, black book lying open on Ketha's lap. Either it approved of Karin's idea, or it was ready to smite her to a pile of cinders. Karin flapped a hand at the tome, and the flow ceased abruptly.

"Without adding extraneous details"—Karin blew out a long, hissing breath—"your plan is to approach the sea people for help."

"Why not?" Ketha furled her dark brows. "There have always been Shifters who lived in the sea. At least there were before the Cataclysm."

"Aye, 'tis exactly my point." Zoe was still on her feet. "One of them, anyway. Aside from the fact there's never been any love lost betwixt us and our sea-dwelling kin, how can ye know the Cataclysm didn't imbue the Nereids and mermaids and whale Shifters with evil?"

"I don't." Ketha's tone was terse. "But we're worse than fools if we ignore a potential group of allies because we're frozen by fear."

"I am not *frozen by fear*," Karin retorted. "Given everything we've run into, though, it's wise to err on the side of caution."

Aura got to her feet. Determination burned in her green eyes and stick-straight posture. "Something started nagging me when Ketha floated her idea about the sea people. While it's not a precise match, the first unfinished prophecy addresses a similar situation."

Karin raked a hand through hair that had totally abandoned her attempt to contain it. "Are you going to tell it to us, or let us guess?"

"Extra commentary isn't necessary," Aura said stiffly.

"Probably not." The sarcasm fled from Karin's tone. "I don't have the prophecies memorized. Not anymore."

"The fourth unfinished prophecy helped us a lot," Moira spoke up. "It wasn't a precise replica of what we faced, either, but it offered direction."

Aura cleared her throat. She clasped her hands in front of her. When the ship lurched hard to port, she grabbed the seat nearest her again. "The first unfinished prophecy deals with the end of days.

It says a great darkness will descend on Earth, sowing destruction. That the darkness will last for half a score of years, which fits, but efforts to eradicate it are doomed to fail."

Recco leaned forward, not liking the sound of things at all. Of course, the fourth prophecy had included two Archangels, and they'd only had one, so maybe he shouldn't take her recitation too literally.

Aura continued speaking in a sing-songy voice, likely regurgitating something she'd memorized long ago. "Keep in mind, these prophecies are unique to Shifter social order. The first unfinished prophecy points historians to the fourth, which leads me to believe they're linked. It picks up after that point and states the world is still in grave danger of sinking beneath the yoke of evil."

"Do ye have the exact verbiage?" Zoe asked.

Aura nodded. "Wickedness poured in through a rent between worlds. The sea rose up and smote any who dared darken its surface. Old allies came to the fore, but neither easily nor willingly."

"Does it detail who those old allies are?" Karin spoke up.

Aura shook her head. "We do have history with Poseidon and Amphitrite. And the Nereids and whale Shifters."

"The whale Shifters have never been our friends," Zoe muttered. "Nor the dolphins. Mayhap 'tis what the part about neither easily nor willingly means."

"Why haven't they been your friends?" Recco asked.

Eleven pairs of eyes swiveled to fixate on him, and he wished he'd kept his mouth shut.

"'Tis a decent question, and one I doona know the answer to," Zoe said.

"Nor do I," Ketha murmured.

"My grandmother would have known." Aura frowned. "All she told me was it was a distant branch of Shifters, and we'd had a falling out millennia ago."

"It's a long time to hold a grudge—unless they blame us for what happened," Karin said.

"They might." Ketha nodded. "I blame us, so it's hardly a quantum leap."

"Nothing ventured, nothing gained. The worst thing to happen is they say no," Daide said.

Karin leveled her copper gaze his way. "Would that it were so simple. They're plenty capable of sinking the ship. A pod of whales swimming beneath it could tip us without breathing hard."

"Our best bet"—Zoe scanned the room—"if we go that route and raise them, is to accept full responsibility for the Cataclysm and make it clear we're doing everything in our power to set things right."

Aura tossed her head back. "While I'm certain they know how the Cataclysm came to be, they may not know we're who made inroads into its chokehold on the oceans. Goddess only knows where they were hiding out for ten years, but they're able to move about now. Assuming they didn't all die out."

"What makes you so certain you'll be able to communicate with them?" Recco asked, still sorting how Shifter magic worked.

"We'll go through the animals," Ketha replied.

"Does their world have oceans?" Daide asked.

"'Tis a magical world. It has whatever is needed," Zoe replied. "The laws of physics don't apply there."

"What about the people who are bonded to the whales?" Recco turned his hands palms up. "I hate to keep asking questions, but I need to know how this works."

"Before you answer him," Daide chimed in. "Are whales and dolphins the only ocean life to form Shifter bonds?"

"No. Whale Shifters always kept to themselves, though," Aura answered. "Insofar as I know, their human bondmates never set foot in North America, but I could be dead wrong. They never took part in our council meetings or any of our joint events."

"If they were so invisible, how'd you know they existed?" Recco asked.

"Anecdotal evidence," Ketha mumbled. "We read about them. No reason to assume they weren't real."

"From what I recall, the only type of sea life to form shifter bonds were cetaceans. Whales, dolphins, and porpoises," Karin added.

"Interesting. Their closest land relatives are hippos," Daide said, followed by, "Never mind. Not relevant."

"Focus, people." Ketha tapped on a table in front of her. "Either we do this, or we don't. If we don't, I'm flat out of Plan Bs."

"Does the prophecy say anything further?" Tessa directed her words at Aura.

"Not really. It's one of the unfinished ones, remember?"

"I did, but I'd hoped for more in the way of direction."

"Yeah. They don't often cooperate with what we hope for." Aura chewed on her lower lip. "My best guess is we go with it, though, and let the chips fall where they will. Lot of ocean between us and Siberia. If we can't even make New Zealand without courting disaster, the odds of traveling ten times the distance don't look good."

Recco didn't bother pointing out her ten times estimate was short by thousands of nautical miles. Instead, he said, "Viktor and Juan need to weigh in before we do anything to maybe jeopardize the ship."

"We're not there yet." Ketha's golden-hued gaze traveled through the room. "Have we talked enough to vote?"

"Not sure. Does anyone have anything pertinent to add that hasn't been said yet?" Karin asked.

"Does this have to be an all-or-none approach?" Recco spoke up.

"What do you mean?" Zoe turned to stare at him.

"Ketha indicated you'd communicate through your bond animals. Is it possible for them to feel out the whales? Float a what-if scenario?"

Zoe shook her head. "They'd see through it quick enough, and chalk us up as sneaky. Nay, if we do this, we must go hat in hand.

The only thing to see us through is humility and acceptance of whatever shit they want to heap on our heads."

"We're not the ones who came up with the half-brained scheme to rid the world of Vamps by turning them into Shifters," Daide protested.

"True enough, but Zoe's correct. We'll be tarred with the same brush," Ketha said, and then added, "What's your pleasure, people. Do we do this, or not?"

As if she'd asked the book still open across her lap, colored lights flared around it in a mesmerizing corona.

"I vote yes," Ketha said. "I need to hear twelve more votes."

Daide elbowed him and whispered, "Guess we get a voice too."

A chorus of yesses ran through the room, followed by an aye from Zoe after a long pause.

Ketha slapped the book shut and stood. "I'll talk with Vik and Juan. Stay tuned. If we're going to do this, we need to move fast."

A staunch roll to the right underscored her words.

Zoe made her way toward where Recco and Daide sat. "You're looking better," she told Daide.

"I am better. Words won't excuse my actions, but I'm very sorry for barging into your cabin and the subsequent harangue. It won't happen again."

The solemn look left her face, replaced by a smile. She extended a hand, and Daide shook it. After he let go, he stood. "I'll leave you two alone. Maybe I can do some good in the galley. It must be time for a meal. Even if it's not, I'm starving."

"You would be," Zoe said. "Battling evil is a huge power hog. Burns calories like nobody's business."

Daide tipped his chin and walked out of the auditorium.

"Feel like a drink or a snack?" Recco asked her.

"Snack first, so I don't pitch head down into my whiskey."

"It could be arranged. Let's follow Daide to the galley, and we'll come up with something. It's been a long time since I stood over leftover cold breakfast and stuffed it into my mouth."

"There might be something hot," Zoe said. "Didn't Vik ask someone to get dinner underway?"

"Now you mention it, he did."

Recco tucked a hand under her elbow. "It feels right having you next to me."

"Keep the schmaltz coming." She leaned into him as they walked out of the presentation room, fighting the ship's motion.

"Schmaltz isn't Gaelic," he protested, laughing.

"Nay, but German's a kissing cousin."

"Good to know. It's not schmaltz. I meant it."

"You feel pretty damned good next to me too. Before we go there, we need to talk more about Ketha's plan. I'm hoping she's laying this part out for Vik and Juan. Do you recall the story about the Hatfields and McCoys?"

"Sure, from North American television."

"It's a close approximation to how we view our ocean kin. And vice versa. They'd as soon spit on us as talk, and we weren't much better."

"Maybe it's changed."

"Given the Cataclysm, more likely 'tis grown worse."

"Whichever way the wind blows, we'll figure things out." He held the dining room door for her, wanting to believe his words.

"Hang onto your optimism. I fear you'll need it and then some afore we reach the far side of this."

Several tables were occupied, mostly with the humans from McMurdo and Arctowski. Poor bastards. The Arctowski bunch had no choice after the Polish research station blew up around them. The McMurdo group could have opted for safety, though, and stayed put.

Zoe shook her head and leaned close. "We'll wait to tell them until Viktor and Juan come to a decision. No reason to put them off their feed for naught."

Recco followed her into the galley, his mind racing a million directions at once, but always returning to the same place. They had to survive. No matter what it took. He'd be goddamned if a sanctimonious whale or dolphin Shifter would stand between them and safe passage. If they had help to offer, by God, they'd pony up and do the proper thing.

"*Pretty words,*" his wolf piped up. "*Any idea how to turn them into something more than hot air?*"

IT'S MY SHIP

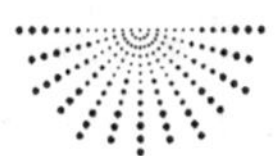

Zoe left the dining room with Recco; they walked up one flight to Deck Three and stopped in the corridor outside their cabins. They'd made small talk over a meal where they ate with one hand and hung onto the table with the other. The ship pitched so abruptly, a few plates had ended up on the floor. At least she'd gotten to know a little bit about the four researchers from McMurdo. Luckily, they were decent sailors, or they'd have been curled into miserable balls in their bunks. She offered a silent prayer to the goddess for ensuring her own stint with seasickness had been short-lived.

"Interesting folk," Recco said. "I particularly liked Aidan."

"The zoologist?"

Recco nodded. "The paleontologist—Jennifer—was a bit stuffy. I suppose studying dead things lends itself to a different world view."

"Eh, she was probably always reserved. Who we were before we went to college plays a huge role in what disciplines attract us. Beyond that, I've been expecting Ketha to show up. Kind of worried she hasn't."

"Do you suppose she caught some flak from Viktor and Juan about our plan?"

Zoe shrugged. "Let's head up there and find out."

"It's the right thing to do," he agreed affably.

"And the wrong thing would be?" She glanced his way.

Instead of answering, he stabilized himself against a wall and closed his arms around her. The heat of his mouth on hers stole her breath, and she melted into him, clinging as they fought to remain upright. The ship's motion forced their bodies against one another. Heat washed through her, and she gripped his high, tight ass. The length of him grew, pressing into her. She wanted to rip his clothes off, touch him, explore him with fingers and mouth and the empty, aching place inside her.

She was starting to know his kisses, anticipate when he'd nibble or suck or bite. Both of them tasted of the dinner they'd shared washed down with a raw, red wine well on its way to becoming vinegar. The stubble on his cheeks tickled her as he kissed his way down her neck. He pushed clothing aside as he moved to the hollow between her collarbones. She wriggled, spreading her legs to straddle his thigh. The contact with her sensitive center sent her heart into overdrive, and sexual heat shivered through her.

Zoe laughed. "Damn all these layers of clothes. It's amazing the Eskimos had any children, bundled against the cold like they must have been."

Recco pressed his hips into her and lifted his mouth from the deliciously sensitive skin between her neck and shoulder. "It's not as if they had to take everything off. A few minor adjustments, and voila."

"Maybe for you. Although I can see the allure of skirts. They're far easier to work around than trousers."

"Um-hum." He jiggled the thigh she was rubbing herself against and pushed a hand between them, inserting it so his fingers cupped her crotch. She writhed against him, the desire for release so urgent she couldn't think about anything else.

His cock bucked against her belly, and she cradled a hand around its thick, hard length, stroking fast. They should move out of the hall, but the semi-public aspect added heat to her arousal. He closed his mouth over hers and plunged his tongue inside. She sucked on it, pretending it was the cock twitching and jerking in her fingers.

Her nipples pebbled, and sensation spilled through her. Without words or direction from her, he knew exactly how to touch her. How hard. How fast. Her hips thrust against his fingers in a rhythm with only one outcome. Sexual waves rioted through her, pushing her upward until orgasm broke over her and she shuddered against him, wanting the exquisite awareness to last forever.

He stifled a groan, and his cock pulsed against her palm. Panting and straining, they ground their bodies together as their passion peaked and wound down. Recco broke their kiss and smiled at her, still breathing hard. "At first, I wanted to move us somewhere more private, but then—"

"It didn't matter," she finished his sentence. A blush added heat to her already-warm cheeks. "We were worse than a pair of randy teenagers in the back seat of an old jalopy."

"I'm sorry. Next time, we'll find a proper bed. I want to strip you naked and worship you, not imagine what your body looks like. That quick peek I had after Daide's meltdown wasn't nearly enough."

"I wasn't complaining." She grinned because she couldn't hold her joy inside. "About imagining. It cuts both ways. This"—she squeezed his still-hard cock—"deserves the light of day."

Recco snorted. "Right now, it deserves a good cleaning. Damn. I haven't come in my pants since I was fifteen."

The ship yawed, and she grabbed a railing. It brought reality crashing home. "I've got to get to the bridge. I was worried about Ketha before, but she should have marched by us."

"Not necessarily. This boat has more stairways than whales have baleen."

"Now there's an intriguing analogy."

"Have you ever looked inside a whale's mouth?" He kissed her once more and disentangled himself from their embrace.

"Can't say as I have."

"Well, there are thousands of strands of baleen. It's how they filter krill and small fish. Aside from the zoology lecture, would you like me to join you on the bridge?"

"Yeah. We probably all need to be there if Viktor dug in his heels. And I can envision him doing that."

"See you soon." Recco ducked into his cabin.

Zoe fought her way up three flights to bridge level. Outside *Arkady*, the storm raged on. Wind howled like a herd of Banshees, and the windows rattled. Each one she passed was coated with spray, making it impossible to see much of anything. The ship labored, sliding from front to back and side to side as it crawled to the crest of waves and then slid into the troughs between them.

Her chest tight from tension—would the next set of waves unhinge their ability to remain upright?—she lurched through the door and onto the bridge. Ketha stood ramrod straight, knuckles white where she clung to the railing beneath the windows. Her back was to Viktor, which had to be significant. Had things deteriorated to the point she couldn't even look at her husband?

On the other side of the bridge, Viktor hung onto the wheel. His expression was carved into grim lines. Juan and Aura huddled to one side, deep in conversation.

"If you've come to have another go at me, don't bother," Viktor ground out.

Zoe tried to stand straight but gave it up for wasted effort. "No one summoned me with telepathy, if that's what you're inferring. So long as you brought it up, though, why are you dead set against asking our sea kin for help?"

Ketha turned around and shook her head. "You won't come up with any argument I haven't already tried."

"Why don't any of you have a scrap of faith in me?" Viktor

growled. "I know these waters. I can guide *Arkady* to Invercargill. Might take ten days, but we'll get there."

"Invercargill is only our first stop," Zoe said. "Do you honestly believe we can get all the way from here to Siberia if the weather doesn't cooperate a wee bit more than it is?" She crossed to him and planted herself as close as she could get and still have something to hang onto, so she didn't end up sprawled on her butt.

"We take it as it comes. Most storms don't last more than a week. Two at the most. By the time we get to New Zealand's South Island, we should have smoother waters."

"Aye, should." Zoe lapsed into Gaelic, and then switched back to English. "Sorry, I think better in my native tongue. What you say might be true were this a normal storm, but 'tisn't. It's magically driven. I feel it and smell it and taste it, and it ices me to my bones."

"Tried to tell him the same thing," Ketha muttered.

"Has your raven had aught to say?" Zoe persisted, still staring at Viktor.

"It's cut from the same cloth as the rest of you," he snapped.

Zoe's temper surged, and she shook a fist at him. "In case you've forgotten, you're part of us now. Unless you wish to sever the bond with your bird, which will leave you in far worse shape than you were as a Vampire. Half a person, forever mourning an ill-conceived, hasty kneejerk reaction."

"Enough," Viktor thundered. "Leave now."

"Ye canna order me about." Zoe faced off against him. Dignity was in short supply when remaining on her feet turned into a moment-to-moment proposition.

"Fine. Please leave. We've nothing more to say to one another."

Breath rattled through her teeth. "At least tell me why you're so dead set against—"

"It's a bigger risk than us taking on the seas between here and New Zealand. From what I dragged out of Ketha, your sea-dwelling kin hate you, and the feeling is mutual. I'll eat my socks if they don't blame you for the Cataclysm. It probably killed bunches of them and sickened hundreds—or thousands—of others."

Fury narrowed her throat. She wanted to hurl insults at Viktor for being so narrowminded. A quick glance at Ketha showed how torn she was. The man she loved wasn't supporting a decision she'd suffered over.

Recco bounded into the bridge. The smile on his face vanished fast. "Jesus. What the hell is going on up here?"

Zoe shook her head and searched for words to punch a hole through Viktor's mulishness. He'd taken a stand, one hard to back down from and save face.

"If there's one thing I've learned from archaeology," she began, "'tis nature doesn't make mistakes. Sometimes it takes centuries or even millennia, but every single bird, animal, human, or magical creation is here for a reason. I canna describe how many times I've knelt over a scrap of something and puzzled as to why it existed. A few times, years passed afore I had one of those 'aha' moments where it became clear."

Without giving Viktor a chance to tell her to shut up, she forged on. "We're at a disadvantage without our libraries detailing Shifter history back to its roots. Our animals know some things, but certainly not everything pertinent. Shifters evolved in two distinct groups for a reason, and if the reason isn't so we can help one another, then us traveling separate paths for so long makes no sense."

"Evil's had a taste of freedom," Ketha said in a dull, dead voice that scarcely sounded like her. "More than a taste. The Cataclysm did far more damage than any of us suspected. Meh. We've covered this ground."

"Aye." Zoe jumped in. "We were fools to believe whatever's driving the current run of wickedness would stand by while we sailed ten thousand miles to confront it. Far simpler to cut us off long afore we got anywhere close. We may not see ourselves as worthy adversaries, but we blew up the Cataclysm."

"Surely it was more than enough to make every nasty, dirty, evil thing in the world sit up and take notice. And circle their wagons against us," Aura said. "This isn't a time to let old hurts stand between us and potential allies."

"Because you see it from that viewpoint is no guarantee the whales and dolphins and sea gods will," Viktor said. He sounded more tired than angry, and it gave Zoe hope.

Juan walked to where Viktor stood, blond brows raised into question marks. Viktor raked a hand through his thick hair. "Unless these sea creatures can hold back the storms, we'll have risked alerting them to our presence for nothing."

"They can't stop the storms," Aura said, "but they can weave their magic in with ours, which means it could extend our power down to the waterline. Maybe it will ease our way. Maybe not. Regardless, it's a possibility that doesn't exist right now."

"How bulletproof is the ward you built?" Viktor aimed his words at Ketha.

"Not very, but at least we'll know if something evil breaches our borders before it gets out of control like it did earlier."

"What about the humans?" Juan asked. "Can dark forces borrow their bodies?"

"Nay. 'Tisn't like the movies," Zoe said. "They can be held in thrall, but magic attracts magic. 'Tis why the sea dragon picked Daide. For his magic. The humans are safe enough, so long as the ship doesn't sink. Naught says their energy can't become cannon fodder, like happened with the sorcerer on Arctowski."

A loud crack blasted her, and one of the bridge's windows blew inward, followed by a gush of seawater, and then two more. Juan raced to the back wall of the bridge and grabbed a sheet of plywood, wrestling it across the room.

"Take these to him." Viktor pointed at a drill sitting in a charging cradle and grabbed a handful of screws.

Recco scurried forward, drill and screws in hand. "What about caulk?"

"It'll take too long." Juan strained to hold the wood over the broken window frame. "Besides, it won't set well."

Zoe crossed to the broken pane and leaned her weight atop the wood. Waves hammered against it, their strength shocking, and she figured it was only a matter of time before the rest of the dozen windows lining the bridge shattered too. The drill droned as Juan drove screws into the sheet metal surrounding the broken window. Water trickled around the fix-it job once he was done, but waves weren't spraying through anymore.

Recco walked the drill back to its cradle and placed the extra screws in a drawer. "We could go back to McMurdo," he said, "or maybe Ushuaia if we could reach it."

"And then what?" Viktor asked.

"And then we'll wait out the end of the world. I suppose eventually everything will mirror Arctowski, replete with monsters and evil overlords."

Juan sent a pointed glance skittering Aura's way. "It's almost exactly the same thing you told me."

She shrugged. "Does hearing it twice make it feel more true?"

"Hearing it twice gives me the heebie-jeebies," he muttered.

Waves crashed against the wood with a hollow booming. Zoe shivered. It sounded like their death-knell, the bell that tolled for thee.

Aye, and where's Hemingway and a nice cuppa when ye have need of them, eh?

"Your wheel." Viktor moved from behind the helm, and Juan took his place. He crossed to where Ketha still stood. Water blew between the board and the window casing, wetting her hair. He extended a hand. "You're getting wet."

"Doesn't matter. I'll be a hell of a lot wetter if we capsize." Despite her harsh words, she let him lead her away from the glass.

Zoe hissed out a relieved breath. She'd been worried the window behind Ketha would explode and take her head along with it.

"I'm sorry I didn't jump on your idea." Viktor's voice carried.

"You think I was being bullheaded, but I weighed the options, and you hadn't offered anything that gave calling the sea Shifters a clear advantage over doing nothing."

Ketha skewered him with her golden eyes, a carryover from her wolf form. Some Shifters absorbed their animals' natures in visible ways. "I can't force you to do anything," she said. "And I lack your years of experience at sea."

"By the same token, my magic is green and untried. My raven has been giving me twenty kinds of hell, so I'm ready to try it your way. We could turn back, but the seas won't be any gentler, which is another reason I opted to press forward."

"Not very forward." Juan threw his two cents into the ring. "We're making three-and-a-half knots."

"At least we're not moving backward. Been there. Done that," Viktor shot back. He stood easily, compensating for the ship's motion without apparent effort.

"Thanks for trusting me." Ketha gave him a quick hug.

He hugged her back before letting go. "It goes beyond the personal," he told her, his voice solemn. "My ship is in your hands. Do not scuttle her."

"I'll do my best." Ketha tipped her chin at Aura and Zoe and left the bridge, using telepathy to summon the rest of them back to the presentation room.

"Why there?" Zoe asked, hustling after Ketha's retreating form.

"It's closest to the water, and we want to make this as attractive as we can."

"What if they don't snatch up the bait?" Zoe walked into the auditorium on Ketha's heels with Aura bringing up the rear.

"All we can do is try." Ketha stumbled to the front of the room, grabbing passing chairs and couches for support.

The other women filed in. "We should form a circle," Karin said. "On the floor since I don't trust chairs not to tip over, and our attention will be elsewhere."

Zoe scooted to the front and sat cross-legged, extending her hands on both sides. Her stomach twisted into a knot of anxiety, and she swallowed around a thick place in her throat. She'd lobbied for this, but she had no idea how it would pan out. If their sea kin had been tarnished by the Cataclysm, they were about to invite death onto *Arkady*. Once invited, they'd be harder than hell to get rid of.

Kind of like Vampires. Once you invited them in, you were stuck with them, except it was an urban myth. In truth, they could go anywhere they wanted, invitations be damned.

Zoe's mind was wandering as a hedge against a pervasive sense of foreboding. They trod a precarious road. Optimism could make or break them. She had to get hold of her fears, funnel them in a positive direction.

Magic flickered through their circle, enhanced by their linked hands. "Talk with your animals," Ketha urged. "Ask them to petition the sea Shifters on our behalf."

"What if they can't find them?" Moira asked.

"Keep trying," Aura replied. "No more talk."

Zoe shut her earth eyes in favor of her third eye and offered her coyote free rein. It was excited and apprehensive, but it understood —maybe more clearly than she did—the risks they ran. Tension filled her, feeling like high voltage electricity. It had great potential to either help or burn everything in its path to a lump of expended coal.

Time hung heavy around them. It might have stopped, for all she knew. The air she breathed felt sticky—Rip Van Winkle air that could put all of them to sleep forever. Panic tore through her, and she tightened her grip on Karin's and Aura's hands to center her here in this room. Not goddess only-knew-where, mired in the ether threatening to suck them into oblivion.

Ketha surged to her feet. "I feel you," she cried. "Show yourselves."

The sensation of choking where the very air spun tendrils

holding her in place lessened. Light flashed, golden then silver then pure, bright white, and two figures shimmered into being.

The man wore a robe made of glistening, silver fish scales, belted in gemstones woven with hammered silver. Blue-gray hair fell to his feet, and his eyes reflected the sea, shifting from gray to blue to silver as he regarded them. His companion's gown sparkled in mother-of-pearl shades. Pearls draped around her neck and dripped from her ears. Snow-white hair was braided with glittering multihued gems and lay close to her head. Silvery eyes regarded them solemnly.

"We are the guardians of all that lives in the sea," she announced.

Zoe scrambled to her feet and bowed low. "'Tis an honor Amphitrite and Poseidon." She spoke in old Gaelic, grateful she could match their language. Perhaps they would view it as a sign of deep respect for their heritage.

The other women mirrored her actions and paid obeisance to the king and queen of the sea.

"The Shifters you've summoned have not fared well," Poseidon said in a clear, ringing voice.

"We have taken the few who remain under our protection." Amphitrite tilted her chin and raised an accusatory finger. "Their plight is your fault."

"We accept full responsibility for our kinfolk's actions," Ketha said. "Even though we didn't know until it was too late, it doesn't excuse us."

"I would be harder on you"—Poseidon's deep voice resonated like the sea— "were it not for the fact you've suffered as well."

Zoe met his unsettling gaze and took a chance. "Once we understood it was a Shifter casting gone awry that created the Cataclysm, we took steps to correct the problem."

"Corrected one part, but made others worse." Amphitrite's musical voice quivered with sorrow.

"We're doing our best to fix the secondary fallout too," Karin said. "We unearthed evil's primary gateway. If we can get there, we'll do what we can to shut it forever."

"You'll never get that far," Poseidon said.

"Not on our own, mayhap," Zoe replied, "but if all Shifters banded together, we'd be stronger." Her heart thudded hard. Had they done all this for it to come to naught?

The air between Amphitrite and Poseidon took on a sickly, greenish hue. Worry twisted the goddess's beauty into something harsh. "I told him not to come."

"As did I." Poseidon shook his head.

Breath caught in Zoe's throat, and she sucked hard to move air into her lungs. What was about to break through? Worse, would it emerge with blood in its eyes?

The salt smell of the sea intensified. A coruscation formed, alternating shades of brightness and dark. When it cleared, a dolphin lolled on the floor. Kneeling, Poseidon stabilized it. "You didn't have to do this, my son."

"I did," it croaked.

When Zoe looked closer, she saw large areas of its skin were marred by wounds, and pity cut deep. The creature must be in constant pain.

"Look well, land Shifters. This is what has become of us," the dolphin intoned. "After a decade of living in waters poisoned by bad magic, I can no longer shift. My skin burns and sloughs off my bones. I am one of fourteen of us left. Within the year, we will be no more." A gasping wheeze cut off its last few words.

Zoe crawled forward, head bowed. "I'm so sorry."

"Sorry won't offer us a second chance at life, coyote Shifter." It shook itself, showering her with blood and sea spray.

An idea formed, and she looked up. "Please don't take this wrong." She moved her gaze from one monarch to the other. "Have you tried aught beyond magic to cure your Shifters?"

"What might such a thing be?" Amphitrite scoffed. "If magic can't fix a magical creature, neither can anything else."

"You have no reason to trust me," Zoe told the dolphin, "but you have naught to lose, either."

It turned its head and regarded her with one red-rimmed eye. Zoe took it as assent to move forward. She focused a thread of magic outward and used telepathy to summon Recco and Daide.

"Brilliant." Understanding lit Karin's lined face. "Their veterinary skill and my magic just might fix this."

"Aye, and if we can make the sea Shifters stronger—" Zoe didn't finish her sentence because the doors at the end of the auditorium burst open, and Recco and Daide ran through.

18

PICK YOUR POISON

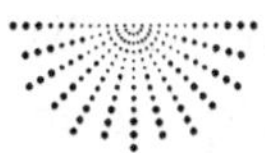

Recco had almost bitten his nails down to the cuticle, worrying about what was happening in the bowels of the ship. Viktor and Juan hadn't made things any easier between pacing and muttering the odd curse in Spanish. He'd wanted to come along with Zoe, but the women made it clear it was only them. Somewhere along the line, Daide joined him on the bridge.

When Zoe's summons blasted through, he couldn't scramble down six flights fast enough.

"What do you suppose they need us for?" Daide asked.

"We'll find out." Recco shoved the doors open hard enough they slapped against the walls. When he caught a glimpse of the trio sheathed with brilliant light, he stopped dead.

"Come forward," the robed man with hair like living fog commanded.

Recco did, flanked by Daide.

"I am Poseidon, king of the seas. Can you help my Shifter?"

Recco bowed reflexively. So did Daide, who replied, "May I examine him?"

"I can talk," the dolphin said dryly. "I'm not that far gone."

"Excellent." Recco smiled. "It puts you head and shoulders above most of our other patients."

Daide knelt next to the dolphin and ran his hands gently over its hide, poking and prodding.

"What do you need?" Recco asked his friend.

"Everything," Daide said tersely and bent to lay his ear over the dolphin's rib cage.

"I'll gather supplies," Karin said. "Whatever you alter, you'll need me to bind things together with magic."

Recco hunkered next to the dolphin. "What's your name?"

"Leif comes closest to what you'll be able to pronounce." He coughed and groaned.

Recco placed his hand on a flipper. "Leif, this man"—he glanced at Daide— "is Dr. Diego Vegas. He used to be a world-renowned expert on treating cetaceans. If anyone can cure you, it's him."

The dolphin barked, and Recco realized he was laughing. When his mirth subsided, he said, "Never thought I'd end up in a veterinarian's hands."

"There are worse places to be," Daide murmured. "Now, hush. I need to listen to something."

Karin rushed back into the room and dropped two black leather medical bags next to Daide. "Take a quick look to see if I got everything. Once I link to the dolphin with my magic, it will be best if I don't leave."

Daide rustled through the cases, extracting a stethoscope and a few other items. "Looks complete enough, but I could use a microscope and an assortment of basic reagents, so I don't have to shuttle between here and the lab. Bring whatever you have for injection antibiotics too."

"On my way." Ketha hurried from the room.

Recco grabbed another stethoscope and moved to Leif's other side, probing and listening while reminding himself what he knew about dolphins. Marine mammals, they were susceptible to many of the same diseases that attacked humans.

"What are you doing?" Poseidon stood behind Recco, so close the scents of salt, kelp, and marine life surrounded him.

"Examining him."

"I'm not stupid, land Shifter. What have you found?"

Recco rocked back on his heels, still squatting next to Leif. "I have a few ideas. Let's see what Daide thinks. While he's working, I do have a question."

"What?" The word rumbled from Leif.

"If you can't shift, why are you in your animal form?"

Understanding flared from the dolphin's eyes. "It's primary for us. Not like you, where your human form grabs ascendency."

"It's a pretty big difference," Daide said and looped the stethoscope around his neck. "Without lab tests to confirm anything—"

"I'm back with one of the scopes and slides and stains," Ketha called from the doorway, sounding out of breath. "And drugs."

"This isn't the human world," Leif huffed out. "Absent laboratory results, what's your assessment? I'm not going to sue if you get it wrong."

"I'm not in the habit of getting things wrong." Daide's nostrils flared in annoyance. "What I believe happened is this. The Cataclysm knocked holes in your immune system, leaving you open to major parasitic infections."

Recco nodded. When he'd listened to the dolphin's chest, he'd been almost certain the creature was infested with lungworms. Trematodes could have attacked its digestive system too, from liver to pancreas to stomach and intestines, raking off nutrition before the dolphin could make use of it.

"Parasites? It can't be quite so simple," Leif protested. "They don't kill their host. If they did, they'd lose their food source."

"True enough," Daide agreed, "if you only had one type of parasite, but they're opportunistic little bastards, and I suspect you have both lungworms and trematodes, which means two of your major organ systems are compromised. The only reason you're still alive is it's not in their best interest to kill you, but left unchecked…"

He didn't finish his sentence. He didn't have to. Leif knew he was dying.

"Can you fix it?" Amphitrite hovered next to her consort.

"I can knock out the parasites. At least I think I can. I haven't looked through what we have for drugs." Daide spoke slowly. "Not sure how to address the original issue, which is a non-responsive immune system."

"Which is where I come in," Karin said. "If magic destroyed it, I bet I can come up with a counter spell."

"It's not only me," Leif cautioned. "I'm one of fourteen. Five whales and eight other dolphins."

Karin joined the group on the floor. "If we can fix what's amiss with you, we simply do the same thing for everyone else. How do you feel about being a guinea pig?"

"If it means you learn enough to save everyone else, I'm game." He thrashed weakly.

Daide regarded him. "You need to be back in the ocean, fellow."

"Agreed, but you can't treat me there."

"Sure I can—so long as they have dry suits and oxygen tanks on board. Recco, could you—?"

"On my way, *amigo*." He dashed from the room, remembering all the times he and Daide had donned diving gear and taken care of marine life. Of course, it had been in somewhat warmer waters. Surely, Daide was expecting Recco to join him. He hadn't said as much, but when they worked underwater, it was always as a team. Otherwise, manipulating instruments and medications in an aquatic environment was close to impossible.

He burst onto the bridge. Before he could get a word out, Viktor and Juan peppered him with questions. Boris and Ted were on the bridge too, listening to his replies and trading incredulous looks, particularly after he told them the king and queen of the sea from Greek mythology were onboard.

"Hate to cut you off." Recco broke into Viktor's never-ending stream of questions. "The reason I'm here is we need polar diving gear. Do you have any onboard?"

"What on earth for?" Juan asked. "I thought you said the dolphin was inside."

"I did, and it is, but it's not doing very well. It needs to return to the sea, and the treatment Daide has in mind requires time to run medication through an IV. It won't be very comfortable, and the dolphin—Leif—will fare far better if his rib cage isn't being half-crushed by his own weight."

"We used to have gear," Juan said. "Keep your fingers crossed the dry suit seals haven't dried and cracked. You can't be in these waters without a fully encased suit with lots of layers underneath. It's too cold."

"I know. Let's have a look at what you've got."

"Come on." Juan moved fast as he left the bridge.

Recco had a hell of a time keeping up with him and fighting the rolling, pitching ship. "Do you have a protected way in and out of *Arkady*?" he asked. "Or will we need to brave the gangway?"

Juan came to a halt in front of one of many metal storage lockers and spun the combination dial until the lock sprang open. "Good question. There's an airlock system we could use on the far side of the engine room, except it hasn't been opened in ten years, and I'm not sure about the integrity of the seals. They're fine now when everything is shut tight, but—"

"Never mind. We'll figure something else out." Recco rooted through the cabinet pulling out dry suits in large sizes and O2 tanks.

"I'll take the tanks and make sure I can pressurize them." Juan walked to a wall-mounted nozzle inside a locked glass cabinet and dredged a key from beneath it. Once it was open, he looped hosing out and flicked a switch. The distant hum of a compressor flared to life.

Recco bent over two suits, examining them for telltale cracks that could fail. One looked okay. The other one didn't, so he dug through the pile in the huge locker and came up with another promising candidate, adding two masks to the pile.

Juan looked up from the compressed air tanks and their attached pressure regulators. "Still good, although I'm not certain how. Regulations require these be replaced every couple of years, whether they've had a problem or not." He cast a sidelong glance at Recco. "Please tell me the two of you are certified divers."

"We are, but even if we weren't…" He shrugged.

Juan narrowed his eyes. "Did the dolphin or Poseidon and what's her name say they'd help us in return?"

"Amphitrite. No, they didn't." Recco tucked the suits under an arm, gave the masks to Juan, and made for a stairwell. "No guarantees on either side. We might miscalculate with the dolphin Shifter. He's weak, and he's not just a dolphin. Daide will have to guess at the dose of medication. And then Karin's timing will need to be spot-on. If she can't undo the magic that tore holes in his immune system to begin with, Leif will be in a worse place from where he started, and a new batch of parasites will rush into the breach."

"Why worse?"

"Antibiotics to treat parasites work on the theory they kill the bugs before they kill you. A working rule of thumb is lowest possible dose for shortest possible time, but we don't have that luxury here. Daide will have to guess right on dosage. Too much will kill him. Too little won't have much effect."

Juan paced him. "You mentioned Karin. You don't have three suits. And I only brought tanks and masks for you and Daide. Will she dive too?"

"Since she'll be working with magic, I'm hoping she can do her part from inside the ship." Recco stopped shy of articulating he and Daide would have to work damned fast. Their time underwater was limited. Cold water meant a higher air consumption rate. They'd expend more energy and become fatigued faster. Cold would also decrease their manual dexterity and eventually erode their mental processes, making them sluggish.

"Do you want me or Vik to come along?"

Juan's question broke into Recco's thoughts. He considered it but couldn't justify putting a third man at risk, particularly one who was instrumental in piloting the ship. "Probably not."

"Then I'll rig cable. Something easy to follow if you become disoriented. And a way we can haul you back topside."

"Not necessary—" Recco began.

"Yeah. It is. You'll have twelve minutes. Fifteen tops. If you're not back on the platform by then, I'm reeling you in."

They reached the auditorium, and Recco pulled the doors open. Poseidon and Amphitrite were still there. Leif was gone. Daide was packing the last of several large ampoules into a box. He stood and headed for Recco and Juan.

"What happened to our patient?" Recco asked.

"It took too much magic for him to maintain himself, and he was fading. I suggested he wait for us outside the hull." Daide took one of the suits from Recco and a mask from Juan. "I'm relieved you located these. I was afraid we wouldn't have a way to work on him in the water."

Zoe walked to Poseidon and his queen. "It's storming so fiercely, it will be dangerous for Daide and Recco to exit the ship so they can reach your Shifter."

"We will create a perimeter of clear water," Poseidon said. "We already discussed it, recognizing the need."

"Hurry," Amphitrite urged. "Leif isn't recovering as quickly as I'd hoped. I told him not to join us in here. He didn't listen."

"It's what makes him a good alpha for his people." Worry turned Poseidon's eyes to midnight blue. "We will be in the sea, awaiting your arrival."

"Do the best you can for our dolphin," Amphitrite murmured. Light flared bright around her, and she and the king transformed into colorful beams as they left the same way they'd arrived.

Recco was careful pulling the hooded dry suit on atop his insulated clothing. A tear could spell disaster. From long habit, he checked the seals on Daide's suit, and Daide did the same for his.

"Meet me at the gangway on the port side," Juan said. "I'll bring the tanks and set up two cables."

"Do you have a communication system?" Daide asked.

"Use telepathy," Karin snapped, sounding like her surly self. She stood. "Once the water calms down, I'll be at the bottom of the gangway along with Juan. It will be an easier reach for my magic, and Leif can swim next to the platform as he recovers."

Karin might have harsh edges, but Recco silently blessed her for her faith in them. That the dolphin was so weak he couldn't remain inside didn't offer much in the way of hope. Animals passed a point of no return where they kept sinking no matter what you did.

"Ready?" Oblivious to Recco's concerns, Daide flashed a grin. "Damn, it feels good to be back in the saddle."

Recco grinned back. He'd been too worried to let himself enjoy being a vet again. Trust Daide and his unflappable nature to put a positive spin on things. The ship's motion quieted as they moved to Deck Three. When Recco stepped outside, he was thunderstruck and stopped moving as he absorbed a scene out of a Hollywood movie.

The storm still raged from a sky heavy with black clouds. The wind still howled. In violation of reason and physics, a fifty-foot perimeter around the ship yielded calm water beneath gray skies.

"It's impossible, but I'll take it." Daide sprang ahead and loped down the gangway steps.

By the time Recco got there, Daide had his oxygen equipment strapped in place and his mask on. Juan was clipping him into a harness attached to a length of cable wrapped around a stanchion.

"Here's yours." Juan dangled another harness.

Recco got ready as fast as he could. Despite the relative calm, it was bitterly cold, and he worried about how their fingers would fare. Both of them wore thin, neoprene gloves tucked beneath the dry suits' wrist seals. Beefier gloves would interfere with their tactile ability.

Karin joined them and sat on the bottom step. "Quicker is better," she said. "I'll link to Leif with my magic while you're doing your IV meds. It'll be like a one-two punch. I'll be able to hold him on this side of things while your medication takes hold. In case it's not a good match for his physiology."

"All set," Daide said. "Same plan as always. I'll get the IV in place, and you hand me ampoules."

Recco nodded. He tucked the drugs Daide had parceled out into a dry sack, sealed it, and tied it to a loop on his suit.

Zoe worked her way down the gangplank and gave him a thumbs-up before hugging him fast and hard. "Be careful. I'll help Karin with the magic parts."

"We'll be all right." He tried to reassure her. "You don't have to be out here." It was hard to let go of her.

"Aye. I do. You do your work, and I'll do mine."

Karin patted the step next to her. "Sit. Don't ask too many questions, and open your power to me."

Pleasure spilled through Recco because Zoe cared enough to keep watch, sitting in the freezing cold. He cinched his mask, tumbled backward off the platform, and followed the glow from Daide's headlamp. At first, his regulator didn't seem to be working; he fiddled with it until oxygen flowed.

The water was warmer than the air had been, which wasn't saying much.

Leif swam to them. *"Let's get moving. I didn't realize how weak I was until the stint inside almost did me in."*

"Apologies. My telepathic skills aren't great," Daide said. *"I'll be as gentle as I can, but this is a big needle. Once the medicine starts flowing, it will burn like nobody's business."*

"I understand. Just get it done."

Daide patted Leif's flipper, moved into position, and slid the IV into place.

Recco fumbled in the sack and handed him a glass vial. His fingers were already losing feeling. He laid a gloved hand on Leif's flank. *"Steady. This will hurt. Do not move. If you dislodge the needle, we'll have to start all over."*

The sea churned like a mad thing. Recco was afraid Poseidon and Amphitrite's spell was fading until he looked around them. Dolphins closed from every side, and whales swam below. The sea Shifters formed a protective circle about them and warmed the ocean water a few degrees.

"Karin. Can you hear me?"

"Of course."

"All the sea Shifters are here."

"Sure and we know," Zoe answered. *"We called them, but I suspect they'd have circled the wagons anyway. Leif is their alpha."*

Daide held out his hand, and Recco gave him a second vial of medicine. Leif bellowed and groaned but held still as Daide had instructed.

A lighter-colored dolphin swam closer. *"You're hurting him."*

"It's all right," Leif grunted between bellows.

"What are you doing to him?" a whale asked from below.

"Talk with them, amigo," Daide said. *"I have to concentrate so the drug doesn't enter his system too fast. This is nip and tuck as it is."*

Air bubbled from Recco's regulator. His face was numb outside the mask's perimeter. All that frozen skin would hurt like a bitch when he got back inside the ship. He focused on the sea creatures. *"Your immune systems were attacked by the Cataclysm."*

"Is it a name for the bad magic that held the sea in thrall?" the light-colored dolphin asked.

"Yes. It's our name for it. I'm sure there are others. Without functioning immune systems, you all fell prey to parasitic infections. Normally, they don't kill you, but you lost the ability to fight them off."

"What are you doing to Leif?" the dolphin persisted.

"My friend is injecting medicine to kill the parasites. Other Shifters

from the boat are addressing Leif's immunocompromised problem with a counter spell."

Recco handed Daide another vial. Lief thrashed weakly, but he'd stopped bellowing. *"Let's wait on more drug,"* Recco said, worried by how lethargic the dolphin had become.

Daide looked up from where he'd been intent on making certain he didn't lose his placement in a vein. *"Hang onto this,"* he said and swam around Leif poking, prodding, and listening intently.

Recco capped off the IV line. It would stay put. *"Karin. How's it going on your end?"*

"Not well. Reach into his chest with magic and clear his airway." Her voice was terse. *"Do it now. Dead lungworms are clogging his bronchi and stealing his air. Support him to the surface so he can cough them out."*

"I heard her," Daide said curtly. *"There's no way the drug could have worked so fast killing the bronchial parasites. Except it appears it did. Further, I have no idea how to doctor with magic. And it won't be easy getting Leif to the surface without a sling."*

"Sure, if we had to lift him, but we have other resources," Recco replied and turned his attention toward the sea Shifters. *"Did you hear the woman talking with me?"* he asked the whales and dolphins."

"No," the nearest dolphin answered.

"We have to get Leif to the surface. Now. Dead parasites are filling his lungs."

"Move out of the way," a whale trumpeted and blasted upward, balancing Leif on his broad back.

Displaced water knocked Recco sideways. Once he recovered, he followed the whale to the surface. When he got there, Karin and Zoe were bent over the gangway platform, jets of blue-white power gushing from their hands. Leif lay across the whale, not moving as the women's magic buffeted him.

Daide's head broke the surface next to Recco. "Damn it," he sputtered. "I'd figured at least three vials of my mixture. I had no idea he wouldn't tolerate even two. Or it would work at ten times normal speed."

"Epinephrine to kickstart his heart?" Recco asked. His best guess was magic mixed with antibiotics were responsible for the quick reaction, but they could sort it out later.

Daide swam to the whale and began to clamber onto its back. A growl shook the water, and Daide backed off. "Please. I can help him."

What you've done so far hasn't been much help," the whale's deep voice resonated through Recco's skull.

"Yes. Sorry." Daide paddled next to the whale. "I can see how you'd interpret it that way, but medicines can be additive…"

"I've got it," Karin crowed. "Found the right combination. Finally." Her voice shook, revealing how close they'd come to losing Leif.

Recco hauled himself onto the gangway platform, water streaming from him as he ditched his mask and O2 tank. His teeth were chattering, but he'd be damned if he'd leave before he was certain the dolphin was out of the woods.

Daide joined him and withdrew a syringe fitted with a long needle and a vial of epinephrine from a dry sack tied to his suit. "Sure we won't need this?" he asked Karin.

She nodded, and he put it away and shucked his own tank of compressed air, leaving it next to Juan along with his mask.

"Thanks for not dragging us out of the water at the fifteen-minute mark," Recco told Juan.

"Thank Karin. She told me everything was under control."

Leif thrashed from side to side on the whale's back. He hacked and coughed, and a stream of gray worms blasted from his nostrils and mouth, followed by bloody spumes. Recco gaped as gallons of lungworms poured from the dolphin. This many would be surprising in a whale, let alone a dolphin.

"Amazing he was still alive," Daide said.

"No kidding." Recco shook his head as the worms kept spewing.

Leif coughed and rasped, "I can breathe. Finally."

"It will keep on getting better," Daide assured him. "You'll have some gut cramps too, as the trematodes die off and you expel them."

"I'm all right," Leif told the whale. "You don't have to support me anymore."

"Are you sure?" Concern rumbled through the whale's deep voice.

"Quite."

The whale's huge dorsal fin sank slowly.

"I need to do one quick thing," Daide said, "and remove the needle."

Leif turned around, and Daide lay on the platform on his belly to withdraw the IV. Bright blood followed, and he pinched off the vein.

"Got it." Karin bent over him. "Sealed it with magic. You can let go."

"How about the rest of your magic?" Leif twisted to gaze at Karin. "Were you successful?"

"I believe so. Your aura feels whole to me, which means you should be able to finish the healing yourself."

Three dolphins surfaced, forming a half circle around Leif. "You were who poisoned the oceans," one said, staring at the group crowded onto the gangway and its small platform.

"Rotters. Bastards," another yelled. Its blue-gray skin was more mottled than Leif's.

"Aye, 'twas our kin who were at fault." Zoe held eye contact with the dolphins, and Recco was proud of her. "Verra few of us, mind you, hatched up a nefarious plan in secret, but the result was still devastating, and we are deeply sorry."

"It's not enough," the third dolphin screamed. "Thousands of us are dead. Because of you."

Leif spun in a circle in the water, making it whip around him. "They went out of their way to save my life."

"So?" the smallest dolphin countered. "They're the reason we're sick."

"They owed it to you. To us," another screeched. Surging

forward, it closed its jaws around Daide's arm and pulled him off the platform and into the ocean.

Daide yowled and punched the dolphin in the snout. It let go, and the two of them squared off, snarling at one another.

"Leave the animal doctor alone." Leif positioned his body between Daide and the others.

Recco reached into the water and hauled Daide onto the platform. He snorted water and shook himself, eying the gash in the arm of his dry suit. "Think I liked it better when my patients couldn't talk," he muttered.

"Imagine all the names they've called us over the years." Recco tried to laugh. Instead, shivers racked him.

"You'd be welcome inside." Daide bowed formally at the circle of dolphins. "All of you, but no biting allowed."

"Will you help my brothers and sisters?" Leif asked.

"Of course," Daide replied.

"What if we don't want help from them?" A dolphin tossed its head and dove for the depths.

"I'll talk with them," Leif said. "They'll come to their senses. At the least, perhaps we could get some of the medicine and use our own magic."

"However you wish to proceed." Recco tipped his head. "You just let us know."

Juan hefted the tanks and trudged up the gangway. Daide followed with Karin behind him.

"Get moving. Ye'll shake the gangway to splinters." Zoe nudged Recco gently.

"Look." Recco angled his gaze outward. Fins cut the surface where whales circled the ship. "It appears they're not letting us out of their sight."

"We've done all we can for now. You dying of hypothermia won't alter the outcome."

"Should we talk with Poseidon and Amphitrite again?" he asked as he dragged himself up the gangway, shocked by how much the cold had weakened him.

"Doesn't work that way." Zoe nodded to Juan who activated the switch to raise the steps. "They're gods. If they want to talk, they'll find us."

19

BARGAINS

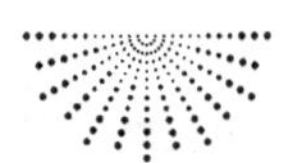

"**G**et moving. Ye'll shake the gangway to splinters," Zoe nudged Recco and did her damnedest to push past the fear that had gripped her when the dolphin nearly died on them. She still tasted the bitter aftermath of an adrenaline surge. They'd come within a hairsbreadth of the sea Shifters turning on them and sinking *Arkady*. All the nice words about *do your best*, had been mere words. Leif was the alpha, and alpha deaths were always avenged.

Because she'd held her magic wide open for Karin to tap into, she'd witnessed the dolphin's acute distress when the medicine entered its system. Apparently, the Shifter's physiology was quite a bit different from animals the men were used to treating. She'd kicked herself for summoning the other sea Shifters to observe, but at the time she'd hoped Recco and Daide's intervention would forge positive links between the two estranged branches of Shifter-dom.

Och aye, and they would have shown up regardless. 'Twas hubris on my part to believe my puny invitation carried aught in the way of weight.

She knew better than to ask Karin even a single question while she redirected energy patterns, patching healthy parts together and gluing them with her own magic, in hopes they'd be enough to counteract the mass parasite die-off. It had begun immediately. Cells burst, depositing wee beasties throughout the dolphin's body. Miniature horrors that would have done a nightmare dreamscape proud.

Because Zoe wasn't familiar with any aspects of medicine, at first, she'd thought it was a normal reaction. Karin's drawn expression crushed that hope, ripped it out by its roots. Offering up her own magic was little enough, and she'd felt helpless. Juan had sensed something was seriously wrong and asked about reeling in the cables, but Karin shook her head, too embroiled in magic to answer with words.

The dolphin's life force had flickered and dimmed. Cursing in Gaelic, Karin moved from the steps to the platform, power arcing from her fingertips. Zoe joined her, and Karin grabbed her to strengthen their linkage. She exhorted the men to move the dolphin to the surface, but Zoe was afraid they were too late. No matter how hard they tried, the ocean muted their power, made it reverberate in unexpected ways.

When Leif's limp form broke through atop the whale's broad back, she figured he was already dead. Karin didn't bother with anything as elegant as an assessment. She blasted the dolphin with magic, altering the pitch and timbre of her working endlessly until its heart lurched into rhythm again.

Zoe had always known Karin was a gifted healer. Today elevated her respect to a whole other level. Engaged in hand-to-hand combat with death, Karin had been indefatigable and refused to accept defeat. A very much alive dolphin Shifter was the result. She'd tried to articulate her admiration to Karin. The other Shifter waved a dismissive hand and told her it was all in a day's work.

"Look." Recco's voice broke into her replay of how closely they'd skirted disaster. He angled his gaze outward. Fins cut the surface where whales circled the ship. "It appears they're not letting us out of their sight."

"We've done all we can for now. You dying of hypothermia won't alter the outcome." Her words were sharper than she would have liked, but the aftermath of terror left her shaken. Whales circling the boat was disturbing. Maybe she was making too much of it. They might be anchoring Poseidon's spell to keep the sea calmer.

"I already told Daide this," Juan said as they passed him. "Stop by the galley and drink something hot. Then take a hot shower and get into warm clothes."

"Thanks." Recco slapped him across the back. "Not my first rodeo with hypothermia, *amigo*."

Juan snorted. "It's mine with magical talking sea creatures. My bondmate is thrilled. Me? I'm just in awe."

"They're beautiful, aren't they?" Zoe glanced over the railing hoping for another glimpse of the dolphins and their aquatic ballet moves.

"And deadly." Juan nailed her with his hazel eyes. "They'd have retaliated if Leif had died, wouldn't they? My bondmate was quite clear in that regard."

"Aye, they would have." She nodded slowly.

Recco's eyes widened. "Damn. Good thing that wasn't spelled out. Double good my wolf kept quiet. Might have made Daide and me so nervous, we'd have decided the risk wasn't worth it."

"And then Leif would have died for sure," Juan said. A corner of his mouth twisted downward. "Not today or next week, but soon. Sometimes you have to take risks. Get moving. Soup. Coffee. Shower."

"Aye aye, captain, sir." Recco rolled his eyes and walked through the nearest door with Zoe right behind him.

"How about this?" she suggested. "I'll get a meal together for us, and you can run through the shower and meet me in the galley."

"Sounds perfect. Teamwork at its finest."

She patted his shoulder. The dry suit was still wet and clammy. "Nay. Teamwork was you and Karin and Daide."

"I can't speak for Karin, but Daide and I were shooting from the hip. Cowboy medicine. We should have run labs, taken the time to check the effect of the drug cocktail on Leif's physiology." He grimaced. "We tossed the dice and got lucky—barely. The dolphin who dragged Daide into the water had every justification to be angry with us."

Zoe tilted her head to one side. "Since you brought it up, is punching your patients standard procedure?"

"Um, yeah, it is. When you deal with animals outweighing you by hundreds of pounds, you have to establish dominance. It's something they understand." He hurried on. "It's not the same situation at all here, though. Daide could have talked with the dolphin, tried to reason with it. Instead, he reacted."

"Naught to be done about it, and the dolphin did back off."

"When its alpha ordered it to, although I have no idea how strict their social order is."

She stepped away from the puddle his suit was making on the floor. "I don't, either. Get moving."

"Christ! You and Juan are worse than nagging parents. See you soon. Dinner's almost as good as having you join me in the shower." He winked, teasingly.

"With you half-dead from exposure? Nay. Once you're clean and fed, we can address the nonessential items."

"Love is never nonessential. Why the ancients lived on it. Look at their poetry. Their statues."

Zoe laughed. "Don't let our dinner get cold. I may begin without you if you're not front and center when 'tis ready to serve."

Blowing him a kiss, she spun and headed down one flight to the galley. She'd already thought about offering to shower with him, but he needed hot food and drink along with the shower. If she got into soaping his body, exploring every nook and crevice, he'd never make it to the dining room. At least not today. The hard truth was she needed sustenance as well. Her magical reservoir was dangerously low after Karin's incursion into it.

Love. The laddie said love, her inner voice piped up.

Doona make over much of it, she answered back.

Still smiling, she strode into the galley and tossed canned and powdered ingredients into something palatable. Tuna, noodles, and milk turned out a reasonable casserole. She put a cup of freeze-dried vegetables in water to rehydrate. She'd add them to the casserole once she removed it from the oven. Cornbread and biscuits sat on the countertop from earlier in the day or maybe the day before. Heated and split, they'd make a decent base to spoon dinner over.

She'd just put the finishing touches on two plates when the galley door swung open, admitting a smiling Recco. His dark hair glistened wetly, and he'd combed it away from his face. He'd shaved and wore thick, gray sweats and Wellingtons. A waterproof parka and bibs were slung over one arm along with a life jacket.

Zoe cast a guilty glance at the pile of outerwear she'd offloaded as a hedge against the kitchen's heat. "Do you suppose we should dress for dinner?" She arched a brow.

"Not necessarily. Mmmm. Smells wonderful." He brandished a bottle from behind him. "Stopped by the bar on my way down here."

"'Twasn't precisely on your way," she retorted. "You started on Deck Three. The bar is one floor up. Galley's one floor down."

"It was worth the trip. What's dinner without wine?"

She wanted to skip dinner and throw herself into his arms. Instead, she addressed the clothes question. "Did you see anyone on the way down here? Were they still all duded up?"

"No. Didn't see a soul, but nor did Viktor withdraw his orders about being fully dressed to move about the ship."

Karin, a tired-looking Karin with deeper lines around her eyes and wet hair spilling down her back, joined them in the kitchen. Not only was she not sporting waterproofs, she didn't even have them with her. "Thank the goddess you made dinner. I'm ready to pitch facedown on my bunk and sleep for days. There's enough for two more, right?"

"Aye." Zoe peered around Karin. "Who's the fourth?"

"Bet it's Daide," Recco said and squeezed around Karin,

probably to scan the dining room. "Yup. He staked out a table. I'll bring those plates with me. And I'll run down a corkscrew and glasses for the Bordeaux." He draped his parka and bibs atop Zoe's. "At least we'll know where these are if the boat starts pitching again. And if Vik gets annoyed, he can throw the book at all four of us."

"You're a bad influence." Zoe elbowed Karin and snatched two more plates from a cupboard.

Karin shrugged and went to work loading the plates with food. "So, shoot me. Sorry if I ruined your plans for a cozy, intimate meal." She trained shrewd eyes on Zoe.

"It's all right." Zoe hugged the other Shifter. "We had a hell of a go out there. Probably, the best thing is for all of us to process it."

"My thoughts, exactly." Karin stepped out of Zoe's hug and dug silverware from a drawer. "We haven't seen the last of the sea Shifters. As Leif improves and isn't fighting for every single breath, the others will want to be cured as well. We have to have a system in place that works better than what we did. There's no way in hell we'll be as lucky as we were with Leif. If he'd been an angstrom weaker, we'd have lost him for sure."

"I know. I had a ringside seat. Remember?"

Karin narrowed her eyes. "Must have been hell for you to watch."

"Och, sure and 'twas. I've never felt so helpless. I ached to do something with every iota of my being."

"You did do something. I never could have managed without your magic."

"At the time, it didn't feel like I contributed much at all. I did see something interesting in Leif's mind, though. Mayhap the reason he allowed us to experiment on him."

"What was it?" Karin picked up the silverware and a plate. "I was far too occupied to split my attention."

"He believed he and his Shifters had been abandoned. 'Twas only recently Poseidon and Amphitrite showed up, and he harbors bitterness they didn't come sooner. Before so many of his kinfolk died. Watching them suffer and wither and die must have cut deep."

"I'm sure it did. As alpha, he carried a link to each member of his pod, which would have made the deaths much worse."

"How come we're not organized similarly?" Zoe asked.

"Long ago, we were. I'm not certain when we discarded the alpha structure. Or why, but I bet Juan's cat would know. Grab your dinner, and let's join the men. I'm sure they'll be interested in what you just said."

Zoe crossed the dining room, thankful the ship was still chugging along quietly. Extending the calming spell all the way to Siberia was unlikely—no one had that much power, not even the sea gods—but she'd take what she could get. Setting her plate down, she slid in next to Recco.

"Go ahead. Dig in," she urged. "'Twill be best eaten hot."

For a while no one said much. Zoe was hungrier than she'd realized, and after the first few bites, she scooped food into her mouth as fast as she could chew and swallow.

Karin took a brisk swig of wine, and then asked Zoe, "Did you pick up anything else from Leif's mind?"

"Anything else besides what? I want to know," Recco said.

During the meal, he'd edged closer until his thigh pressed against hers, and she appreciated his solid presence. "Basically, he believes Poseidon abandoned him and the other sea Shifters. He and Amphitrite only materialized after the Cataclysm receded, and Leif thinks it's because they went to ground during the worst of things— to save their own hides."

"Aren't they immortal?" Daide asked.

"Supposedly," Karin replied. "Who knows exactly how their immortality works."

Zoe set her fork down and sipped her wine. "If Leif feels his Shifter pack—or pod—was forsaken, perhaps he'd be more willing to work with us to heal the schism between our two peoples."

"Before we go there," Daide said, "I owe all of you a major

apology. The bunch in the sea are about as far from normal dolphins as we are from…from Vampires. I never should have taken even one shortcut, and I took several. We're doing full lab work—as full as our limited resources allow—before we treat anyone else. If Recco hadn't said something, I'd probably have injected a third ampoule and killed Leif. I didn't notice how lethargic he'd grown."

Recco nodded thoughtfully and drained his wineglass. "Off the top, I'd say half the amount of antibiotic—"

"With an antifungal and a steroid," Karin cut in.

"And a staged approach," Daide said. "So we don't end up like today with boatloads of dead and dying parasites gumming up the works as they head for the exits."

"Was that what they were doing?" Zoe asked.

"Yup. The prime directive for any species, and it includes parasitic ones, is survival. Those lungworms, and probably the trematodes too, although their egress is far less dramatic, recognized they'd been targeted."

"How long can they survive outside a host?" Zoe glanced at the empty plates. "Shall I bring the casserole dish out? There's some left."

"Yes on the casserole," Recco said.

"In terms of survival, some parasites go into long-term stasis between hosts," Daide said. "But these varieties aren't among them."

Zoe hustled into the galley and returned with the casserole and a serving spoon.

"Feel like more wine?" Recco tapped the empty bottle with an index finger.

Zoe's belly was full, and her head buzzed pleasantly. "If I were certain we wouldn't be called back onto the front lines, I'd say sure, but—"

The dining room door swished open, admitting a man she didn't recognize. Blue-gray hair fell to his knees, shrouding a tall, broad-shouldered body with pale skin. Eyes the shade of a restless ocean met hers, and Zoe knew who it had to be. She shot to her feet. "Leif. Please. Join us."

He hesitated. "Do you have clothes I might borrow? I'm not cold, but I lived as a man long enough to know human customs."

"Of course." Daide stood. "Come with me. We're about the same size, and I'll get you set up."

"Before you leave…" Zoe walked to him. "Do you eat as a human? If so, are you hungry?"

The corners of his unusual eyes crinkled at the corners. "Do you eat as a coyote?" When she nodded, he went on, "Then you have your answer. I'd be honored to share a meal with you."

"I'll heat it up a wee bit."

"You needn't bother on my account."

Daide crooked a finger. "Come with me. You can catch me up on how you're feeling."

Zoe detoured through the galley to grab another plate and utensils before returning to the table. Karin blew out a noisy breath. "Nothing like laying eyes on someone I was worried about. He'll be better than fine."

Recco chuckled. "Knowing Daide, he'll at least have a listen with his stethoscope. I'll heat some water and make tea if we're done with wine for now."

Karin bent close to Zoe. "The dolphin is here to ask a boon."

"My take too. Do you suppose 'tis a good time to make a pitch for unity? We'll need all the good magic we can scare up once we get to Wrangel Island."

"Let's see what he has to say." Karin pressed her mouth into a thin line. "I don't want him to feel we're taking advantage of him."

"We're not," Zoe protested. "'Tis in everyone's interest to close the gateway. So long as wickedness has an access point, we're all at risk."

"I was referring to his perception, not the reality of how bad things are." Karin rubbed the bridge of her nose between a thumb and forefinger. "I swear, it's grim enough I shy away from thinking about it most of the time."

Daide and Leif walked into the dining room looking like twins in black fuzzy pants, stretchy long john tops, and insulated, brightly-colored jackets. Daide had a stethoscope looped around his neck, and he was smiling. And apologizing. Zoe caught the tail end of what was probably a much-longer conversation.

Recco brought a carafe of hot water to the table along with mugs and tea bags and sugar packets.

Leif broke into a grin. It lightened his somber expression and brought his defined cheekbones and square jaw to the foreground. "I adore tea. Most of my time in human form was spent in London."

"How'd you end up here?" Zoe asked. Once he'd sat down, she poured hot water over a tea bag, and then dished up the remaining casserole, placing it in front of him.

"How else? We were trying to find a stretch of ocean that wouldn't kill us on contact," he replied between bites. "Thanks. This is good. Unfortunately, many from my group—most of us—died en route. We finally found an isolated pocket of water not far from Antarctica still capable of supporting life. Other sea Shifters weren't so lucky. Many died in distant oceans. Whale song carries thousands of miles, and for years the songs have held nothing except sorrow."

"Words are inadequate, but I'm so sorry," Karin said. Reaching across the table, she patted his hand.

"Thank you." Leif glanced up from his empty plate and inclined his head. He stirred sugar into his tea and drank deeply. "I am here on behalf of my lieges, Poseidon and Amphitrite, as well as my pod."

Zoe buried surprise deep before Leif could pick up on it. Probably best if he didn't know she'd mined secrets from him while he lay near death. Either he'd come to terms with his bitterness, or more likely he'd found a way to coexist with it.

"We'll help any way we can," Recco murmured.

"Yes," Daide concurred. "Like I reassured you when we were in my cabin, we learned enough from working on you I'm certain treatment for your pod will proceed far more smoothly."

Leif's nostrils flared. "It would have to since I almost died. I felt my spirit hovering, trying to break free from my body." He eyed Karin. "You're who kept me together."

She nodded solemnly. "One of my better moments as a healer, but you had strength. If you hadn't, all the doctoring in the world wouldn't have mattered."

"Does your offer to cure the rest of my pod still hold?" Leif's gaze settled on each of them in turn.

"Of course," Daide said. "Maybe we could tackle the rest of the dolphins first. We'll need to do careful calculations for the whales."

"Poseidon suggested holding off on the whales until we see the ship safe to Invercargill. They used to have a cetacean institute with specialized deep-water byways to treat larger marine mammals."

"Perfect," Recco smiled warmly. "By then, we should have the fine points worked out."

"We offer safe passage to New Zealand's South Island in return for—" Leif began.

"No need to bargain," Karin broke in. "We'll take care of you, regardless. One thing you will want to take back to your lieges and your pod, though, is this. We told Poseidon and Amphitrite we were on our way to the Arctic to do what we could to address a rent in the ether. It's allowing evil access to Earth, and we must find a way to close it off."

"We know about it," Leif said. "The thing you call the Cataclysm ripped it open—and killed all the sea life between Wrangel Island and the thirtieth parallel." Anger turned his gaze a deeper blue.

"Between here and northern waters," Karin went on, "one of our primary tasks is to gather as many magic-wielders as we can."

"If no one except yourselves signs up, will you still confront the darkness standing guard over the fissure?" Intensity shimmered around Leif, turning the air blue.

"Aye," Zoe said. "We will do what we must. 'Twas our blood who started this."

"And it's our responsibility to end it," Karin spoke firmly.

Leif finished his tea and set down his cup. "I can't speak for any beyond myself, but I will stand with you."

"Thank you," Daide said. "After my blundering, we don't deserve your loyalty."

"You may have blundered"—Leif smiled—"but your heart was in the right place. It's what counts." He stood. "I'll leave your clothes and return to my people. When will you be ready to cure another dolphin?"

"As soon as you bring me a blood sample and I can do some calculations," Daide replied.

"Fine. Give me a syringe and I'll get you what you need. Thank you for the meal. And the tea." Leif stood and bowed, a formal, old-fashioned gesture that warmed Zoe's heart.

"Join us any time. Your pod are welcome as well. I'm looking forward to getting to know you better." She stood too, along with Karin and Recco and Daide.

"You as well, coyote Shifter." Leif bowed slightly and then walked toward the door with Daide behind him.

"Turn right," Daide said. "Might as well show you where the lab is. It's where I'll want you to bring the blood."

"Intriguing that you, er we, are human most of the time, while their primary form is the animal one," Recco murmured.

"Aye, they're also far stronger magically than we are," Zoe said.

"Probably why any of them are left at all," Karin noted. "I'm encouraged he committed to join us. It bodes well for the others. They'll probably follow their alpha's lead."

Zoe began piling dishes into a stack. Karin slapped her hands away. "You cooked. I'll clean up. Besides"—she leered knowingly —"I'll bet the two of you would like some time alone together. Daide and I crashed your cozy supper, so why don't you find a nice, private location where you're not likely to be disturbed."

Zoe's cheeks warmed. "Yes, Mom."

"So long as I'm Mom, take your outside clothes with you. I'm not expecting a ship's emergency, but they should be close to you in case something goes south."

Recco threaded an arm around Zoe's waist. "How about a second bottle of wine?"

"Nah. How about just you and me?"

Karin picked up the pile of dishes. "Time for me to exit stage left and let you lovebirds sort out the fine points."

Recco's coppery skin colored with a blush. "Your cabin or mine?"

Zoe grinned. "Yours. It's closer."

He tightened his arm around her. "I like a woman with clear priorities."

She hip-butted him. "Aye, they're verra clear."

"I'll grab our things from the galley. Bet I catch up with you in the corridor."

"Bet you don't." Zoe sprinted from the dining room. If she timed it right, she'd greet Recco naked as the day she was born. Desire surged, annihilating everything else.

Soon. Very soon she'd lay claim to her heart's desire—and never let him go. Deep within, her coyote yipped and yowled.

"Thanks for being happy for me," she told it.

"Happy? I'm ecstatic. I never thought you'd settle down. This is one time I'm delighted to be proven wrong."

Zoe sent a jet of magic to open the door to Recco's cabin. "Oh come on," she retorted. *"I wasn't as awful as that."*

"Not awful." The coyote's reply was slow and thoughtful. *"But nor did you expend any effort to find an appropriate mate."*

"And now we know why. I was waiting for this one."

The coyote yipped and chittered while Zoe stripped off clothing, folding it as she went.

2 0

LOVE CLAIMED

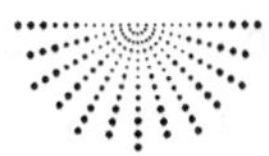

*R*ecco hustled into the galley and snatched up an armload of waterproof outerwear and two life vests. Karin turned from where she'd been bent over the sink and shook a finger his way. "We've been through so much. Do not hurt her."

"No worries on that front. I love her."

"Have you told her?" Karin furled her white brows.

"Um, by inference."

"Not good enough." More finger shaking, but this time Karin was smiling.

Recco nodded. "I was thinking the same thing, about what I need to tell her before we're so caught up in one another talk is the last thing on our minds."

Karin's copper gaze bored into him. "After I'm done in here, I'll run Viktor down. The Sirens cursed us, and we have a few loose ends dangling, items that might tempt fate. It's high time Juan and Aura formalized their mating. Maybe we can make it a double wedding."

Joy beat a path through Recco, brimming with hope, determination, and potential. The small distance between him and Karin sparkled with crystalline clarity, which meant magic was in

255

play. "Save your compulsion spell, Doc. I'd like nothing better. So long as Zoe says yes. I've known for a long time she was the woman for me. I haven't wanted to crowd her."

Karin snorted. "Crowd away. We women like to know we're wanted."

"Thanks for the tip." Recco spun and loped from the galley, out through the dining room, and up the nearest flight of stairs. He yanked the door to his cabin wide and strode inside. Zoe, a buck-naked Zoe, grinned at him from where she perched on one of the bunks.

Breath caught in his throat, and his cock jumped to attention in the blink of an eye, hard as it ever got. He'd known she had to be stunning. Reality surpassed his imagination many times over. Red curls cascaded down her shoulders, snaking around perfect globes of breasts tipped with strawberry nipples the size of silver dollars. Hips flared around a flat stomach. Where she'd crossed her legs under her, a triangle of copper-red curls graced the vee between her legs.

She arched her shoulders back, making her breasts bounce forward. "Are you planning to stand there gawking with the door open?"

The door. He'd forgotten all about it. A swift backward kick seated it firmly in the jamb. "Dear God, you're gorgeous."

A slow smile lit the bottoms of her brown eyes and made its way to her mouth. "Thank you. What kept you so long? You were going to catch up to me—before I got here."

"Karin had a few words of motherly advice."

"Aye, 'twould be verra like Karin. Such as?" Zoe angled her head to one side.

Recco hung the pile of clothing in his arms over a hook and toed off his Wellingtons, using the boot jack in the corner. He unzipped his warm top and dropped it on the desk.

"Good start." She pointed at his recently discarded jacket. "You have a way to go to catch up. Also, you didn't answer my question about Karin."

Recco dragged the room's only chair until it faced where she sat on the bunk. Sitting down, he placed a hand on her knee. The simple contact had an electric effect. Heat and urgency traveled up his arm and straight to his groin, but he had things he needed to say. Recognizing it as a losing battle, he did his damnedest to smother the waves of desire rioting through him.

Her smile faded, and she closed her teeth over her lower lip. "Oh-oh. You've a serious look about you. Is this where you tell me I'm a nice lass, but you've rethought—?"

"Not at all, darling." The temptation to crush her against him was overwhelming. He held back. "I love you. I've loved you for months now, but I've done my best to offer you space to warm to me." He shrugged, feeling uncomfortable. "Maybe too much space. I'm babbling, but Karin wanted to make certain my intentions were honorable. If she didn't know, then probably you don't, either." He stopped to suck in a breath. "Anyway, I wanted to make certain you realized how I felt. Damn it, Zoe. I want to protect you from every bad thing in the world. Put you in a bubble and stand guard over you."

The corners of her mouth twitched. "Neanderthal sentiments aside, you said honorable intentions? Sure and is this a backhanded marriage proposal? You haven't even sampled the goods. You might not like—"

"Zero probability. Jesus, I can barely breathe with you naked and only a few inches away. I would love it if you'd marry me, Zoe. It would be the greatest honor of my life if you said yes."

Her eyes sparkled with mirth, and longing flared in their depths. "Best proposal I've ever gotten. Also the only one, but 'tis beside the point. Aye, I'll make an honest man of you. Now could you get those clothes off? Or should I do it for you?"

His face heated. She may have said yes, but he was making a total botch of things. More like a shuffling schoolboy than an experienced lover. Inside, his wolf whuffled what was probably laughter. *"Sincerity will win the day. It always does."*

"My coyote is so happy it's yipping." She laid her hand over his. "It also called me a hussy."

"My wolf is laughing too. And you can be a hussy so long as your hussiness is all mine." He let go of her long enough to free both hands to drag his top over his head. The heat of her gaze seared him, made him self-conscious. Was his body still attractive? His gym years were a long way behind him.

Zoe uncurled her lithe, long-legged form and stood, eyes never leaving his face. Reaching between them, she undid the fastenings on his pants and gave them a push. They slithered down his legs, and she closed a hand over the unruly appendage jutting from his body. The heat of her hand was intensely erotic and made it seem as if his shorts weren't even there. His cock had never been so sensitive. Delight spilled through every cell, creating a pulsing vortex of lust so intense it took all his self-control not to toss her on her back and plunge into her as deep and fast as he could.

He threaded his arms around her and teased her back and shoulders with his fingertips, reveling in her soft, silky skin. She smelled heavenly. Cinnamon, amber, and the musk of her arousal. Weaving his fingers into her lush hair, he drew it back and away from her face.

"Has anyone ever told you your hair is like liquid fire? It shades from cherry to amber to copper to gold."

"Nay, but when I was verra young, Rowana used to tease me. She'd tell me dragons were waiting to spirit me off to grace their hoard. Because my hair was like dragon's fire, they'd covet it, want it for their own."

"Not going to happen on my watch." Possessiveness surged through him, surprising in its fierceness.

She slid the elastic waistband of his underwear over his erection and pushed the cotton shorts down his legs. They joined his trousers in a heap around his feet, and he stepped out of them. Zoe leaned back against the circle of his arms. Spots of color rode high on her cheekbones, and her nipples formed peaks.

He brushed his thumb across her full lower lip before bending his head and settling his mouth over hers. She nipped his lips in a string of biting kisses, and he scrubbed his tongue over her lips until she opened for him to dive inside. He loved how she sucked on his tongue, and he withdrew to encourage her to tongue-kiss him.

Magic pulsed around them, forming colorful streamers that made him shiver with longing when they stroked his naked flesh. He ran his hands down her long, straight spine, settling them over the curves of her ass and drawing her against his aching hard-on. Where she stroked his back, digging in with her nails, he caught fire with lust so pervasive it drove everything except the woman in his arms from his mind.

He strung kisses across both cheeks and down her neck before dropping an arm low enough to scoop it beneath her knees and lift her onto the narrow berth. Before she could drag him down next to her, he filled his hands with her breasts, working the nipples between his fingertips.

Zoe made little mewling noises as she writhed beneath his touch. The magical motes of light continued their arcane dance, heightening his pleasure wherever they touched him. Her legs fell open, and she squirmed, rotating her hips in unmistakable invitation.

Recco traded his lips for his hands and took a nipple into his mouth, suckling her. His body was so tightly strung, he almost didn't recognize the sensations bombarding him from all directions. To center himself and keep from coming, he focused on her breasts, switching from one to the other and back again.

Her breathing quickened, and the color dotting her fair skin deepened to a lovely rose. Letting go of her breasts, he drew his mouth down her rib cage and across her flat stomach to hover above the mat of red curls, spiky with her arousal. She made a grab for his cock, but he evaded her. If she touched him, he'd explode.

Kneeling between her splayed legs, he let his mouth hover half an inch above her distended nub. She bucked upward. He kept his mouth out of reach as he breathed on her. Two of the colored streamers wrapped around his cock, hot and teasing.

He got the picture. She was using magic as an enhancement, not that he needed the slightest bit of any kind of boost. As it was, his heart pounded against his chest, and he fought to breathe.

A volley of Gaelic was followed by her hands on either side of his head, pressing him downward. He licked her clit, just one fast swipe. She mewled and pulled his head lower, clearly as lost in lust as he was. He drew his tongue up one side of her sensitive center, and then up the other. Up. Down. Around. While he pushed between her legs and buried two fingers inside her.

She ground herself against him, hands tightening where she'd woven them in with his hair. Her clit, firmly inside his mouth now, quivered, and her muscles clamped around his fingers. She moaned low in her throat, and the sound joined everything else, merging into an erotic ballet. He drove his fingers into her and sucked hard on her nub until release crashed over her, almost carrying him with it. The streamers tickled, teased, and slapped, like mini-BDSM accomplices.

He didn't back off until he was certain her orgasm had played itself out, and then he raised himself until he knelt, straight-backed between her legs. She curved a hand around his cock and licked her lips. "I can return the favor." Streamers bobbed around her, awaiting her commands.

"Later," his voice came out in a rasp, "I want to know about these." He batted a streamer.

"Aye, and do you like them?" She grinned coquettishly.

"Aye," he aped her brogue, "but I like you better. Spread your legs, wench. I'll take a rain check on, well on everything else."

He disentangled her fingers from his shaft, dragged a pillow over, and lifted her hips onto it. The sight of her sex spread before him was deliriously tantalizing. He still tasted her on his tongue.

The sensory mélange pounded through his veins, and he positioned his cock at the entrance to her body. Her labia were hot, slick, and enticing, and he slid inside slowly, savoring the scorching heat of her core as it closed around him.

At first, he stayed quiet, engaging small muscles to make his cock twitch inside her. She snugged herself around him, twitching back. Arching her spine, she raised her legs, wrapping them around his waist. He drank her in. Red curls spread across the pillows, eyes hot with desire. Nipples puckered into inch-long peaks.

He reached for her clit, flicking it with his fingers. "Touch yourself," he ground out.

She moved a hand from his thigh and placed two fingers over her nub, rubbing in small circles. "Like this?" Her tongue slid across her passion-swollen lips.

"Yes. Exactly like that. Touch yourself while I love you."

He'd always liked to watch, but watching Zoe existed in a whole different universe. He withdrew inch by inch before plumbing her again. Long, slow strokes gave way to faster ones until he pounded into her. She was rubbing herself harder now, eyes glazed with lust. The streamers wound around both of them, heightening sensation until he growled his need and delight.

His balls tightened. He rode a ragged edge of control. She would come again before he did, goddammit. Jamming his fingers over hers, he displaced them and teased her slick mound, alternating hard and soft touches. She dissolved around his cock in a wave of heat that crashed hard around his rigid flesh. The rhythmic demand of her peak was impossible to evade. Semen shot from him in jets so intense the edges of his vision hazed to gray.

Gasping and panting, they writhed against each other. Bending low, he kissed her, sealing their lovemaking with their mouths. Recco held her close as their bodies quieted. Her legs were still twined around him, and he remained buried deep in her body. When he moved his mouth from hers and opened his eyes, the streamers were nowhere in sight.

He smoothed stray hairs off her face. "You were amazing. Thank you."

"Nay, 'tis I who should be thanking you."

He smiled. "The colored ribbons, where'd they come from?"

She grinned back. "A wee bit of magic from the old country. My granny, she had a Gaelic counterpart to the Kama Sutra. She kept the book well hidden, but I'd sneak-read it whenever I could."

"Bet you were a young hellion." He ruffled her curls.

"Och, I gave granny more than one anxious moment."

"Did she raise you?"

"Aye. Mum and Da weren't around much. They were archaeologists too. World-renowned at that, which meant they were always off on some dig or other. What about your people?"

"Poor as dirt, but lots of love to go around."

"Someday"—her expression turned serious—"maybe I could meet your family, and you could meet mine. If any of them are still alive."

He turned them onto their sides in the narrow bunk and cupped the side of her face. "My family would love you, but I don't hold much in the way of hope they survived the Cataclysm."

"Juan found lots of people when we scanned Buenos Aires during our joint trance." Concern spilled from her, and he respected her for caring.

"People, yes, and lots of destruction, particularly in the poorer sections of town. He and I talked about it later and concluded it would be a miracle if our older family members had survived."

She spread her fingertips across his back, kneading tight muscles. "I'd enjoy lolling around here for hours, but we probably should see what everyone else is up to."

He wound a curl around one finger. "What? The honeymoon's over already?"

"No, silly. It's only a few hours until bedtime..." Her eyes widened. "Damn. I believe I have bridge duty at twenty-two hundred."

"Why damn? I'll keep you company. Besides"—he lowered a hand to squeeze her ass—"we might have it all to ourselves."

"Nay. We won't. Juan or Vik will be there. It's fine." She wriggled out of his embrace, dislodging him from her body as she crawled over him, and then walked to the sink.

"I'll just rinse off." She ran a washcloth under hot water, wrung the water out of it, and tossed it his way. "Here's one for you too."

"Thanks." He wiped his hands and face before wrapping the damp cloth around his semi-erect appendage. "While we still have some privacy, can we talk about something?"

Zoe rinsed her cloth and hung it over a hook. "Sure. Anything."

He swung his legs over the side of the bed and made a grab for the clothing he'd discarded. "Did something strike you as odd about Leif's visit?"

She drew her brows together until a vertical line formed between them and plucked clothing from a neatly folded stack he hadn't noticed before. "Now you mention it, some of what he said seemed a wee bit staged. The part bothering me most, though, was the discrepancy between what I saw in his head and his actions. He truly hates Poseidon, yet he told us he was here on behalf of his lieges."

Recco fastened his trousers. "Are such reactions so unusual, though? Don't most commoners dislike royalty?"

Zoe slid her vest over her top and put her boots on. "Shifters don't report to royalty. We never elevated any of our own to that position. The gods knew about us, but it was more a relationship where we coexisted, not one where we owed them fealty."

"Could it be different for sea Shifters?"

"I don't know. Leif seems decent and sincere. I tested him with magic while he was on board."

"You're full of surprises."

"Nay, just not verra trusting. Wasn't only me. Karin checked too. I felt her distinct brand of power."

Zoe walked to him and held out her arms. He walked into them and hugged her back. "We won't solve this one today," he murmured. "Did you mean it when you agreed to be my wife?"

She tilted her head back and met his gaze head-on. "Did you mean it when you asked me? Still time to back out."

"I don't want to back out. I want you. More than ever."

"Good, because I feel the same way." She laid her cheek against the hollow between his neck and shoulder.

He tightened his hold on her as emotion sluiced through him. "You've made me a very happy man. We face a phalanx of unknowns, but we'll get through them better together."

A shadow crossed her face. "I hope so. 'Twould be a hell of a cosmic joke to find my one true mate and have him ripped away because one of us died."

"Hey." He tipped her chin up. "I'm not planning on dying."

"Neither am I," she said, sounding fierce.

"You look like one of those female warriors. Harsh. Beautiful. Foreboding. Sure glad you're mine."

"Aye, that I am." She leveled her gaze his way, said something in Gaelic, and followed it with. "Never forget the street cuts both ways. Ye're mine as well."

"How could I ever forget? It would be the same as forgetting you. Shall we?" He nodded at the door.

"Aye."

Hand in hand, they walked from his cabin into the corridor beyond. The same, yet not. Recco had never been married. Hell, he'd scarcely had what he considered a girlfriend who lasted more than a few months. Walking by Zoe's side, he vowed to do whatever it took to be a good husband. To love her, support her, and protect her.

"Keep those thoughts flowing," she murmured, chuckling.

Recco smothered a snort. "I forget you gals and your mind-reading proclivities. You'll have to teach me how to sneak into your thoughts."

She twisted to face him. "What? And have you privy to all my secrets? I think not. If you want to know how to mind read, you'll have to learn on your own."

He nudged her. She nudged back. Laughing, they started up the stairs to the bridge.

You've reached the end of *Abandoned*. Please take a moment to leave a review for *Abandoned*. It doesn't have to be fancy. A line or two will do. Reviews help so much! Thank you in advance.

If you're still in a reading mood, a sample from *Betrayed*, next book in the series, is just below.

ABOUT THE AUTHOR

Ann Gimpel is a USA Today bestselling author. A lifelong aficionado of the unusual, she began writing speculative fiction a few years ago. Since then her short fiction has appeared in several webzines and anthologies. Her longer books run the gamut from urban fantasy to paranormal romance. Once upon a time, she nurtured clients. Now she nurtures dark, gritty fantasy stories that push hard against reality. When she's not writing, she's in the backcountry getting down and dirty with her camera. She's published over sixty books to date, with several more planned for 2018 and beyond. A husband, grown children, grandchildren, and wolf hybrids round out her family.

Keep up with her at www.anngimpel.com or http://anngimpel.blogspot.com

If you enjoyed what you read, get in line for special offers and pre-release special reads. Newsletter Signup!

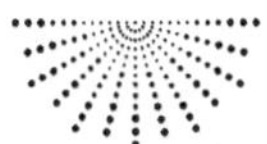

Karin's watched magic ebb and flow over her long life. A healer by nature, as well as a wolf Shifter, she fixes what she can and buries her personal needs deep. In a race against time, she and a small group of Shifters and humans are sailing toward a gateway in the Arctic. If they can't close it, Earth will be doomed.

Daide's a scientist, first and foremost. Once a world-renowned expert on treating cetaceans, his skills are rusty. Ten years as a Vampire altered a whole lot, and he's still analyzing his brand-new Shifter magic. Karin caught his eye before they left Ushuaia, but she seems to be in love with a dolphin Shifter. Immersed in jealousy, Daide considers walking away, but he can't give up. The only woman he's ever loved is worth fighting for. Consequences be damned.

Vampires, Witches, high-handed gods, Kelpies, and a host of others all want either the ship or the Shifters' magic. Even the simplest tasks grow thorny edges, and misunderstandings threaten to destroy everything.

BETRAYED, CHAPTER ONE, OVERSIGHT IN JUDGMENT

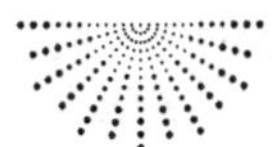

Karin Carson had been relieved the lab on Deck Two was empty. It wasn't likely to remain that way, so she hurried up, fussing with the controls on the darkfield microscope. Nothing changed on her slide. Not the way she wanted it to, anyway.

"Yeah, right. Why would it? Sheer wishful thinking on my part," she mumbled.

Dragging herself upright, she moved to a prep area, stabbed her finger with a lancet, and made three more slides. Even though she worked automatically, fatigue dragged at her. A weariness so pervasive, it was tough not to curl up in a ball on the floor and close her eyes.

"What did you find?" her wolf asked.

"Not sure," she hedged not bothering with telepathy. Magic of any kind took energy, a commodity she couldn't spare right now.

"What do you think you found?" her bondmate pressed. *"Must be something, or you wouldn't be making more of those glass things."*

Instead of answering, she prepped the new slides with different reagents. She'd suspected something was amiss when she hadn't bounced back from healing the dolphin Shifters' alpha. It had been significantly more than just healing, though. The creature died, and she'd held its spirit with her magic, urging it back to this side of the veil. It had drained her resources down to bedrock, so she hadn't thought much about it when she didn't have her usual complement of energy afterward.

Working with Daide, one of two veterinarians aboard *Arkady*, she'd gone on to cure eight more dolphins, feeling slightly worse after each one. The last dolphin had been two days ago, and she'd expected her depleted energy to stage a recovery. It hadn't. If she were honest, she felt worse now than she had after they'd finished the dolphin.

Her bondmate had noticed. How could it not have? She was here in the lab she'd helped set up on Deck Two, assessing what could possibly be wrong with her, because of its urging. She tamped back a wry grin. Nagging, wheedling, and cajoling came closer than urging. Her wolf had a relentless streak, one of many things she loved about it.

The slides were as ready as they'd ever be. She walked them over to a normal scope, set one on the stage, and bent over the binocular eyepieces. The same dyscrasia she'd seen earlier was even clearer here. It fit with her white count being off the charts high, but what made no sense was how she'd developed what looked like a precancerous anomaly in her blood over a few weeks timeframe.

Bodies didn't operate that way.

Apparently mine did.

"Are you going to tell me?" the wolf demanded.

"Something is wrong with my blood." Karin straightened from her hunched position, not bothering with the other two slides. They'd contain the same information.

"Can you fix it?" Her wolf punctuated its question with a howl.

She scrunched her eyes shut to rest them and rubbed her temples to ease the headache that rarely let her be.

"Well, can you?" the wolf persisted.

"I don't know. The dyscrasia—wrongness—has to be a

byproduct of magic, but I don't get it. The dolphins are Shifters too. Their magic should be similar, nothing that would attack me, but it's the only logical explanation."

"What is? I'm your bondmate. Why are you making me drag things out of you?"

"Sorry. I don't mean to. There's this lethargy, and it drags at me. Makes it hard to think, and then I panic. If I don't figure this out damned soon, I fear my capacity to reason things through will desert me."

Yeah, and then I'll be totally screwed. She kept that last thought to herself, but the wolf probably culled it from her mind.

"What's the only logical explanation? I get the lethargy part, but you never answered me from before."

"I absorbed something from when I healed the first dolphin shifter. I was far closer to him than the others since I forced his spirit to remain when it would have departed. I patched him back together with magic and cells from my body. It's impossible to do that without cross-contamination."

"Tell Ketha," the wolf urged. *"And Recco and Daide. Working together, maybe you can—"*

"Not yet," she cut in. "I appreciate you're worried, and that you care about me, but we'll be in Invercargill soon. Goddess only knows what we'll face there. My problems are trivial by comparison. I'll dose myself with something and see if I can't fix this on my own."

The wolf's silence was significant. Clearly it saw through her words as the false assurances they were meant to be.

After another glance at the slide, she quickly slotted the next two into place and muttered, "Same story, different verse." Because Ketha, a microbiologist, and the men would recognize what was on the slides, she ditched them in the biohazard waste bin and marched to the cabinet where they stored their limited supply of pharmaceuticals.

Antibiotics weren't the answer. Neither was anything else in the cupboard. Maybe one of Invercargill's hospitals would have a selection of chemotherapy agents or immune modulators. It was possible. Even if the town was in as bad a shape as Ushuaia had been, drugs that disappeared from clinics were items like opioids and benzodiazepines. No one wanted chemicals that made you puke and lose your hair.

She bit down hard on her lower lip. A precancerous condition that sprang out of nowhere didn't bode well. Meant it would progress fast and not be particularly amenable to standard treatment approaches. She'd have to engage her immune system to have a prayer of winning this battle, which meant she had to get her magic back online.

When she assessed the reservoir where her power dwelled, it was just as empty as it had been the day before. Why wasn't it bouncing back?

If I could figure that out, I'd be able to fix what's wrong with me.

Ketha trotted into the lab, coffee mug in hand, and stopped abruptly. Dark hair shot with red and gold strands fell in braids to her waist, and her golden eyes—byproduct of her wolf bondmate— narrowed. "Jesus. You look like hell. Are you sick?"

Karin shrugged. "Maybe. I'm sure I'll be right as rain after another night's rest."

Ketha covered the distance between them and splayed the flat of her hand across Karin's forehead. Before she could duck from beneath Ketha's touch, a jolt of power rocked her. The other Shifter's eyes widened. "Holy crap. You're running a fever. Your blood pressure is dangerously high, and your respiration rate—"

"I already know all those things." Karin dropped back a couple of steps to avoid Ketha's questing fingers—or magic.

"If you do, why aren't you doing something about it?" Ketha set her cup in a holder and crossed her arms beneath her breasts.

"Maybe because doing the wrong thing would be worse than doing nothing."

"What have you tried so far?"

Karin shook her head. "How about if you let this go for now? I'm sure it's nothing—"

"Well I'm not. We're never sick. Maybe you should shift. Your wolf heals faster than you do."

"If it comes to that, I will."

Ketha dropped her hands to her sides and angled her head. Her forehead creased into worried lines. "Why haven't you done it already? It's our first line of defense."

Karin turned away and closed the drug cabinet. When she turned back, she pasted a reassuring smile on her face. "I'll take care of it as soon as my magic's done recovering."

"But it's been two days since you and Daide finished with the dolphins," Ketha protested.

"Enough." Karin marshaled what little energy she had into that one word and strode out of the lab. In truth, she didn't have enough magic to shift—at least she was fairly certain she didn't. If Ketha kept picking at things, she'd be bound to discover how depleted Karin was. Once that happened, all bets were off and everyone aboard the ship would be focused on her instead of what they should be thinking about, which was Invercargill.

What would they find there? It was a reasonable bet the natives would pose problems. If any remained. No one had responded to their radio calls. She dragged herself up one flight of stairs and along the corridor to her cabin, wishing she could lock herself inside. So far, Ketha hadn't followed her, but she would given time. Hopefully, she wouldn't round up reinforcements.

Of all the times to come down with a mystery ailment, this wasn't a very good one. Not that any occasion existed when it wouldn't be problematic to operate at less than a hundred percent. Karin slumped into the room's single chair, weariness crashing over her in waves.

She steepled her fingers, pressing the tips together to force a point of concentration. Maybe she was onto something with her incompatible magic theory. Zoe had been right there with her, but

Karin had absorbed the dolphin's essence, shielding it so Leif's primary form wouldn't die.

Her wolf was quiet, but she felt it prowling within her. "Do you know when our line diverged from the sea Shifters?"

"What exactly are you asking?"

"Not whatever we argued about that created the schism. It's not important. Do you know when they took to their sea forms while we stuck to the human ones? Also, when did we abandon a social structure where alphas ran things."

"Long ago, your primary form would have been mine. All Shifters were animals first, humans second, until the Romans made it dangerous for wolves and coyotes. They were captured and tossed in pits to fight. Hawks and eagles were trapped and forced to hunt."

Karin frowned. She thought she knew Shifter history, but she'd never heard about this part. "Why wouldn't they have fought back?"

"When they summoned magic to win contests in the pit—and save their lives—it revealed what they were, and many of our ancestors were hanged or burned."

"So someone decided we'd be safer in our human bodies. Makes sense."

The wolf growled. *"Like all solutions, some things improved, but others grew worse. We lost a goodly share of our magic during the tradeoff."*

"Which explains why the sea Shifters are more powerful than us." Karin mulled it over. "Might also explain why their magic is different. You'd asked what is wrong with me, and I only gave you a partial answer. I'm convinced a disparity between my power and Leif's created the problem. His magic fought mine, and remnants of it are actively sabotaging my power. It's the only explanation that makes sense."

"So get rid of the remnants. Seems simple enough."

Karin twisted her mouth into a grimace as she recalled the patchwork quilt she'd created where she wove her power with Leif's fading energy. He'd been ill for years with parasitic infections and was nearly at the end of his strength, so she'd borrowed liberally from her own magic and used it to shore up his. If she hadn't, he'd be dead.

But because she had, her own demise was staring her in the face. If she couldn't reverse the process eroding her tissue and organ systems—and damned soon—there'd be nothing left to salvage.

"It's not simple," she told her wolf. "This is like an autoimmune disorder where my body is attacking itself. A healthy immune system sorts friend from foe. When I joined with Leif, I confused mine, and its turned on me."

"Can you fix it?" The wolf asked again.

"I don't know. If I grow much weaker, I won't be able to do anything."

"If you're too depleted to shift, do you want me to break through? I can force a shift."

Karin shook her head. "I thought about that, and it's too dangerous for you. If I'm developing the sea Shifters' pattern, you could end up stuck. Instead of being able to return to the animals' world, you'd die here, and I won't do that to you."

"You don't know that."

"Oh but I do. If those dolphins and whales could have returned to a world like yours when they fell ill, they would have. They were stuck here." She swallowed around a thick spot in her throat. "I love you too much to have you sacrifice yourself."

"How about if I love you too?" the wolf countered. *"This is both our choices, not just yours."*

Karin blinked back tears.

Her door flew open, and Ketha marched inside, face twisted with pain—and anger. She kicked the door shut. "I dug your slides out of the trash. Why didn't you talk with me?"

"We have bigger problems than me right now." Karin kept her words simple, mostly because it was all she was capable of. "We're stopping at Invercargill at least long enough for Recco and Daide to make use of the cetacean institute's pools to work on the five whale Shifters. It will be a miracle if something doesn't attack us while we're there. You need to be planning for contingencies, not worried about me."

"I will not focus on contingencies while you wither and die on us." Ketha plopped onto the bunk nearest Karin. "Christ! You're an MD. I don't have to interpret what I found on those slides for you. Your white count is astronomical. Your body is destroying itself—"

"I know what's wrong. At least I believe I do," Karin protested. "What I'm less certain of is how to neutralize it."

"Maybe we can get hold of some immunosuppressant drugs in Invercargill."

"Already thought about that. It might slow things down, but it won't work over the long haul. Immune modulators might, but chances of finding them in Invercargill are almost nill. The parts of Leif I absorbed when I saved him have to stop fighting me. I assumed our physiologies would be compatible, or I'd have made certain to establish a few degrees of separation."

Ketha shook her head. "You were in full savior mode. I know you, and when you go there, the last thing on your mind is your own safety."

"Your point?" Karin spoke stiffly.

"Not sure I had one. Can you shift?"

"No. Not enough magic, and before you suggest having my wolf circumvent that problem, I won't place it at risk."

"At risk, how?"

Breath rattled through Karin's teeth. "I just explained this to my bondmate. Do you think the dolphins and whales remained in a poisoned ocean voluntarily? Hell no, they didn't. They couldn't return to whatever borderworld they live in, or they would have. If I'm correct, and I'm changing into something more like our sea kin, my wolf could be trapped here and die."

"I can fight this thing off. I know I can." The wolf chimed in.

Karin wanted to wrap her arms around its lush pelt and hug it, something she'd never been able to do.

"I heard that." Ketha's voice was soft. "Why not give your wolf a chance?" Without waiting for Karin to answer, she continued. "Have you spoken with Leif?"

"Of course not. He was my patient. I took chances that didn't seem risky at the time, and—"

Ketha waved her to silence. "He might know a way to intervene. Those dolphins haven't had their human forms long enough for me to get to know any of them, but there could be a healer in the bunch. Their magic is stronger than ours." She turned her hands palms up. "Worth a shot."

Karin straightened, horrified by how much energy it took. "It is worth a shot. And if it doesn't work, I'll let my wolf shift for us."

A delighted howl ripped through her.

Ketha placed her hand on Karin's leg. "I'm going to find Leif now. If he has any ideas, I'll bring him back here."

Karin swallowed hard. "Thanks. I'll throw some cold water on my face. I'm burning up."

"Take some aspirin or Ibuprofen." Ketha quirked a brow. "Physician heal thyself."

Karin smothered a snort. "Awk! Since when did we stoop to quoting scripture? Christians would just as soon burn us as look at us, or have you forgotten?"

"Nothing holy about it. Just a phrase. Back very soon, I hope." Ketha sprang to her feet and bolted out the door.

Karin struggled upright and tottered to the sink. Cold water on her face and hands helped, and she dry-swallowed three aspirin. She came close to breaking into a litany and telling her wolf how much she loved it, how much its presence and undeviating loyalty had always meant, but it knew. They'd been together for over two centuries.

Karin rarely told anyone how old she was. In the first place, it didn't matter. In the second, she feared it would insert artificial distance between herself and the other women she'd ended up with in Ushuaia. Rowana had known, but she was the only one.

And now Ro was dead. She'd died a hideous death in Karin's arms, racked with pain but absolutely certain it was her time to go.

"Damn, but I hope I can exit with a tenth her grace and style."

You are not going anywhere, the wolf said, steel in its voice.

The sound of running footsteps alerted Karin moments before her door swung inward. A worried-looking Leif burst through with Ketha right behind him. The dolphin shifter was naked and still dripping ocean water. The salt scent of the sea clung to him. Blue-gray hair shrouded his tall, broad-shouldered form to knee level, and he trained sea-blue eyes on Karin.

"Apologies," he said. "Finding clothes took a backseat to Ketha's summons." He placed a palm across Karin's forehead, and she felt a jolt of rough magic, glass shards and pepper flakes. He moved his hand from her face to her upper back and then her chest across her collarbones. Each place he touched her tingled unpleasantly, but the crippling inertia eased too.

"Well?" Ketha hovered behind him. The door was shut, so presumably she'd closed it.

Leif drew his brows into a thick, gray line and skewered Karin with eyes that had shaded to gray. "Why didn't you call me sooner, wolf Shifter?"

"I kept thinking this would improve."

"Mmph. Would have been far easier to intervene a few days ago. I must summon the other dolphins. This will equire all of us."

"What are you going to do?" Karin and Ketha asked at almost the same time, their words tripping over each other.

"Reclaim the parts within the Shifter doctor that do not belong," Leif said. "And hope to hell we don't injure her in the process." He blew out a tight breath. "This would have been simpler right after it happened, before our essence put down roots trying to displace land Shifter magic."

"At least it explains why I have no power," Karin muttered.

Leif leveled his gaze at her. "If we do not intercede, nor will you have a life. Sea Shifter enchantment is trying to convert you, except our two types of magic have grown incompatible over the centuries. Left unchecked, there's but one way out of this."

A knock was followed by dolphin shifters filing into the cabin. "We need a bigger space," one of them said.

"Aye, no room to maneuver in here," another voice chimed in.

"What in the hell is going on?" Daide boomed from somewhere in the hall.

Karin tried to tell him it was nothing, but her head whirled crazily. It might have been the three aspirin, since she rarely took anything at all. It might have been so many people crowded into her cabin. It might have been fear she wasn't going to make it through what lay ahead. Desperate to hang onto a semblance of control, she made a grab for consciousness. Did her damnedest to hang onto it, but it eluded her, and she fell ass over teakettle into a deep, black hole.